Blooms in the Fall

by

Micki Miller

Blooms in the Fall

Cover Art by *Debbie Taylor*

The Wild Rose Press, Inc.
PO Box 708
Adams Basin, NY 14410-0708
Visit us at www.thewildrosepress.com

Publishing History
First Edition, 2021
Trade Paperback ISBN 978-1-5092-3631-2
Digital ISBN 978-1-5092-3632-9

Published in the United States of America

So there she stood. Facing the soft wind, breathing in this world, and letting it hold her in ethereal arms.

It occurred to Letty how Nature's earth was an immense sundry and quite enduring when left in Her competent hands. It looked after itself, picked up after itself, without neglecting or overthinking the ways of days. All seasons served a purpose.

Even now, when the flowers of summer were fading, and the leaves were falling from the trees to their deaths, and all seemed hopeless and headed into permanent desolation, the land understood it was nothing more than a hiatus. It didn't fear the transformation. It didn't struggle against what it couldn't change but rather flowed with comfort from one stage of life to the next, knowing by instinct spring would come again.

Letty gazed around again before kneeling beside a broad patch of the lavender, daisy-like flowers. She picked a good handful, careful to spread out her trimmings and leave enough so the field would look undisturbed by a human hand.

Previous Releases by Micki Miller

THE MARSHAL'S PURSUIT
THE DARKEST SUM
A SCANDALOUS REQUEST
A BANDIT'S REQUEST
AT HER REQUEST

~

A Bandit's Request was nominated for a Readers' Choice 2020 award.

Dedication

To Claire Jacobson.
If everyone had a mother like you,
the world would be a better place.
Love you forever.

Chapter 1

The music caught Cole Holloway as he wiped the narrow stream of blood from the corner of his mouth.

For a moment, he wondered how hard Darrell hit him. No way he could be hearing music way up here on his Montana mountain. He shook his head to clear the punch-fog. The music was still there. The strumming of a guitar and a heralding voice like a composite of earth, air, and spirit, divine enough to make him forget the pain in his jaw, and at least for one blissful moment, ease the infinite torment to his soul.

And then it stopped.

Beneath the endless azure sky and a broad scattering of cotton-ball clouds, Cole stood as still as the massive cottonwoods and ponderosa pines staking his world. The depth of intensity with which he listened left every pore of his body open, waiting, hoping, and even wishing with childlike naïveté for the solace of that sublime sound to come back.

In the distance, the unmistakable call of a loon. Envy was rife in its elongated wail. A nearby sparrow chirped a few brief notes before ceasing its efforts as if knowing its own lovely singing could never equal the heaven-sent sound of that voice.

A sudden breeze brushed Cole's skin, making him aware of the goose bumps rising on his forearms below the rolled-up sleeves of his brown and green flannel shirt. Leaves swayed on their branches in a brief dance without the music for which he could swear the entire Pine Bluff mountain range begged.

When the air stilled, Cole waited to hear her voice again. The divine, mournful sound had captured all the world's suffering and offered to carry it far away. But this world was bereft of such a phenomenon. No doubt it always had been. The music was naught but a dream of his imagination, the covetous trickery of a hangdog man.

The uncouth knocking of a woodpecker broke the last strands of the spell. Cole shook his down-tipped head, eyes closed tight, ashamed of his silly bent of romanticism.

He touched his lips again and glanced at his dry fingers. The cut on the inside of his mouth had stopped bleeding, but it would be a source of pain for days. He damned Darrell Clayton for poaching on his land; damned him a second time for the fistfight. Good God, he was at a time in his life when things like fighting should be a memory, and not a recent one.

At fifty-two years old, Cole was in good health and good shape, and it was rare he felt his age. He was, however, too old for such a ridiculous schoolyard brawl like the one he'd just had with Darrell.

A sardonic smile tugged at his lips. He and Darrell had been fighting over one thing or another since the third grade. Cole wondered if someday they'd be trading blows with their walkers, ramming each other like a couple of stubborn old elk. He almost grinned at the image it conjured as he bent to brush the dirt off his clothes. His large, work-worn hands swept across the legs of his jeans, and Cole found a tear in the knee. He damned Darrell a third time.

From not more than ten feet in front of him, a gray squirrel caught his attention as it scampered about the patchy carpet of leaves and twigs and a million strands of elk sedge softening the slopes. Cole stuffed his hand into his pocket and scooped out a peanut, which he then tossed toward the squirrel. The small critter snatched up the treat with impressive speed and stuffed it into its mouth before scurrying away. The little guy would appreciate the tidbit later in the year when the ground was hard with ice and snow.

Cole took a moment to survey his surroundings, scented with the smell of clean dirt. Yes, clean dirt. Every day of his entire life, he'd been out here somewhere on his land, and the mountains and woods never changed. Yet it was always so fresh, so revitalizing. How could it be anything else?

The land he owned and protected was unpolluted; the water in the lake near his spacious, log house and the running streams throughout were clean, clear, and pristine, the way nature intended. Many thousands of trees as old as time purified the air he breathed. Up here, his mountain land existed in bliss, free of the countless noises of man and machine agitating so much of the rest of the world.

Except for the house in which he lived and nature's constant growth, the land was much the same as it had been when his great-grandfather bought it more than seventy years ago.

Cole never tired of this property, quite the opposite. He couldn't get enough of it. These eighty acres of prime Montana land were an appendage, no less important than the others thriving on his will and his blood, and in return supported him. He'd already arranged for his burial here, beside his mother and father. It wasn't something done in most cases, but with enough money and enough pull, a man could get whatever he wanted.

Well, almost.

Cole closed his eyes and breathed in deep the pine-scented air. It always cleared his head and settled his thoughts, and even to a certain extent, his heart. Like the animals born and living here, he could smell as much as hear the water running nearby. He loved the gentle clash of leaves against leaves as another cool breeze swept through. The gust traveled on down the mountain, heading for town, maybe to freshen it up some. A pleasant thought for sure.

Then the music sifted through again.

Cole didn't open his eyes right away for fear of losing it. Imagined or not, it was more beautiful than anything he'd ever heard in his life. A full minute passed. The music continued, the voice in harmony with the gurgle of water flowing over river rock, the soft clatter of leaves keeping tempo to the strumming of a guitar. The tune was sad, ethereal, almost more feeling than sound.

Cautious, as if to sneak up on it, he opened his eyes. The song still played. It wasn't his imagination. It was real, and it was coming from somewhere on his land.

Cole turned his head in a slow revolution. Pinpointing anything heard could be difficult out here. Hills, valleys, streams, trees, and a wide variety of woodland creatures all worked to displace sound. The soulful music wove through the woods, becoming a part of it, or maybe vice versa.

Craning his neck, Cole took a scan up a low-grade rise, which led to a rocky cliff. Focused on the direction, he listened with rapt attention. Yes. Yes, it was coming from up there. He was sure of it. Stepping with quiet intent, he made his way up the rise.

As he neared the edge of the tree line, Cole caught his first sight of her. He had a good view from her left side. The girl was young, early twenties, maybe even in her late teens. Long blonde hair, wavy, rather unkempt, hung down her back to the bottom edge of her shoulder blades, where it formed a vague U shape. She wore jeans and a plain brown T-shirt that was small yet still hung loose on her, so narrow was her frame.

She sat on the edge of a large, flat rock jutting out, her sneaker-clad feet dangling over, strumming the guitar she cradled in her lap. Her head bowed down toward the guitar, but from his side angle, Cole could see her lips moving as she continued to sing her heart-wrenching song.

Cole stared in utter fascination, transfixed by the sight and the angelic voice filling the welcoming valley below her as she then tilted her head upward until she faced the sun. Her eyes were closed. A tear slid down her face, and Cole placed a bracing hand against the rough bark of an ash tree, so sad was the sight.

He had a powerful notion to hold her like a child, as he had his own son not so many years ago, to soothe her as if he could somehow free her of the pain flowing through her song and clenching his heart. But he stayed where he was.

She drew out the lyrics. They were melodic, metaphoric, keeping the severe points of truth from marring the beauty of the music while leaving no doubt they were there. All the sadness in the world, all the harsh injustices were contained in the symbolisms in her song.

As Cole lowered his hand and leaned his shoulder against the sturdy ash, the thick trunk supporting his body while his mind wondered about the song, he was humbled to witness this sight and sound. *This moment will remain in my mind.* Even after the passing of years, decades, what he was seeing and hearing at this very time, in this very spot, would be with him forever. Cole was old enough to understand the value of a beautiful memory.

It turned out to be a short one.

Her mouth closed, her hands stilled upon the strings, and he could believe the valley wept with the loss, holding on to the fading echo as long as possible. With her small, delicate fingers, the girl wiped the tear from her face. She sucked in a good lungful of fresh mountain air. When she released it, she nodded twice, appearing to have resigned to something. It was clear from the rounding curve of her skinny body, the deflation crying of surrender.

The girl stood, careful not to scratch her guitar on the rocks. She backed up several paces, held her instrument's neck with her right hand, and wiped the right side of her face with her left hand. Cole assumed it was a tear out of his vision. Her song had been very personal, full of her own pain. It was so real it was almost as tangible as the wilderness surrounding them.

Emotion like that was incapable of deception, he well knew. It was too raw to carry off the subterfuge popular today with people angling for sympathy.

Besides, as far as the girl knew, she was alone. Cole's wish to soothe her, to ease her burdens, took hold of him again, yet he remained hidden.

The varied green and brown plaid of his shirt blended in well with the scenery. It was so unlike him to *want* to feel camouflaged here. This was his land, and he would go where he pleased when he pleased. To approach her, though, at this very private moment, would be too intrusive, no matter his right.

The girl straightened. With a very sudden, very angry burst of energy, she jerked her arm back far enough to twist her body some and then thrust it forward. A small grunt escaped her as she flung the guitar over the edge of the cliff.

Cole shoved away from the tree, shocked and appalled at what she had done. Though neither of them could see it, the sound of the instrument crashing and splintering echoed throughout the canyon. Jagged rocks plucked the strings from their bindings. The violence reverberated, ugly and profane.

At last, it ended, landing somewhere far below them, no doubt a useless pile of trash now. A unified silence followed as if the entire world had stopped to mourn.

Standing there, staring at the girl, baffled by her actions, Cole suddenly knew what she would do next. It turned the blood in his veins as cold as a winter storm.

He would never be able to say how he knew such a thing. Maybe it was the tightening of her stance. Or the slight dip of her head. Maybe it was a sense of her surrender turning to determination or the way her eyes focused when she stared in the direction in which she had sent her guitar.

Whatever the reason, in the very next second, Cole's instinct proved right. Never in his life had he so wanted to be wrong.

The girl pushed off with one leg and stretched out the other in one long leap toward the edge of the cliff. Another stride like that, and it would be too late for Cole to do anything. As her foot hit the ground, her knee bent in order to gain the necessary propulsion. Cole sprang from the shadows and grabbed for her.

He wasn't close enough.

He leaped again. This time he caught her in mid-air, no more than a second or two before she would have gone over. They spun around and crashed down together onto the hard ground. Cole landed on top of the girl. Air rushed from her lungs, and in an instant, he rolled off her and sat up, worried he'd saved her only to crush her to death.

Cole's heart pounded a wild tempo all the way into his head. Terror, clashing real against the surreal, speared through to his core at the knowledge of what had almost happened right in front of him.

He stared down at her, relieved to see all he'd done was knock the breath out of her. The girl's stunned eyes were wide, bewildered as she sucked in air, trying to comprehend what had happened, he was sure. Cole imagined he bore the same expression. Finally, her gaze met his.

"Why did you do that!" she shouted. The silk of her voice was gone, replaced with raw outrage. She fixed her glare on him, waiting for an answer.

Cole stared down at the girl. She didn't look familiar. Whoever he didn't know in town, he had at least seen, and he was sure he'd never seen her.

No makeup adorned her oval face, not even that dark stuff around the eyes so many of the young girls in town liked to use. The scattering of freckles across her nose made her appear even younger than she probably was. She hadn't ironed out the waves nature had put in her hair, and her clothing was as basic as it got, plain, brown T-shirt, jeans, sneakers.

The girl was pretty, in an uncluttered, unpretentious sort of way. The rage through which she viewed him at present, though, made her about as welcoming as a riled porcupine.

Cole scowled at her. "What do you mean, why did I do that? What was I supposed to do, let you jump?"

"Yes." She maneuvered into a sitting position on trembling arms. "This is none of your damn business!"

In an instant, Cole got over his rush of emotions, no longer enchanted with her. She'd just taken ten years off his life. His fear became a whip of anger, and he lashed out at her with his words.

"This is my land, and whatever happens on my land is my business."

"I didn't see your name on that cliff."

Cole barked out one chuckle, the release of nervous tension he supposed. "There are *no trespassing* signs all around *my* borders," he told her. And, of course, a good amount of *no hunting* signs, but he didn't see any point in mentioning those.

Cole rose to his feet and brushed the dirt off his jeans for the second time in less than ten minutes. Not because he cared about his ruined pants, but he had to do something with his hands to keep from grabbing the mess of a girl and shaking some sense into her.

The girl stood, too. Dust and twigs fell from her

clothes, but she didn't bother brushing off any of it. It took her too long to find her balance, and for a moment, Cole worried she might topple over. But she managed to stabilize. The challenge appeared to have raised her anger, and Cole soon believed she'd gotten her mind and body together for the sole purpose of turning her fury on him.

Although the top of her head didn't quite come up to his shoulder, the girl tilted her head back and glared at him as if they were eye to eye. "It's not like I was stealing your stupid cliff."

Cole was beyond incredulous, and for a moment, all he could do was stare at the girl. She was very young, had so much to live for, had so many years to overcome whatever it was that had her upset enough to jump off a cliff. The waste of life was disgusting and pitiful.

Sympathy diluted his anger, and he asked, "Why would you want to do something like that anyway?"

"That's none of your damn business!" Her shouted words echoed down the valley, pounding on the walls of rock until the ground took them in.

She slapped her palms over her eyes. Cole figured she was either shutting him out or holding back tears. He scrubbed a dirty hand down his clean-shaven face. "And here we are, back to square one."

The girl dropped her hands and huffed out a sigh, deflating before his eyes. As she stared at the ground, Cole took note of her size. He was a big guy, three inches over six feet, broad shouldered and thick across his chest, but even taking his own size into consideration, the girl was too thin for her height of about five, six. He'd bet an acre of barley she didn't even weigh a hundred pounds.

"What's your name?" Cole asked.

Her head snapped up, and she was glaring at him again. "None of your business, that's my name."

Cole sharpened his gaze. "Is that your favorite phrase?"

"No," she shot back. "This one is; goodbye."

The girl spun away from him. She bent down and grabbed a navy-blue backpack and a denim jacket he hadn't noticed before off the ground and then stood upright again, ready to walk off in a huff. She lost her balance, and this time, was unable to regain it. It looked to him as if she'd decided to go sit down on a nearby boulder, but she wasn't going to make it. Her backpack hit the ground with a heavy thud, and she swayed deep. Cole caught her before she could fall.

He was appalled to find she weighed even less than she looked. The girl wasn't much more than bones wrapped in skin. She tilted her face toward his, appeared to have trouble holding her head up. It took her a moment before she was able to focus on him.

"Put me down," she said, but her voice wasn't strong enough to summon the demand for which she strove. She must have used up the last of her energy yelling at him. Her palm half shoved, half fell, against his chest, her fight giving way to what was inevitable.

"When was the last time you had anything to eat?" Cole asked as he scanned her, seeing her clothes were indeed small yet too big on her. She had the appearance of one whose body was wasting away, and a horrible thought strode into his brain. Maybe she suffered from a serious illness. Maybe she was dying and had chosen a faster, less painful route.

Though she lacked the strength to pull it off, the girl still managed to sound indignant in her short struggle. She tired in seconds, surrendering to the weariness, allowing her head to rest against his chest. Her eyes were heavy, and she didn't expend much effort to keep them open.

"I don't remember."

"Yeah, that's what I thought."

Cole settled her into his arms and started the hike back to his house.

"Where are you taking me?" she asked.

Her eyes remained closed. Her lips moved no more than necessary, sleep already claiming her. He responded anyway.

"No matter how determined you are to die on my land, I'm more determined to prevent it."

Chapter 2

Somewhere along the way, Letty had fallen into a heavy sleep. Like everything else in her life these days, it had been inescapable.

Though she'd gotten a motel room last night in some little town close by, she hadn't slept a single minute. After her wasted efforts to drift off watching television, she'd given in to pacing her agitation in the confines of her room. Her tired legs carried her from the locked door between her and the outside world, to the tiny bathroom, back to the door, back to the bathroom, again and again, while some late-night talk-show host made jokes about news she hadn't heard.

Around two a.m., her legs weakened under the weight of her plight. Her wavering strides shortened. The passion of her gait had played out.

Letty had no choice but to surrender to the physical limitations she had brought on with her own neglect. She'd turned off the television and spent the next several hours lying on top of the thread-shedding, nylon bedspread, staring at the nicotine stains on the ceiling, listening to the blaring silence of her life.

Every so often, she closed her eyes in an effort to fall asleep, but her turmoil was too boisterous, too demanding of her attention. Sleep hadn't yet the power to overcome. Her mind kept busy dwelling on a past she couldn't change and then planning her short future.

It was the only thing left she could control. As it turned out, someone else restricted even that.

As she slipped from the respite of sleep, Letty kept her eyes shut in hopes of remaining in the blissful haze encompassing her. For the moment, the past existed in a muddled condition, and though the details were still groggy with residual sleep, she knew it was better that way. Much better. With minimal movements, Letty snuggled farther into the blanket. Consciousness dragged her, though, waking her thoughts, and worse, her memories.

She held still, thinking she might get lucky and drift off again. But, like everything else in life that was good, reality had to crash down with its usual brutal fist. Letty didn't know where she was, but now awake in the darkness behind her eyes, she was with perfect clarity aware of where she had been and of what the cruelties of fate had done.

Though she was still very tired, sleep once again mocked and refused her. With great reluctance, Letty opened her eyes, snipping the last tenuous thread of slumber.

She was on a soft bed, curled on her side beneath a patchwork quilt made in many shades of pink, still dressed except for her shoes. Waking up in her clothes made Letty think of when she was sixteen, and she and her friend Kathy had snuck a bottle of peppermint schnapps from Kathy's parents' kitchen cupboard. They'd spent the night in Kathy's room, drinking, giggling, dancing, and eventually on the bathroom floor wondering how something that tasted so good going down could be so vile coming up.

She'd awakened in Kathy's bed the next morning,

still wearing all her clothes, except then her head pounded, and her stomach was a toxic dumpsite. It was the last time either of them drank themselves drunk.

Deep western light shone through the bedroom window. How long had she been asleep, and where was it she'd been dozing? She had a vague memory of telling the big man to leave her alone, that she was tired and wanted to sleep. Apparently, for once, she had gotten what she wanted.

On the lace-covered table beside the bed sat a yellow ceramic plate holding a sandwich. Plastic wrap covered the plate, and a tall glass of water sat beside it. Seeing the water brought forth Letty's realization as to how dry her mouth was. It was as if she needed a visual to remind her of the necessities for survival.

With more effort than she would have guessed necessary, Letty managed to get into a sitting position. The amount of energy such a simple act required was frightening. The irony wasn't lost on her.

Last night, in the sick yellow light that must be standard in all dreary motel rooms, where no doubt others had decided on the same fate, as the room inspired little else, Letty made the decision to end her life. Now here she was, feeling fear at the way her life's energy was leaving her.

Maybe starving would have been a better way to do it. She hadn't been hungry anyway, which was why she'd lost all the weight in the first place. It would have taken far less effort. Later, she'd give the idea more thought. Right now, all she wanted was a drink of water.

Using both hands, Letty picked up the glass and managed to get it to her lips without spilling any. It took a good deal of concentration. Her hands shook, sloshing the water precariously close to the lip of the glass. The loss of strength was stunning, as was the rapidity at which it had come upon her. Apparently, she'd drained the last of her energy on her trek up the mountain.

After swallowing half of the water, Letty revived to a better condition. In fact, hunger got her attention for the first time in weeks. Just then, her stomach made a noise so loud she'd have been embarrassed had anybody else been in the room. It was shocking how something so normal like feeding her body had been incinerated by a fire lit before she was even born.

After setting the glass back on the table, Letty eyed the sandwich. She could see peanut butter and what looked like strawberry preserves oozing from between two pieces of wheat bread. Her stomach grumbled again, even louder this time, and ground, as though it was turning in on itself, sucking in hard to get her attention. Maybe starving to death wouldn't be so easy after all.

Using both hands, Letty brought the plate to her lap and peeled back the plastic. The nutty, creamy smell of peanut butter and sweet jam wafted up and enticed her more than any fancy restaurant dinner could have. A good ole PB and J always held a special kind of magic. It filled an emotional void as much as a stomach, the part of a person longing for the simpler days of childhood, the days before life's inevitable complications.

And the not-so inevitable.

The smell of the sandwich did that for Letty, reminding her of all of the peanut butter and jelly sandwiches her mother had made for her when she was a little girl. At the thought of her mother, however, Letty's sweet memories soured.

Her mother, the woman who had given her life, and in doing so, had cursed her to damnation.

Letty's stomach grumbled again, and she was able, at least for the moment, to set aside all those thoughts and their offshoots. She focused on the simple enjoyment of the sandwich. Her teeth sank through the layers of bread and peanut butter and preserves lumpy with fruit. She ate it with the relish of a gourmet taste-testing a fabulous new delicacy. The first bite was heavenly. The next was no less wonderful. Her stomach growled with effort as if it couldn't grab the food fast enough. Letty almost laughed. Now her own body was scolding her.

While she chewed, Letty took a visual tour of the room. Light pink paint covered the walls, the same color as some of the patches on the quilt covering her. A simple brass footboard completed the queen-size bed. The ballcaps on the end poles were large and snowy white. Her jacket hung from one. Letty glanced behind her to see if the headboard matched the footboard. It did.

Facing her across the modest-sized room was a dresser stained in antiqued shades of mahogany, buffed soft and shiny clean. A squat, copper vase of colorful dried flowers sat upon it, centered on a lace doily. The mirror above the dresser was also clean of streaks and dust. Its frame matched the dresser.

In regard to personal touches, it was sparse. She had another glance around, searching for books, or photographs, or some sort of item suggesting this room belonged to anybody in particular. The two pictures on the wall were generic renditions of a bluebird in a tree and a sun-drenched meadow. Letty had seen the same pictures in a bath and linen store back home. Still, it was a pretty room, welcoming with soft comforts.

Leaning a little over the edge of the bed, Letty peeked at the blond wood floor polished to a high gloss and patched with an assortment of braided rugs, unmatched but well-coordinated with each other and with the room. The toes of her sneakers poked out from under the bed.

White lace curtains adorned the single, opened window. Occasionally they fluttered inward, nudged by a cool breeze drifting in to brush fresh against her face.

The air puffing in through the window carried the scent of natural pine, which air fresheners strained so hard to copy but never could. Letty took another bite of the sandwich and closed her eyes while she took her time chewing, letting the unsoiled air envelop her outer self while the food gave solace to her innards. For the moment, she knew peace.

The sandwich was half-gone when Letty's attention swung to the boy standing in the doorway holding her backpack. She didn't know how long he'd been there. He was so still, so quiet, almost a part of the inanimate world around her. It was as if instead of walking into the doorway, he'd appeared by magic, a fresh character in the gothic novel of her life.

The boy looked to be about twelve with a lean build, fair skin tinted with outdoor play, and soulful blue eyes that shouldn't be familiar but were. His face was young, sweet, solemn, and uncertain, bearing the uneven growth of puberty. His hair, thick, bronzed, and a little long, fell past his ears. A wide lock hung heavy over his right eye in a way that might be deliberately careless if he was older. His jeans were well worn but clean. He wore a white T-shirt with an American flag across the front and several thin bands of different colors around his left wrist.

His posture was good. An odd thing to notice, and maybe she wouldn't have except for the incongruity between the dignified stance of his body and the downward tilt of his head. It was as if his body were determined to own the dignity his head was denied.

The boy's eyes shifted from her to the floor, twice down the hall, and then back to her again.

"Hi," Letty said after half a minute passed, and the boy still said nothing.

His left hand crossed his face and swept back the lock of hair. He took a step into the room. The boy entered with caution, or maybe it was uncertainty. "Hi," he said, in a voice as subtle as his being.

"Who are you?" she asked, not warmly, but without much frost.

"Brett Holloway. What's your name?"

After a breath, she said, "Letty Norris."

"My dad sent me to get this for you," the boy said, lifting the backpack a little, displaying what he meant. "I'm supposed to put it in here without making any noise and make sure none of the animals are bothering you. Are you allergic to cats or dogs?"

"No." Letty scanned the room again in search of a pet. She didn't see so much as a single hair. Turning her attention back to the boy, Letty couldn't help but smile a little at the way he was setting her ragged old backpack on the floor near the wall, all gentle, like it was an expensive piece of luggage.

"It's all right. I'm awake now." She softened her tone as she studied him. His movements were graceful, fluid, yet restrained, a summer breeze in a basement room.

The boy straightened and shifted to face her, though his eyes still struggled to hold hers. "My dad said he found you up on the ridge. You were asleep when he carried you in. Are you sick?"

Yes. Sick had more than one meaning, however, and she knew to which the boy referred, so she replied in all honesty. "No. I just haven't slept in a while."

"Eaten either, I suppose." He glanced at her body, toward her eyes, and then shifted his glance back to the floor. "You look…hungry."

When her mother commented on the weight she'd lost, it aggravated the hell out of her. From the boy, it was more an observation, and his face showed concern rather than condemnation. That, along with his timid poise, made it hard to get irritated.

"Did you like the sandwich?"

"Yes, thanks," Letty said. "I'm too full to finish it, but it was good."

"I didn't make it. My dad did."

His dad. Must be the big guy, the bully. "Oh," she said, taking into consideration the man was the boy's father. "Well, he makes good peanut butter and jelly sandwiches."

"He should. He gets enough practice. We eat a lot of them. Here," Brett said, going to the nightstand. "I'll wrap it up, and you can finish it later if you want."

He took the plate and covered it with the wrinkled plastic wrap. "Out on a cliff is a funny place to take a nap," he said, slanting a look her way.

In his eyes shone a hint of knowing. The boy was young, but he wasn't stupid. He was aware something wasn't right. At least he was tactful enough not to press. A thread of worry wound through her at the example she'd set. What if he'd been standing there with his dad when she'd tried doing a swan dive off the cliff? At his age, small troubles could seem gigantic. Her solution had been a last resort for her, one she'd come up with on no sleep, no nutrition to speak of, and no real thought past the immediate future. The fact was she didn't really want to die. She'd just wanted the pain to stop.

Letty stared at the patchwork of pink covering her. "I was very tired."

"Good." The voice too big for indoors boomed from the doorway as the big man entered. He glanced at the half-eaten sandwich on the plate Brett still held, his approval souring to a glare as he stepped into the room.

His heavy boots clunked loud on the wooden floor, and his stern bearing filled the room too delicate for such an authoritarian presence. He took another step, this one quiet as his boots landed on one of the braided rugs. Thumbs tucked through his belt loops, he stood as if he were king of all he surveyed. Letty had a disconcerting feeling he was including her in his kingdom.

Letty gazed up at the man who, for better or worse, had saved her life. His skin had the weathered appearance of a man who worked outdoors. Suntanned lines etched in his clean face, muscles testing the seams on the rolled-up sleeves of his flannel shirt. He was solid but not fat. Powerful, in more ways than his physical might, if his display of arrogance was any indication.

In his father's presence, Brett's shoulders lost some of their starch. The boy said nothing, but then something akin to defiance flickered across Brett's face before his head tipped downward again.

Like his son, the big man's hair was bronze, but it was much shorter and salted by his years. Their faces both had the same defined bone structure, the same shape of lips, thinner on top than on the bottom, and the same straight nose. But where the father was an unbendable oak, the son was a mere sapling, fragile, green, susceptible to the elements.

****

Cole took a quick glance around the room and gave an inward sigh.

Frilly curtains floated about the sash window to his right; a lace-covered table served as a nightstand beside a bed covered in pink and pink and pink. Several times in recent months, he'd considered redecorating this room. This was a house of two males, and it was way too feminine a room. Then again, so was the bedroom he slept in every night. He hadn't been able to change that either, though he had no doubt it would be for the best.

To continue hoping his ex-wife would return was irrational and more than embarrassing to a man who valued his pride. Danielle had made it quite clear she would not be coming back. After almost two years, though, he still wasn't ready to believe her.

Turning his attention, Cole focused again on the young woman sitting upright in his guest bed. Her stormy blue eyes were on him, haunted, angry, appearing too large in her gaunt face. In the voluminous folds of the comforter, she didn't look any thicker than a drawing of a stick person. The girl needed to get some weight on her, and soon.

With the quilt his ex-wife had sewn gathered around her tiny waist, she looked like a neglected child, bony, breakable, too vulnerable to be out in the world all alone. Hell, she wasn't much bigger than his son. He fought off the sudden and prodding worry that someday Brett would be so troubled he might want to end his life. The thought was far too horrible, so he crushed it like an enemy and flung it into the pit of nonexistence where it belonged.

Losing Danielle had almost finished him. Losing his son would complete the job. For that instant, though, thinking of life without his boy, his only child, Cole could understand the kind of torment that would drive a person to suicide.

"I'm glad to see you put something in your stomach," Cole told her, though he still frowned. "Otherwise, I was going to have to drive you to the hospital, and I hate those places. Brett, give the plate back to her," he said without looking at his son. "I want you to eat the rest."

Though Letty had finished just half the sandwich, her insides bulged as if she'd eaten three. Her stomach had shrunk over the previous weeks, and it took much less to fill her. Brett handed her the plate, but she held up her hand to block it.

"Thank you, but I'm full."

"On that?" Cole asked with no attempt to mask his incredulity. "A squirrel could eat more."

"Then give it to a squirrel. I *said* I was full."

Cole cast her a brief stare and then set the topic aside for the moment. He had issues of more importance to take up with the girl. Frankly, he was glad she'd eaten at least as much as she had. He meant what he'd said about taking her to town if she didn't eat. They might well end up there anyway. He would avoid it as long as he deemed it safe.

On the walk home, in her sleep, she had snuggled childlike in his arms. She'd looked so helpless, so alone. The thought of her in a cold, sterile hospital sent a chill up his spine.

The way she was now, small and snippy, the girl reminded Cole of an injured animal. He'd seen his fair share, living way out here. He'd taken care of them, too. Hell, old Ray Shriver, the town's vet since forever, had probably paid off his house from all the bills Cole had paid over the years for the treatment of some animal or another.

He should have at least called Leon, the sheriff of Pine Bluff. The town down the mountain was just big enough for a sheriff and a handful of officers. Cole trusted Leon. They'd gone to school together, been friends most of their lives. But he didn't call the sheriff. First, he would know what he was dealing with. If the girl was in some sort of trouble, he might be able to help her. Helping would be a whole lot easier now than if she got into the system. Before he could help her, though, he had to get her to talk.

"You ready to tell me your name yet?" Cole asked.

Brett looked up at his father, innocent and knowing. "Her name is Letty Norris."

They both flashed a glare toward Brett, his father's mingled with exasperation, and the boy cringed.

"Brett, go put the rest of her sandwich in the kitchen."

"Yes, sir," Brett said and then pivoted.

"Hey," Letty said when the boy was almost to the door. He glanced back over his shoulder, an apology in his eyes.

"Thanks. You're a good guy."

Brett's lips curved into a smile. Letty surprised Cole by smiling back at his son.

"After you put that away," Cole told Brett. "You get back to your homework."

The boy nodded and left the room.

No sooner was Brett out of sight than their plump, golden tabby strolled into the room. His yellow eyes gleamed. Part of his right ear was missing, and an inch-long scar crossed his head where fur would never grow again. The cat entered the room without any trepidation whatsoever. His impassive expression held a trace of curiosity.

"Out, Spencer," Cole said. His voice was harsh, but when he lifted the cat and turned him away, he was gentle with the animal. The cat curved its body around the doorway and left, his tail straight up in the air.

"Well, Letty," Cole said, facing her again. "I'm Cole Holloway. That was my son, Brett, in case he forgot to make a proper introduction. Is there someone I can call for you? At least let them know you're okay, maybe your mother or your father?"

Letty shook her head before shifting her glance to look out the window. "I don't want to speak to my mother."

"What about your father?"

Letty's eyes filled with tears, but she managed to

blink them away before they fell. A dour laugh slipped out ahead of her soft words. "No, not my father."

"You want to tell me why you tried to kill yourself?"

Her face hardened, and she swung a glare toward him. "No. Look, I'm sorry if I disrupted your day. I'll be going now, and I won't bother you again." She threw the quilt aside, but before she could get up, Cole was beside the bed, blocking her way more with his presence than with the application of gentle pressure to her shoulder.

"You're not well enough to go anywhere," Cole said.

"I'm fine," Letty said, but she couldn't quite meet his eyes when she said it.

Cole yanked the blanket back over her, took a step back, and slipped his thumbs through his belt loops again. "I'm not going to let you walk out of here all by yourself."

Fire flared in her eyes, and she spat her words. "You can't keep me here. That's like kidnapping or something. It's illegal."

"So is suicide. You want to call the sheriff and see which one of us gets hauled away?"

Letty's head drew back, and her mouth dropped open enough to see the straight lines of her teeth. "You would do that? You would have me arrested?"

No, he wasn't going to see her taken away by the law. Nor could he allow her to walk out his door when she might well go straight out to that cliff again or find another one or another method to end her life. Blackmailing her with the threat of arrest sounded like the best way to keep her safe.

"I'll make you a deal," Cole said, tempering his stance with a softer tone in hopes of gaining some ground. "You stay here and rest for a couple of weeks; get your strength back, and then you can leave without fear of being arrested. My word." With any luck, by then, he'd find a family member or a friend to come and get her.

Letty didn't like him, not one little bit. It was obvious in her shifting scowl, the way she must have been searching her brain for an escape. It was Cole's good fortune to not care whether she liked him or not. As her head made a small swivel from left to right and then back again, they made brief eye contact. She yanked away first, angry but cornered into his care.

Cole resisted the urge to smile at her childlike frown. She made him think of Brett whenever he was called away from something he wanted to do and ordered to get his chores done. Her frown might well be about to deepen, as he wasn't finished with her yet.

"Another question and I want the truth," Cole said, pinning her with a steady gaze. "How old are you?"

Letty released a hefty sigh. "Twenty-two."

"Do you have any illnesses?"

"Why would you ask such a thing?"

"You're staying here, under my roof, with my son," he said, assuming he'd won the discussion about her staying with them. "I have a right to know a few things about you."

Her response was accompanied by a narrow-eyed glare and plenty of attitude. "No diseases. I'm perfectly healthy."

He shot her a dubious look.

Letty rolled her eyes, this time sighing into a

slouch. "I know I'm a little underweight. That's all, though. Honest."

Cole nodded. "Okay. Where do you live?"

She huffed, getting ready for some more arguing, he assumed. But what little verve the girl had worked up on ire and half a peanut butter and jelly sandwich was fizzling. "I live in Nevada."

"Do you have any weapons or drugs in that bag?" Cole asked, nodding at her backpack.

She looked him in the eye and answered without hesitation. "No. I don't have any weapons, and I don't do drugs, never have."

Cole relaxed a little, feeling better in his decision to keep the girl at his house. Not because he was worried about her being a minor or any of the other things he'd questioned her about. He'd already given a thorough search to her backpack and knew the answer to almost every question he'd asked.

The first thing he found was her wallet zipped into one of the inside pockets. Most of the information he sought came from her driver's license. He knew she lived in Las Vegas, Nevada. He knew Letty was short for Loretta. And he already knew her age. He knew she didn't have any drugs or weapons in her backpack, and her cash supply totaled ninety-two dollars and change. She had one credit card. Whether it was maxed or not, he hadn't a clue. What made Cole feel better about the situation was the girl hadn't lied.

Cole nodded as if he had taken her word. No point in losing trust before he could gain it.

"All right. Fine. You rest. The bathroom is across the hall. If you're feeling up to it, you can come down to the table for dinner. If not, Brett will bring your plate up here." Cole turned and left the room without waiting for a response. One wasn't required.

Walking at a slow pace toward the stairs, Cole passed by the linen closet and stopped at the closed door on the other side of the hall. His son's room.

A vertical sign hung from the doorknob reading *Brett's Room*. Pictures of racecars, animated and whimsical, surrounded the bulbous words of varying colors. The sign had hung there since he was five. Brett celebrated his twelfth birthday a few months back. Cole had the unsettling feeling any time now, his son would notice the forgotten sign and realize he'd outgrown it. Thinking about it put an ache in his heart and kept him lingering outside his son's door.

Secured to the middle of the door with a blue thumbtack hung another sign. This one was thin, laminated, and without frivolity. The black print on a white background read, *No Parents Allowed*. Cole didn't know where it came from or when it had gone up on the door. He'd first seen it a couple of weeks ago. The sign irritated him, but he'd allow the boy to keep it. The door didn't have a lock, and they both knew no sign or closed door would keep him from entering his son's room if he wanted to go in there. He'd tolerate Brett's silent shout of rebellion, but he would not acknowledge it.

Music played a little too loud on the other side of the door. Some of that god-awful music his boy was so fond of lately. Alternative music, heavy metal, some other classifications Brett had referred to, but Cole couldn't remember. To Cole, it all sounded like music designed to annoy parents. When the hell did screaming into a microphone become a talent? A pissed-off bear was more melodic.

Cole rested his hands on his hips and shook his head. Melancholy tugged on him again. It wasn't so long ago Brett was listening to children's songs and welcomed his father into his room. Kids grew and changed. It was normal. Cole hated change, though, which didn't bode well for Brett's upcoming teenage years.

Brett was supposed to be doing his homework. He wasn't allowed to play any kind of music while studying, and the boy well knew it. After placing his hand on the doorknob for a few seconds, Cole let his hand drop. Maybe Brett was cleaning his room before he got busy with his studies. More likely, he was reading something from his stack of comic books. But he would give his son the benefit of the doubt today. He wasn't up to another confrontation with a youth.

Cole's feet dropped heavily as he descended the stairs, his boots making muffled thuds on the royal blue carpet. He hated royal blue. It was as elitist a color as there ever was. Every time he walked over the carpeting Danielle had chosen, he had to fight off the decorous urge to take off his shoes, lest he upset the queen. He would change out that carpet someday.

After a brief stop in the kitchen for a cold bottle of beer, Cole strolled out to his front porch and sat on the swing he'd hung years ago with sturdy chains, all done for his wife's birthday, and acted like he was watching the birds at the feeders. He feigned interest in the scampering squirrels. He pretended to look over his land, searching for anything out of place, anything needing his attention. Cole had gotten very good at this pathetic routine of fakery.

Yesterday, he'd said it was the last time he would gaze down toward the short stretch of dirt road that for some bureaucratic reason was never paved, watching for the rising trail of dust kicked up by the rare car heading toward his driveway. He'd repeat the same falsehood again today. Why would this day be any different from all the other days since his wife put a suitcase in the trunk of her car and drove away?

Yet, no matter the want, he couldn't let go of the belief that someday Danielle would come home.

Early October exhaled a cool but tender breath across Cole's beloved patch of the world, stirring twigs and early-fallen foliage into a short-lived swirl. The air was still mild, but the daytime temperatures had dropped a few degrees, quite a few more at night.

Random scatterings of ash and maple leaves were well into their turn. Reds and oranges and every shade of gold hung from branches like Christmas ornaments, glowing when the sun hit them at particular angles. A small portion of the leaves had already finished their lives on this earth and crunched beneath his boots on his walks. And his vibrant, pacifying fields of poppies, daisies, and primrose were packing for their trip to seed.

Most people claimed spring as their favorite season; some would say summer. Cole always believed fall was by far the best of the four. The land was colorful, refreshing, yet at the same time settling. The crispness in the air wasn't yet severe enough to be uncomfortable, and the inevitable bitter cold of winter was still far enough away so as not to plague him. But winter was on its way.

Winter in Montana could be brutal—subzero

temperatures, icy roads, and snow drifts as high as the house. Even then, however, his land had a bounty of beauty and fun to offer. Everything covered in rolling layers of white, very little of it soiled by the vulgarities of mankind. The season could be brutal, but its splendor was undeniable.

He and his son enjoyed snowshoeing beneath the frosted tree branches, drinking hot chocolate at the window, watching deer eat the feed they'd leave out to attract them.

He'd be indoors quite a bit more. That's what set his dread to a slow burn now. The sun would set earlier, come up later. Sometimes winter's wind bit right through the layers of clothing on the short walk to his pole barn, where he'd spend his days making adjustments and repairs to machinery, readying for spring. Winter meant more time confined with his thoughts. The what-ifs and regrets could suffocate a man when he didn't spend enough time outside where they could air out some.

Before Danielle left, the three of them had always built a monster of a snowman in the front yard, coal for eyes with a carrot for a nose, corncob pipe, branches for arms, a broom in the twigs of his fingers, the whole shebang.

The annual tradition took place after the first heavy snow had begun when Brett was no more than a toddler. Danielle always wrapped a thick scarf around the snowman's neck, telling Brett it was so the snowman wouldn't get cold. Brett accepted the explanation with ease, the way a child's innocence allowed belief in such things.

Cole hadn't thought about the snowman since

she'd left. It was one of many casualties of the divorce, though he couldn't say why the snowman. Maybe this year, he and Brett would build one again. Maybe it was time.

Maybe it would make Danielle smile if she came back during winter.

He gazed across the mowed lawn rolled out broad and long in front of his house, still green, still lush even as the season was fading. Cole pictured the thick blanket of delicate white crystals coming to cover the land in the not-too-distant future.

In his mind, he could see the footprints of man, woman, and child around three stacked balls of snow. The ghosts of their laughter haunted his ears. Was his boy getting too old to enjoy such things? Cole had a hard time picturing the Brett of today laughing about a silly snowman.

Time. It moved too fast and took too much.

Cole finished his beer with no memory of having drunk it. He breathed in deep with all his senses, the gentle creak of the porch swing, the day's last chirps and flights of the birds, the faint rustling of leaves in the evening breeze cooling his skin, the doleful scent of yet another dying season.

Darkness lowered on the day. The sun spread out the last of its deep golden rays over the elevations of his eighty acres as if to cling to the earth a little longer.

Sunset used to be his favorite time of the day. After dinner, until the weather turned too cold, Danielle would sit on the swing with a magazine, glancing up now and then to smile as her husband and child played catch until it was too dark to see the ball.

After they put Brett to bed, he and Danielle would

each have a beer and sit out on the swing together, discussing the farm, their son, laying out plans for all of the tomorrows ahead of them. Often, they'd sit in companionable silence, at peace, his arm around her sturdy shoulders. Danielle was a little on the large side for a woman, but Cole liked that in a woman. Whenever she complained about her weight, talked about going on some kind of diet she'd read about, he discouraged it. Danielle was perfect just the way she was, and he didn't want her to change.

The sun dipped a little more. His irrational hopes followed suit.

No matter how hard he tried, Cole could never scroll back through his memories to spot one single sign that anything in their marriage was amiss. If he knew what had gone wrong, if he'd said or done something to set her off so he could fix it. He was sure he could. They'd had a good life together, a wonderful life. Danielle had been happy. She really *did* seem happy.

Back then, when things were at their best, she didn't care for painted nails or painted lips. Unless they were going out somewhere special, she didn't put on any makeup at all. She didn't need any of that stuff. Cole had told her so many times, and she always appeared to be pleased by his comments. He'd never said it for the sake of flattery, though after seeing her blush, he found it was a nice bonus. Still, it was the truth. Up until those last few months, Danielle was never fancy, but she was always pretty.

His wife enjoyed farm life. She'd grown up with such a life, and she was as strong and as capable as any woman he'd ever known. That's not to say she wasn't feminine. Danielle had the face of an angel. Her large green eyes never ceased to captivate him. She had a smile brilliant enough to catch the attention of a blind man. Cole never for one minute forgot how lucky he was to have her up on the mountain with him. And he saw to it his wife didn't want for anything.

She enjoyed cooking. Well, baking. She made the best cakes and cookies he'd ever eaten. Sometimes she'd decorate things with a variety of frosting tools. However, with foods outside of the dessert category, it was kind of hit and miss.

One time for her birthday, he bought her a set of cookbooks. For some reason, she took it as an insult. They ate frozen dinners for a week after. To this day, he never knew if she made any of the recipes. Her cooking did improve some, not that it had ever been terrible. The table held decent food every night. He had his wife, his son, and a well-built home on his own land. Life was good.

Cole took a deep breath in through his nose and breathed out from his mouth. Sometimes he imagined he could still hear Danielle singing along with the radio, puttering around the house while waiting for some sweet treat to come out of the oven. He imagined her upstairs, taking her bubble bath, getting into one of her simple nightgowns, shutting off the light, and then slipping into bed beside him.

As if no more than a day had passed since her leaving, he remembered the soft warmth of her skin against his. She always welcomed his love. She never ever turned him away, never showed so much as a hint of resistance or displeasure. In fact, his wife was an enthusiastic player in their lovemaking and often was the initiator. Afterward, she always slept in his arms as if she was happy to be there.

Cole wished Danielle would hurry up and sow her wild oats and come home. He was tired of missing her.

He had plenty of things to do, with a houseful of situations requiring his attention. He needed to make sure his son was getting his homework done. He needed to put something together for dinner. He had to figure out what he was going to do about his houseguest. He needed to do anything, anything at all besides sit there like a horse's ass, waiting for a woman who'd had enough of being a wife and a mother and fled to greener pastures.

Blinking his eyes, Cole found he was sitting in the dark, with no visible moon, to help with his game of pretend. Still, he stared into the cooling night. Quieter than it had been, as it was too chilly for crickets. Then the rattle and grunt of a leopard frog hauled him back to the matters at hand.

Cole got to his feet and stood still on his porch for a moment, the swing bumping into the backs of his knees, stopping its movement, stopping the steady creak that had hypnotized him.

After one last look through the thick darkness settled all around him, he walked into the house and closed the door. He didn't turn the lock. Maybe it didn't even work anymore. Cole didn't know. When Danielle had walked out, she'd left her house key on the kitchen counter. He hadn't locked the front door in almost two years.

Chapter 3

While the woman entertained Brett and Letty, Cole's neck was getting an ache from stiffening every time he subdued a cringe. Teresa set down a plate of chocolate chip cookies, still warm from the oven, on the kitchen table where Brett sat beside Letty. Teresa then swung back to the counter to scoop more balls of dough onto a baking sheet.

Letty wore her hair in some kind of fancy braid that made her look even younger than her age. Brett flicked the hanging part of the braid, and she swatted at his hand, both of them laughing the whole time.

The cookies smelled wonderful. Cole, however, stayed where he was, leaning against the counter. Their dogs, Burt, at least half golden retriever, and a smaller, sweet mutt of a dog with brown and white speckles, named Scotty, sat on either side of him. If Teresa knew how much he loved her cookies, she'd give him those ridiculous puppy eyes again, this time with a sated smile, and he'd cringe himself into a neck brace for sure.

In his mind, he referred to Teresa Staten as the widow Staten. The name made her sound too old, especially since she was three years his junior. Her husband Teddy had passed away almost five years ago of a heart attack. He'd been sixty pounds overweight, and his cholesterol was through the roof. After twenty-some years of Teresa's cooking, Cole could understand why. The official cause of Teddy's death should have been "murder by food."

The way she was always shoving her goods down his throat made Cole wonder if the woman was aiming to make him her next husband. He'd suspected such for a while. Or, considering the kinds of food she came over and cooked every Sunday, her next *late* husband.

Teresa was a nice enough woman, decent, thoughtful. Kind of pretty, he supposed, the way she kept her rich brown hair curled about her roundish, pleasant face. She was a bit on the heavy side, and she was aware of how Cole was drawn to a little excess on a woman. The way she so often referenced her size, he was sure Teresa figured it gave her an edge.

But Cole wasn't looking for another wife, since he was still fool enough to be waiting for the first woman he married to come home.

Teresa ran on at the mouth as if paid by the word. What was worse, most of what she had to say was repetitive and irrelevant to anything about which he cared. He once saw her puttering around a cluster of bird feeders, and he could swear she chattered a poor little hummingbird into a coma.

Brett bit into a cookie with all the relish it deserved. The chips hadn't yet hardened, and one left a small chocolate glob on his lower lip. Letty laughed and wiped it off with a napkin. His son, though he acted disgruntled at the motherly act, appeared to enjoy the attention from Letty. The two had become fast friends over the last couple of days. Since he still didn't know much about the girl, Cole wasn't sure how he felt about their blooming friendship.

"So then I said to Bradford," Teresa continued, swiveling toward Letty so she could clarify. "Bradford owns and operates the smaller of the two markets in town. I said, Bradford, why don't you keep another checker on at this time of day? It's always busy. Well, he said the rush hour doesn't last for more than forty minutes or so, and he couldn't see any sense in paying someone to be there for a little spurt of business."

Teresa paused to take a breath, and Cole savored the moment of silence. It was a big one since it was her habit to talk until she wrung the last of the air from her lungs. Sometimes she almost didn't make it, and the ends of her sentences were painful to hear.

Teresa had refueled with another deep inhale and slid the plate of cookies to the edge of the table, in Cole's direction. She added a few drops of sweetener to her voice with a fair-sized pinch of flirtation.

"Won't you have one, Cole? They're fresh out of the oven."

He broke. The damn things smelled too good. Cole gave her a slight nod and a slighter smile before taking a cookie. As he feared, it was delicious. He tried hard not to say so, but he appeared to have no choice. Teresa was staring at him as if he held the secret to eternal joy, and he was about to share it. Brett and Letty slanted wary looks his way, as if he might be so tactless as to hurt her feelings if he didn't like it.

"Delicious," Cole said.

Teresa beamed, gave him a shy "thank you" and those puppy-dog eyes he'd dreaded, before getting back in the groove of her mild tirade.

"Now, where was I? Oh, right, so I stood in line, fuming, of course, because I wanted to get these cookies baked before I made dinner. Oh, I know you all shouldn't be eating cookies before dinner, and I won't have you spoiling my meal, so you can't have any more than one each, just to whet your appetite. It's fried chicken tonight with green beans, dinner rolls; I made some of that cinnamon butter you like, Cole. Oh, and fried potatoes," she said, wiping her hands on her red-and-white checked apron as if they were already greasy.

Teresa faced Letty and said with lifted brows and a knowing smile, "Fried chicken is one of Cole's favorite dishes."

Cole hated fried chicken, especially Teresa's. It was more grease than bird, and he was going to taste it throughout the night. He'd eat it. It had to be better than the garbage he put on the table every night.

Brett and Letty sure looked pleased with the prospect of having something besides the hunks of the shoe leather and hard baked potatoes he called dinner. All Letty had eaten last night was a few bites of her potato and the scraps of iceberg lettuce in a bowl he called a salad.

A month or so after Danielle had left, Teresa started coming over on Sundays to make dinner for them. She stopped by at least one other day during the week to drop off a pie or a cake, sometimes cookies. Cole appreciated it. He did. But sometimes he wondered if it was worth the cost to his sanity, as well as to his arteries.

Cole had to sidestep to get out of Teresa's path as she passed by him on her way to the oven to check on her batch of cookies. The woman was always finding ways to get close to him, or touch him. Sometimes, if no one was around, her moves were awfully close to obvious.

Cole broke the rest of his cookie in half and gave the pieces to each of his dogs, careful that they didn't get any of the chocolate as it was harmful to them. Then, in a covert motion, he shifted his attention to Letty.

She and Brett were whispering and giggling like brother and sister. It was good to see her smile. Brett too, thinking about it now. His gaze changed to focus on his son.

The difference in his boy struck him hard. How long had it been since the house had been blessed with Brett's boisterous laughter? Cole hadn't realized what a somber child he had become until just now. The stark contrast between this evening and the long string of days of the previous two years was stunning.

Brett used to be so playful. To his son, everything was a joy. Everything was fun, interesting. It all changed after his mother left, though Cole couldn't say for sure if it had been a gradual change or all at once. Shame dragged his head downward. His own misery had so immersed him, he'd not taken fair notice of his son's.

After a moment, Cole shifted his gaze from his work-scuffed boots back to Brett's face. For again, his son was laughing. The sound was loud, pure, and bursting with delight, the way a kid was supposed to sound. Cole looked to his houseguest. She was laughing, too.

The first full day Letty was with them, Brett had visited her room twice. Cole didn't know what they'd talked about, but both of them had ended the day happier than they'd begun it. Both being young, having pain, they shared some degree of vulnerability.

It was obvious they took comfort in each other's presence. They could be siblings in any house with the teasing and the silliness. To watch them now, no one would guess they were one child mourning the loss of his mother, and another who two days before had almost ended her life by jumping off a cliff.

Teresa pointed a finger at Letty. "Now, there will be plenty of food, and I want you to have extra. Lord, you look like one of those Hollywood girls, all bones and nonsense." Then Teresa walked by and patted the girl's head.

Cole prepared for an outburst. Letty's defensive attitude would not let such a comment slide. In Cole's short experience with the girl, he found she took offense at the slightest personal remark. But no retort came. In fact, Letty's face lit with amusement, and then she let out a peal of laughter. Brett joined in right away.

Well, how about that? The girl had about jumped down his throat when he'd wanted her to stay at his house and get some rest. Teresa referred to her as "bones and nonsense," patted her head like a dog, and got a laugh. Well, hell. If he lived a hundred years, he'd never understand the female mind.

Teresa had taken to their guest the instant they met. Teresa had a generous soul and was a natural nurturer. Maybe such was an attribute with which only women were born. For as soon as Teresa had seen Letty, she hovered about the girl, talking to her like a loving aunt. It was as if Teresa sensed Letty's inner distress, sensed an urgency, and set about to do what needed doing.

Cole shifted a covert glance at Teresa. Mothering came naturally to the woman. It appeared to him Letty liked and trusted her the same as Brett always had. Cole wondered if he should warn the girl to guard her arteries.

All he'd told Teresa about Letty was she was a distant relative who had come to stay for a while. Teresa accepted the foggy explanation without question. Of course, it was rare Teresa questioned anything Cole told her. Such was a quality he should appreciate, but in regard to Teresa, it dulled her colors.

"I'm going to look for Spencer, get that cat inside before it gets dark," Cole said, as Teresa got the chicken from the refrigerator and prepared to give it a grease bath.

Teresa was the only one who paid attention to his leaving. She gave him what he supposed she believed was a seductive smile. He sent her back a curt nod and fled, the two dogs trotting along with him. He wandered around the outside of the pole barn with the dogs, only half looking for Spencer. The cat always came to the door around dinnertime on his own.

****

"I'll help you fix dinner," Letty told Teresa as she jumped from her seat. For two days she'd done nothing but eat and rest, so she was feeling better. Besides, after working in the kitchen with her mother all these years, she was more than capable of putting together a meal. She was great with side dishes, which to her was the meal since she didn't eat animals or anything that came from them.

Obvious reluctance slowed Teresa's hustle. Letty glanced at Brett for confirmation as to why, but she had eyes and ears, and she didn't need an explanation. Brett had already told her how Teresa was trying to get something going with his dad. It was clear she strove to be the woman of the house, and since she wasn't, Teresa might have some misgivings about someone else cooking part of the meal. No woman wanted another to outdo her in front of the man she's trying to impress.

After winking at Brett, Letty said with a weak shrug and her hands held up in a helpless gesture, "I'd like to feel useful."

The muscles in Teresa's face relaxed, and a breath huffed through her fresh smile. "How are you with vegetables?"

Letty beamed back. "They're my specialty."

For the next hour, Letty and Brett peeled potatoes and cleaned green beans while Teresa handled the chicken. Letty rummaged through the spices and, while she preferred fresh, found everything she needed to jazz up her dishes.

At the dinner table, a bout of silliness overcame Letty, and she made funny faces at Brett until he laughed. He was awkward in the way most kids are at that age, with parts of him growing faster than other parts. Letty liked the way his teeth had grown a pace ahead of his face. It made his smile broad and electric. Brett's ears shared the same growth spurt as his mouth. His head was still working to catch up with the rest of him.

"Stop feeding the animals at the table," Cole said to Brett when he caught his son tossing chicken to Spencer the cat and the two mixed-breed dogs.

"You do," Brett said.

"I pay the bills around here. I can feed anyone I want," Cole said. Brett didn't respond. Then, chewing his food, Cole looked around the table from his seat at the head. His son sat to his right, Teresa to his left. Letty sat beside Teresa. He stopped with a frown when his eyes rested on Letty's place.

"There's no meat on your plate," he said, hard eyes meeting hers.

"I'm vegan."

"Vegan?" he asked, scowling as if already knowing he wouldn't like the answer. "What the hell does that mean?"

"It means I don't eat anything that comes from animals."

"You don't... You..." Cole's fork made a clank on his plate, which then budged forward by the quick thrust of his crossed arms when he leaned toward Letty. The white tablecloth scrunched up before him. A fold curled and almost rolled over the edge of his plate and into his roasted potatoes. Cole's scowl deepened. "No wonder you're so damn skinny. How can you live that way?"

Letty held the gaze of the man she'd come to believe was more bark than bite, and clung to her core beliefs. "I live quite well and with a clean conscience. Do you have any idea what life is like for animals bred and raised for slaughter? Factory farms are hell on earth for animals. It's horrific; their lives are full of pain, fear, and deprivation. They're treated as if they have no feelings, like they're inanimate objects. Then they die a gruesome death. They suffer, beginning to end. I won't be a part of it."

"So you just don't eat any meat? None at all?"

"Or seafood, or dairy." Letty set her fork down, too, and looked Cole right in the eye. "And you can't make me." She waited for and got the inevitable question, the one every vegan gets about a million times.

"What about your protein?"

She had her answer ready, as she'd answered the question more times than she could count. "Protein is not a problem for vegans. Nuts, seeds, nut butter, leafy greens, a wide assortment of beans, legumes, tofu, quinoa, oatmeal, flax seeds, peas, almond milk. Should I go on? There's more."

Cole's frown deepened. "Aw hell, look, if—"

"If what, I want to pay someone to torture animals?"

"Letty—"

The building tension at the table diffused when a green bean bounced off Letty's chin. Everyone at the table turned to a giggling Brett. Two seconds later a green bean slapped his forehead. He already had another bean in his hand ready to throw back at Letty when his father bellowed, "That's enough!"

Facing his son, outraged at such behavior at the dinner table, Cole opened his mouth, no doubt to swing a tirade of another branch. Before he could utter a sound, a green bean hit his forehead with a light thud and then fell onto his lap.

Silence struck the room.

Brett sank back into his seat with his mouth agape, his eyes even wider than his mouth. Teresa paled as if she was about to faint. For a long minute, Cole stared down at the bean lying on the leg of his jeans—the one Letty had thrown. Then, in slow motion, he raised his astonished glare to Letty.

"Sorry," Letty said, but the word lacked sincerity as she was struggling not to laugh when she said it.

"That was meant for Brett."

The act was so brazen, it stunned Cole silent. Letty couldn't help it. And it wasn't like she started the food toss. Brett was the one who pressed her silly button. Cole shifted his stare across the table. Teresa and his son were staring at their plates as if the secrets of the universe were hiding in the potatoes.

"Finish your dinners," Cole said, his voice a growl, flashing a sharp scan across the others. He set the wayward bean on the table before sliding his plate back and picking up his fork.

The foursome went back to eating, Letty, Brett, and now Teresa suppressing giggles. Letty glanced over at Cole and, though she couldn't swear to it, thought maybe he was doing the same.

"Those braids are awful pretty," said Teresa after a few quiet minutes passed.

Letty lifted a hand to touch one of the French braids running back on both sides of her head. "Thanks. Brett did it for me."

Cole's attention flashed to his son in disbelief. Quietly, almost with caution, he said, "You did that? Where did you learn to braid hair?"

Brett kept his eyes on his plate, scooting a chunk of potato around with his fork. He shrugged. Then, as if he knew without seeing his father's expression more was expected, he said, "I guess I saw some girls doing it at school."

The silence in the room took on weight.

"There's nothing wrong with a boy doing hair," Letty said.

Cole ignored her. He was staring at his son as if he didn't quite know him.

When the silence continued, when Brett hunched over his plate, looking ready to crawl under the table, Teresa dropped a spoon full of potatoes onto Cole's plate. "Aren't these potatoes delicious, Cole?" Teresa said. "Letty made them."

Letty caught the drift. "Yeah, it's polite to give the cook a compliment if you like something. You do like them, don't you?"

After another still moment, Cole dragged his gaze from his son to his plate. When he found his voice, he said, "They're very good, Letty."

Eventually, Teresa was able to coax more conversation from Cole, and the dinner picked up where it left off, with Teresa laughing too loud at even a hint of humor from Cole. She was too attentive, too responsive. Whenever Cole was speaking, Teresa hung on his every word by a rope she quite obviously strove to use as a lasso.

He kept polite, but holding back, ducking said rope with the same adamancy with which it was thrown. Teresa's eagerness and ever-adoring looks grew bolder. Cole squirmed in his chair a little. The poor woman was trying so hard to win him over she was defeating her own purpose. Letty didn't know who deserved more of her pity, Teresa for her over-the-top tactics, or Cole for being subjected to them.

She glanced across the table at Brett. When he had her attention, he made a funny face, which she returned. Teresa talked on, pausing when she had to take a breath or ask Cole's opinion. Cole gave her courteous nods, spoke when necessary, and fed more food from his plate to the two dogs and the cat who knew the best place to sit at dinnertime.

The glass chandelier shed soft light over the plates, and bowls, and food. All of it atop the embroidered white-on-white tablecloth Letty had helped Teresa lay over the dining table in the room off the kitchen. Teresa had told her she'd grown up with Sunday dinners being special and it was a tradition she liked to keep.

Letty and her mom usually worked on Sundays. If not catering an event, then cleaning up and reorganizing from one they'd worked the night before. This group, this family setting, was nice. Very nice.

Inserted into the champagne-colored wall of the dining room was a large rectangle of a window. Gold ropes held open the silvery white, floor-length drapes. Letty and Teresa faced it, but only Letty was looking out.

The sun had almost set. Thickening shadows stretched from the wilderness onto the neat lawn as night inched forward to swallow the day. The darkness crept toward her, relentless, bold, and unstoppable. Along the edges of its insistence, though, the light didn't so much wane, as it did rotate to the next turn, as if knowing its absence was only for a shift.

Letty looked around the table and had to smile at the picture they made. If someone were to peer in through the dining room window and see them, they would be the image of the perfect average American family, something out of a 1950's sitcom. Kids were giggling, the woman chatting and advising, the gruff old man who was feeding scraps of food to two dogs and a scarred yellow cat. By the looks of them, the laughter, the appetites, no one would guess such sadness lay in their pasts.

Brett had told her about his mother, how she had

up and left them two years before, how his father had been a miserable sort ever since. He'd told her how the man Teresa had been married to since a month after high school graduation had died, that she was lonely, and how she wanted Cole to take his place.

And of course, Letty had spent the last weeks ground under the monster boot of her own troubles. This evening, though, she'd been able to contain them to a manageable state.

Working in a kitchen had blessed Letty with a feeling of normalcy, and she enjoyed joking around with Cole's son. She liked him. Brett was a sweet kid. Smart, too, with a contagious laugh and a creative mind. They shared a love of books and talked about stories and characters. It was nice. Since she hadn't grown up with any siblings, Letty had gotten a taste of what it might be like to have a brother in her small family.

Family.

Emotions hit Letty like a hard-swung hammer, and for a moment, her lungs seized up on her. The others had risen and were gathering their plates and silverware. She squeezed her eyes shut and made a strong effort to force her thoughts in another direction. The last thing she wanted right now was to break down in front of them.

"Are you all right, sweetie?" Teresa asked.

Letty opened her eyes. The room had gone quiet, and all eyes were on her. Letty forced air into her lungs and then let it out. "I'm fine." She should offer them some kind of excuse, the way they were all looking at her, but she couldn't think of anything to say. So she stood up and carried her plate through the swinging door and into the kitchen.

Forty minutes later, Letty scanned a final look around the kitchen before draping the damp dishcloth over the sink divider. "Well, it looks like we got everything cleaned. I think I'll go upstairs and help Brett with his homework now."

"Sunday night. Nothing like waiting till the last minute," Teresa said, but the remark was spoken with a smile and no hint of reprimand. She wiped her hands on her apron one final time before untying it, folding it, and placing it in one of the canvas bags she'd brought with her sitting near the door.

"I think Cole went out front to sit on the porch swing. Brett told me you always go sit with him after dinner."

Teresa's longing gaze strayed toward the kitchen door which led to the front of the house. Teresa was a kind woman. When Cole wasn't around, she was quite pleasant, relaxed, and normal in her conversation. Her emotions led her astray when Cole was near her. Letty was all too familiar with emotions leading a person astray.

Letty slipped her fingers into the back pockets of her jeans. She'd put back a couple of pounds, but they were still too big; her belt was the only thing keeping them from falling down. Even still, they dropped a bit at her hips.

"You know, Teresa," Letty said. "Back home I knew this guy, Danny. I was so crazy about him I couldn't sleep at night for thinking about him."

Teresa smiled at her, and in an instant their relationship became less generational. Letty scooted out a chair and sat down, folding her hands in loose fashion on the kitchen table.

"Did you feel like you were always wearing your heart on your sleeve, making a fool of yourself at every turn?"

"Couldn't help it."

"Did you ever find out if Danny was thinking about you, too?" Teresa asked. The woman curved another lingering glance toward the front of the house.

"Yes, Danny was thinking about me, too. But I didn't find out until later."

Sliding into the chair across from Letty, Teresa said, "Go on."

"I tried everything to get his attention. I showed up at his house making lame excuses to be there. After finding out the places he liked to go, I would 'accidentally' run into him." She smiled and shook her head and rolled her eyes. "Often."

Letty gave a small, self-conscious laugh. Teresa chuckled in sympathy.

"Once he caught me in a sporting goods store, and I had to buy a stupid tennis racket so he wouldn't know why I was really there. It was so obvious. By then he knew me well enough to know I didn't play tennis. Yet the embarrassment didn't stop me from popping up again. I couldn't help myself."

Teresa tipped her head in commiseration. "Made a bit of a pest of yourself, did you?"

Letty chuckled. "A bit. But he didn't seem interested, and I got tired of feeling foolish, so I gave up. The funny thing was, once I shifted my interest elsewhere, all of a sudden, Danny was making excuses to be where I was. The shoe was on the other foot when I caught him in the lingerie department at Yander's."

Teresa's head fell back with the fullness of her laughter.

Letty laughed too, before saying, "He grabbed the closest hanger without looking at what was on it, you know, trying to look like he meant to be there. It was a crazy lacy bra with matching thong underwear. He actually said, 'Um, I'm just getting something for my mom's birthday.' "

The two women burst out laughing and continued until they wiped tears from their eyes. Teresa said, "And they say women are fickle. So did you get your guy?"

In an instant, Letty's heart crushed within her chest, but she managed to keep a smile on her face. She couldn't tell anyone, not ever. It was bad enough Danny and their mothers knew. She'd die of shame if anyone else found out the truth.

"Yes. I got him," Letty said, rubbing her palms on her jeans.

"Well, how about that."

Teresa took a moment's pause, thoughts crossing her face in full view. She stood up, straightened her blouse, and smoothed her skirt. Teresa nodded. With a firm jaw, she looked across the table before standing.

"Well, I'm rather tired tonight. I think I'll go home, watch a little TV, and turn in early. It was a pleasure to meet you, Letty. Will you be here next Sunday?"

"I think so," Letty said, standing up.

"Good." Teresa gave Letty a big hug. "I'll say goodbye to Cole on my way out."

"I enjoyed meeting you too, Teresa."

"I'll see you next week, sweetie." Teresa picked up her purse and the two canvas bags she had used to tote her goods, and made her way out the front.

****

At the sound of the front door opening, both lazing dogs lifted their heads, and Cole scooted over on the porch swing to make room for Teresa, as he always did. But her steps didn't even slow when she told him to take care and she would see him next Sunday.

She was halfway to her car before she glanced back to where he was sitting. Cole's shocked expression, when he'd already made room for her on the swing, when she'd always without exception sat with him after Sunday dinner, made her smile all the way home.

****

The sound of a closing car door traveled through the living room and into the kitchen, to where Letty had sunk back in her seat. Moments later, the sound was followed by the fading of an engine as Teresa drove away.

Did she get her guy? Teresa had asked. Oh yes, she'd gotten him. The most wonderful guy she'd ever known. The man she loved so much she had planned to spend the rest of her life with him, the man who had once felt the same way about her. She'd gotten Danny all right. And then life had gotten them both.

Letty buried her face in her hands and caught the sobs come again to rack her body. It had been two days since she'd cried. It was longer than she would have believed possible.

Chapter 4

Connie Norris paced through the roomy but unfamiliar kitchen, passing the sparkling-clean, stainless steel refrigerator as she went. She stopped at the wooden cutting board, empty-handed, before remembering she'd gone to the refrigerator to get the celery. Tired, frustrated, tense with worry to the point of pain, she turned and crossed the kitchen once again.

"Joan!" she spun and shouted to the woman setting out the table arrangements in the next room.

Connie leaned her fit body toward the doorway. Not a strand of her dyed-red hair moved, as she had it clipped to the back of her head, and the shorter strands sprayed into compliance. Her skin was pale, and smudges from lack of sleep marred the delicate skin below her eyes, but makeup did a fair job masking the toll these weeks had taken.

From where she was, Connie couldn't see the room where the party would take place, but she was confident everything was being set up the way she wanted. The handful of people who worked for her knew better than to alter her instructions if they valued their jobs. She'd worked too hard building her reputation to allow someone else to damage it.

"Send one of the girls out to the van for the silver platters," Connie said, loud enough to leave no doubt she was heard. At her employee's acknowledgement, she returned to the task before her, or rather, tried.

Over the years she'd become quite accustomed to working in other peoples' kitchens. Running a successful catering business depended on it. Her customers were already running around with pre-party jitters, frantic about something or other. The last thing they needed to see was their caterer looking out of sorts. Over the past few days, however, Connie had long surpassed *out of sorts*.

The weeks after Letty's life had blown up in her face had been horrible. What was worse, nothing Connie could say or do would set things right for her daughter. She hadn't even been able to serve up any words to give her comfort. In fact, every effort she made had the exact opposite effect.

Having nowhere else to vent her raging emotions, Letty had thrown it all at her mother. Danny wouldn't speak to Letty. He couldn't even bear to look at her. His parents were nice, but they too were distraught after that wretched night. While Connie could understand Danny's feelings, her empathy multiplied her daughter's torment. And none of it was Letty's fault.

Connie let loose a weary sigh as she opened the refrigerator. The cool blast of air blew over her pallid skin and revived her a bit. It was a needed blessing since she'd slept very little the past few nights. She was surviving on the short naps she took during the torturous hours she spent waiting for her phone to ring.

Letty had been gone for four long, excruciating days. She'd left her cell phone on the kitchen table in front of the chair she'd always occupied. It was a clear message to her mother.

The argument they'd had right before her daughter

had taken off for who knew where had been hellacious. Letty had made accusations, said terrible things, cutting Connie to her core. Thinking back, maybe she had said some things she shouldn't have, too. But Letty had shoved her to the limit. Her daughter couldn't get it through her head things were not going to be the way she wanted, and she *had* to accept the facts.

The only thing the girl wanted to do was blame somebody, as if blaming could fix anything. Connie had never been one to dwell on the unfixable. If something couldn't be fixed, then go on to the next. Nor would she take hits she didn't deserve. The ugliness spat back and forth between them that last night was even more disturbing because of the contrast to their usual relationship.

Over the years, they'd had the normal mother/daughter arguments; things like when Letty could start wearing makeup, start dating, curfews, etc. As Letty grew out of her teen years, though, their relationship teetered to a pleasant balance. Even the few times they did butt heads over something, the situation never grew too far out of Connie's control. They got on well together. Letty worked hard for their catering business, did what she was told, and wasn't one to take advantage because her mother was the boss. Up until a month ago, their lives had been good and normal.

After what had happened, Connie wondered if her little girl would ever feel normal again.

Little girl. Those two words didn't suit anymore, but her daughter was still her little girl. Letty was twenty-two. Legally, she'd been an adult for four years now. But she was still so young. Too young to make all her own decisions. She needed her mother's help and advice. The girl was just being too stubborn to realize it.

Life had been so much easier when Letty was a child and Connie could alleviate the hardships in a simple manner. A kiss for a bruise, a colorful bandage for a cut or scrape, a warm hug and a cookie could cure almost anything else.

Every mother with any sense at all expected some difficulties. It came with the territory. Twenty-somethings were no more than teenagers with more rights, and more avenues for problems. What happened here, though, this was beyond even the most far-reaching of predictions.

Being a mother had been so important to Connie. Having her own business meant the world to her, but molding a child was an experience she wasn't willing to forfeit just because she didn't have a man in her life. She could do both and do both well. Her daughter had always accepted she was the child of a single parent. It wasn't a subject that even came up very often.

Letty used to be so proud when she'd tell her friends about her mother's business, prouder still when she was old enough to help. Their partnership was a good one, and someday down the road, Letty would take over their catering business. She would pass Norris Catering down to her daughter the same way so many father-and-son businesses had been.

Starting a business and then running it left little time for a social life. After a couple of failed relationships, it became clear she would have to take a different route if she was going to have everything she wanted. Connie wondered if someday Letty might be in the same situation. Would she do what her mother had done? No, of course she wouldn't, not after this.

Connie chopped the stalks from the core and the leaves from the top, washed the celery, and then sliced half of it in a steady, habitual cadence. After sliding the pieces into a bowl, she laid the other half on the cutting board but held still while she reran in her head her conversation with the police.

They didn't consider Letty a runaway. She was too old. She was not a missing person, as she had gone away by choice, saying as much by packing a bag. But her daughter was both those things, yet no one in a position of authority saw it her way. The frustration of it was maddening.

Quiet awakened Connie to the present. She stared at a cutting board full of work, but did nothing. It took her a moment to think what to do next. After zoning out for, she didn't know how long, Connie's hands went back on autopilot. Firming her grip on the sharp knife, she chopped the rest of the celery stalks from their core as if she were decapitating the unforeseeable beast.

Her mind, though, slipped away on a mad rush of a mother's angst.

None of Letty's friends knew where she might be. They were worried, too. They'd worry more if they had any clue about the real reason Letty and Danny cancelled their wedding. But Connie hadn't told anyone. She wouldn't add to her daughter's shame.

Then, breaking into the tempo of her knife clacking against the cutting board, sounded an old-fashion telephone ring. It jerked her attention to the area at the end of the kitchen where the counter dropped to form a small desk. Upon the desk were the homeowners' closed laptop, a notepad of paper, pens in a silver cup, and Connie's purse. The semi-muffled ringing came from inside her purse.

The knife Connie was using clattered to the floor in her desperate effort to get to her phone. She snatched it from her purse in mid-ring. The caller ID registered a phone number and area code she didn't recognize. When she answered the phone and waited through the silence, Connie knew. She knew the way a mother knew. Her daughter was on the other end.

"Letty, it's you, isn't it?"

The crying on the other end was her daughter's. The sound summoned Connie's own tears and sliced her heart into a million pieces.

"Oh, Letty. Where are you?"

"I'm okay, Mom," Letty said through a sob.

Connie slid to the floor and leaned her head against a cabinet. "Tell me where you are."

"I'm okay. I just wanted you to know."

"Come home, Letty. Everything will be all right."

"How can you say that? Things will *never* be all right. My future is screwed, and I can't do a damn thing to change the past that screwed it."

Connie sniffed and wiped her wet face with her free hand. "I know, it was a stereotypical thing to say, but it's not altogether untrue. Your future isn't ruined. It's changed, but not ruined."

"I don't want it changed! I want things to go back the way they were. I want to plan my wedding. I want to have a normal life!"

"You *can* have a normal life. But not the one you thought you'd have."

For a full minute all either of them could do was weep across the miles.

"I love Danny, Mom. I love him. He used to love me. Now the sight of me makes him sick."

"No, honey." Connie wiggled her fingers into her pocket for one of the clean tissues she kept close at hand these days. Tipping her head back, she caught sight of the opposite counter where peach-colored napkins were stacked neat beside the crystal champagne flutes, the polished silver, fine china, and all of the other party accoutrements. It was the first time in years she'd worked a party without her daughter by her side. She worked today for both of them, making sure the business's reputation stayed intact.

"You're going to have to give Danny some time."

"Time won't change what you did, *Mom*."

Her back stiffened at the snide accusation charging Letty's voice. She was a good mother, had been right from the start, and Letty damn well knew it. Being in a position of having to take lip from her own daughter was bad enough, but now Letty was taking advantage of the present situation, making her feel guilty when she'd done nothing wrong.

Connie held her tongue, though, because she had to get her daughter back from wherever she'd gone. Even on her best day, Letty wasn't ready to be out in the world all on her own. She still needed her mother's guidance.

Connie made a galling effort to core the ire from her voice before saying, "You're right, Letty. Time won't change the facts."

"That's not what I want to hear! Tell me there was a mistake, a misunderstanding, a problem someone can fix. Tell me you didn't do this to me!"

"No!" Connie shouted, her fist pounding her

scarce-tethered limit against the cold, tile floor. Her jaw tightened, and she jumped to her feet. One hand squeezed the phone, and the other curled hard and tight, fingernails ripping through the fragile tissue she still grasped.

"Don't you dare think you can keep blaming me for this, Loretta, and don't you forget I'm the reason you're here on this earth at all! I've sacrificed for you. I've given, and given, and given. And in case you forgot, we have a party booked for today that I'm now working without your help, thank you very much. We have a business to run, so you can pack up your troubles and get yourself back here right now!"

"You can't order me around anymore! I'm not a child!"

"Then stop acting like one! Do you have any idea what this is doing to me? How I'm suffering? I'm a wreck! Do you even care?"

"It always has to be about you, Mom, doesn't it?"

"Don't you pull that crap on me, little girl."

"I'm not…"

Then, as sudden as the call had come, the connection died.

Chapter 5

Letty hung up the phone, an old-style deal, Dijon yellow with a lengthy, curled cord, hanging on the kitchen wall. She stared at it for a long while.

It was horrible to leave her mother hanging like that, but right now it was hard to care. Sometimes the woman brought out the worst in her. She supposed it was good she suffered a twinge of guilt at having left her mother to continue to worry. After some thought, however, the edge of her guilt was blunted by the realization her mother was less worried than she was pissed off at her inability to control the situation.

Letty had never before considered the advantages of telling off her mom over the phone. For one thing, not having to face her practiced look of intimidation made it a whole lot easier to say what was on her mind. Nor could she deny the perverse satisfaction of for once wielding the power.

It wouldn't last. Her mother was a force. Sooner or later Letty would have to pay for her offense. She hung her head and made an effort to cast out that particular trouble, but all it did was land on the pile with all the rest.

An idea, sudden and welcome, snapped Letty's head up, and she glanced over at the cupboards in Cole's kitchen. Three seconds later, she was searching.

The pantry turned up zilch. When she didn't find

what she wanted in any of the bottom cupboards, she dragged over a chair to stand on so she could search through the ones on top. At the third door, tucked behind a flowery pitcher, Letty found what she was looking for. She dragged the chair back to the table and sat down. The whole time her eyes stayed on the bottle of whiskey she held in her hand.

The bottle's weight, the bold lettering, and the rich, amber color made it seem too rough. The black label all but said this was a drink for someone of a tougher constitution. She was by law an adult. At twenty-two, she was entitled to all of the privileges and miseries that came with age. This was her right. This choice was one she could make, the decision all hers.

Aside from the one night with her friend Kathy, she'd never been a big drinker. Occasionally, she'd have a glass of wine with dinner. One night, the night Danny proposed, the two of them shared a bottle of champagne. They drank it in bed and loved each other until they'd fallen asleep in a warm, wonderful tangle.

The memory squeezed her heart in a fist empowered by pain and rage until Letty was desperate for relief. Then the bottle of whiskey waving at her through the murk of her watery eyes appeared more inviting than intimidating.

Letty returned to the cupboard, took down a short glass, and carried it back to the table. The bottle was near to full. Like her, Cole must not be much of a drinker. Either that or this was a new bottle to replace one he'd finished off. Who knew? Who cared?

Letty twisted off the cap and leaned over to have a sniff. It smelled like death in a bottle. Perfect. She poured until the stubby glass was almost full to the top.

Raising the drink, Letty paused, wondering if she was supposed to add ice. Although she'd been to a few parties, she'd never had whiskey before and had never paid much attention to how others drank it. Well, melting ice would dilute the liquor. She'd skip the ice.

Letty took a breath and a fast swig. Two seconds later, she could have sworn she'd swallowed lighter fluid, after it had been set on fire.

Her eyes bulged as the whiskey burned its way down her middle like a lit wick leading to dynamite. Her stomach was so outraged it quivered and threw her lungs into a gasping, coughing fit. For a minute, Letty was afraid it would come back up, and she wondered why anyone drank such a foul liquid. She got her answer after a few desperate gulps of air were followed by a wave of mellow bliss. Letty lifted the glass to her lips and drank some more.

****

Cole couldn't say for sure how long he sat there like a lonesome fool on the porch swing after Teresa had gone. It was a while.

Maybe he'd said something to anger her. He had been somewhat distant, maybe even a little rude. But that was nothing new. He figured she was used to it, could be she even expected it. Surely he hadn't been bad enough to cause her to run off the way she did. And why did it bother him anyway? He should be glad for it.

It's not like he'd been sitting out there so very eager for their usual after-dinner conversations. Well, if you could call it conversation. Most of the time it was Teresa talking her head off, jumping from one subject to the next like a stalked frog with no apparent connecting themes. Yeah, he should be grateful she'd left early tonight.

But dammit all to hell, he wasn't. He kind of missed that part of their evening.

Cole crossed his arms, and with a huff of breath shook his head. What was wrong with him? He glanced over his right shoulder toward the door and then shifted back to his yard for a few seconds before slanting a glance at the door again. What had those two women talked about in there, anyway?

Earlier, Cole had almost gone back into the kitchen to find out what was so damn funny. They'd sounded like they were having the time of their lives. It made him curious, and paranoia prodded at him because he wondered if they were talking about him. But right about the time he'd worked up a reasonable excuse to go back into the kitchen, Teresa breezed out the front door like she'd forgotten all about him.

As was their regular routine, Cole scooted over to make room for her on the porch swing. He never sat nearer to one side of the swing, at first. For some odd reason, he liked Teresa to witness his effort, small as it was. He liked her thinking he was considerate. So he slid over to make room for her, and then she had the nerve to walk right past him with nothing more than a hasty "goodbye" and "see you next Sunday." She'd acted like…like she didn't care. Now what the hell was that all about?

All he did was sit there like a dumbstruck dolt, didn't even help the woman carry her things to the car, like he always did when Teresa decided it was time to go home. They didn't have their car-side conversation, as was their every Sunday night routine. It was the time of their weekly visits when the woman calmed down enough, or was worn down enough, to have a normal talk. It was maybe even…well, it was nice.

Teresa got in her car without her usual final smile and wave, started the car, circled around the wide spot in the driveway, and left.

After letting his mind chew on it for a few, Cole had to consider that maybe after all this time Teresa finally noticed how he'd been ill-mannered with her. Frowning, he leaned back into the swing, giving it some movement.

Well hell. His lack of manners never bothered her before. In fact, she'd always come back for more. It's how things always worked for them. Why all of a sudden would it change?

Cole cast a brief glance toward the front door. It was quiet in there now. He straightened and stared out across the land, his mind working. The darkness oozed, stretching and thickening until it smothered the last of the day's light. He stayed where he was until curiosity flexed its might and hoisted him from the porch swing. Cole strode into the house with a purposeful stride.

****

Dragging her index finger around the smooth rim of the glass, Letty gained a new understanding as to why some people drank too much.

The sedation was a wonderful, cozy bumper. Her troubles were still out there, somewhere beyond the protective haze. They lurked about in wait. For now, however, their claws couldn't scratch, and their teeth couldn't bite. Letty could even go so far as to taunt them. What did she care about riling her demons now, when she lay safe in the arms of Mr. Whiskey?

Letty gripped the chubby neck of the bottle. She

was able to lift it, but even though she'd drunk it down a few glasses' worth, the bottle was heavy and wobbled a little in her grip. She cupped her other hand on the bottom corner of the bottle to steady it.

Somewhere in her brain, a dry patch hinted the difficulty might be her body's way of telling her mind she'd had enough to drink. But she'd been at war with her body and mind for weeks now. Screw them both.

It took a fair amount of concentration, but Letty managed to pour some more whiskey without spilling any. She used both hands to lift the glass to her lips. The drink was going down much easier than the first taste. With every sip, her cares diminished a little bit more. For now, at least, the torment in her head was silent. The whole world had quieted.

Even the opening swing of the kitchen door didn't catch her attention.

Chapter 6

Cole shoved through the kitchen door and halted as if he'd hit a wall.

The first thought that jumped into his head was, "Where did the whiskey come from?" He knew she hadn't brought it with her because he'd searched her backpack. Cole was a beer drinker, and so was Danielle. Neither of them ever touched the hard stuff.

But then Cole remembered.

One night after his wife left him, he had been so miserable he'd driven down the mountain to buy a bottle of solace. As soon as he got home, he downed a couple of shots. Then his mind landed on his young son, upstairs asleep in his bed. The boy's mother had run out on him. All the kid had left was his father. The thought of Brett finding him passed out drunk was detestable. So Cole stuffed the bottle in the back of a cupboard somewhere and forgot about it, until now.

The second thought marching through his mind was how Letty was going to feel like hell tomorrow.

The bottle had been close to full when he'd put it away. It was almost a third of the way gone now. Letty was a small-built woman and underweight to boot.

Cole crossed to the table in two decisive strides. With one hand, he picked up the bottle, and with the other, he wrenched the glass from Letty's grip. The girl didn't want to give it up, and while she had the will, she hadn't the strength to keep hold of the glass.

"I'm not done with that," Letty said. Her words ran together, and all of them lacked sober definition.

"Oh, you're done with it," Cole told her in a hard tone no one could misinterpret. Scowling, he took the bottle and her glass to the sink. From her seat at the table, Letty gasped as he poured the remaining contents of both down the drain.

"No! What are you doing?"

"Saving your life, again." Cole twisted the cap back onto the empty bottle and tossed it in the wastebasket under the sink. After running the water for half a minute or so, he faced Letty, ready to let her have it the same as he would if he'd caught Brett drinking. It didn't matter to him if she was legally old enough to drink. She shouldn't be, at least not whiskey, straight, and not all alone at the kitchen table.

It occurred to Cole the scene he walked in on might be what had him most upset. She was sitting in the exact same place he sat the night he'd tried drinking away his troubles, and seeing her like that was an uncomfortable reminder of the pitiful sight he must have been.

The chair facing the wall, the wall with that god-awful abstract painting Danielle had bought, every color of the rainbow splashed onto a canvas like an accident, must be the drinking chair, he mused. Maybe he should throw the chair out with the trash before Brett got any older.

"You're killing me with all this saving, you know," Letty told him with her loose, drunken words. She plopped her elbow onto the table and her temple upon her rolled up fingers.

Cole dragged out a chair and sat near her. Letty's eyes were glossy and red, the fragile skin around them puffy. Her eyelashes were wet and spiked. Her jaw dropped slack, but she drew it up again before rolling her head to look his way. It almost fell off of her fist before she was able to regain her balance. Tomorrow she was going to wish he'd stopped her sooner.

"What were you and Teresa talking about?" Cole asked. Something had launched both women into a tailspin. Less than an hour ago, his kitchen rang with feminine laughter. Then Teresa left as if she'd catch the flu if she stayed another minute, and now here Letty was, drunk.

Letty rolled her body back against her chair enough so she could sit somewhat upright. "Men."

"Do you always run for a bottle when you talk about men?"

Letty ran both hands against the side of her head, closing her fancy braid in one hand for a moment before she answered. "Not all men." Her hands dropped to her lap, and she stared at them. "Just Danny," she muttered.

Cole stilled. It was the first time she'd given him any information outside of the basics. He leaned back and spoke in an easy manner, his voice and posture casual. In the state she was in, she might be able to help him help her.

"Who is Danny?" Cole asked.

Still gazing at her hands, Letty took a deep breath before giving her answer. "Danny. Me. 003421."

Whatever he'd expected to hear, it hadn't been a series of numbers. Cole turned it in his mind for a moment in an effort to make a connection to something, to anything. He couldn't. "I don't understand, Letty. What's that, part of a phone number? Danny's phone number? Do you want me to call him?"

Letty folded her arms atop the table, laid her head on them face down, and wept.

"Letty?" Cole asked, probing for an explanation. She was phasing out. Her sobs weakened, and her body was diminishing to limpness. He didn't have much time before she passed out. He leaned over and laid a hand on her narrow back in between her shoulder blades, the bones of her spine against his palm. "Letty, what's 003421?"

"My father."

"Your... Is your father in prison?"

A sad puff of laughter passed through Letty's slack lips as she sat up. Tears spilled from her drooping eyes. The whiskey had left her unguarded, put the rawness of her misery right out there in front.

"I don't know if my father is in prison," she said. "Maybe. Who knows?" She used her hands to wipe her face and then held her braid for another second or two.

Cole stepped over to the kitchen counter and tore off a segment of paper towel. He handed it to her, and she wiped her face. Cole sat back down.

Letty was quiet again, staring at the wall, at the visual gibberish of painted colors within a gaudy gilt frame. Cole glanced up at the painting. The picture made no sense. Neither did Letty. Cole hated when things didn't make sense. They gnawed at him until he gnawed right back.

Since the road he was on wasn't taking him anywhere, Cole backed up the conversation and steered it down a previous road. "Letty, who's Danny?"

"Danny is the man I love," she said without hesitation, still staring at the picture. "He loves me too...loved, he loved me. Not anymore. Now he pretends he never met me."

"Why?"

Her face tightened, her eyes, filling with tears again, still focused on the painting. "Because...because...003421."

Letty's chin made a slow drop to her chest. She was in a struggle to keep her eyes open, or maybe she was trying to keep them closed. Either way, it didn't look like he was going to get much more out of her tonight. He slid his arms beneath her and carried her up the stairs.

After laying her on the guest bed, he slipped off her shoes, tugged out from under her the pink, patchwork quilt Danielle had sewn, and covered her, the same as he'd done a couple of days before. This was quite a routine they had.

Letty moaned and then opened her eyes. "I feel dizzy."

"Here, you'd better sit up a little while." Cole stacked some pillows behind her and helped her shift into a sitting position. "Better?"

"Yes. The room was starting to spin."

"I bet it was. Do you need to throw up?"

"No. Maybe later."

Cole smiled a little. He'd better bring a bucket in and set it next to the bed. She rubbed her eyes, and when her hands dropped to her lap, her eyes were more alert. Though, she was still drunk. Her words didn't form quite right, but at least she was speaking. He sat beside her on the edge of the bed and stared at her until she looked back. "Letty, what's 003421?"

Subtle pain crept across her face, but she answered the question. "My father." Her eyelids widened, drooped, and then widened again in her effort to focus. "My father was a sperm donor. That's his number."

"Your mother got pregnant with you through a sperm bank?"

Letty nodded. She wiped at her eyes with the paper towel she still clutched as the tears flowed again.

"So you're upset because you never got to know your father," Cole said.

"Mom was honest right from the start. I always knew how my birth came about. From the paperwork, I know a few things about him, height, hair and eye color, education, interests. He was a musician. He played the piano. Really, though, I never gave the man much thought. To me, he wasn't anything more than…than a number." She made an effort to shrug, but her body wasn't working right.

"You're thinking about your father now."

"Because of Danny."

"Your boyfriend."

Fresh tears filled her eyes as she stared past him and into her memories. Guilt flowed over Cole. His goal here was not to make her more miserable, but to help her. However, he couldn't help if he didn't know what was wrong. With the gentle touch of a fingertip, he caught a warm tear as it rolled down her face.

"Danny was my fiancé. He isn't anymore."

"Why not?" Cole asked.

"Because of 003421."

"Danny disapproves of the way you were conceived?"

Her words were still loose but on track. "Well, that would be pretty damned hypocritical," Letty said, with another one of those lopsided shrugs.

"How so?"

"It's the same way he was conceived."

"His mother used a sperm bank, too?"

"The same one—003421."

The truth struck Cole like a fist to the face, and the enormity of her torment about dropped him to the floor. He spoke the revelation aloud.

"You and Danny have the same father."

Letty drew her knees up to her chest and clutched her head. "We found out a month ago. We always thought it was a funny coincidence, how both of our mothers used the same method to get pregnant. The possibility of them having used the same donor never occurred to us. There are so many donors, the odds of them both using the same one must be out of this world.

"Then Danny was helping me pack up my stuff because I was going to move in with him before the wedding. The lease was up on my apartment. Neither of us saw any point in renewing it. We spent almost every night together anyway, at his place or mine, and his was a little bigger, with more closet space. I had a copy of those papers in with some things. Danny saw them, saw the number. He knew right away."

Letty's forehead dropped on top of her knees, and she wrapped her arms around her legs as the sobs racked her body.

Cole sat there, stunned, unable to imagine the emotions of a young couple in love faced with such a devastating blow. Pain radiated from Letty's trembling body; the suffering, the helplessness at knowing no amount of effort or any power on earth could change the state of her biology, or the biology of the man she so loved.

Cole scrubbed a hand down his face and waited for Letty to calm. When she didn't, when he could almost believe she would drain away through her tears, he pulled her close to hold her the same as he used to for Brett after a nightmare. She laid her head against him, and as the minutes passed, her body eased.

When her sobs weakened into some manner of control, Letty spoke. "I still love him, Cole. I still want to be with him. That's how sick I am. I'm not right in my head to feel that way. Someone like me, I shouldn't even be alive for having such twisted thoughts."

Cole squeezed her as he spoke, as if he could protect Letty from her torment if he held her tighter. "Don't you say such a thing," he told her, surprised at his own fierceness. "Don't even think it."

"He's my *brother*."

"You didn't know that."

"I know it now, and I still love him in a way I shouldn't."

"You need time."

"Danny didn't need any time. His feelings changed the second we learned the truth."

"Men are different."

Letty leaned back, her red, running eyes staring at his face. "You're not. Brett told me how you still sit outside every evening waiting for your ex-wife to come home."

Cole sat back and stared at Letty as his hands fell in slow motion onto his thighs. He didn't sit outside *waiting* for Danielle to come home. Disgrace took aim and slugged him yet again. That's exactly what he did. What was shocking to him was how the knowledge was anywhere other than in the cordoned-off section of his brain. How could Brett know? In an instant, Cole answered his own question. Because his son was not a baby, and he wasn't stupid.

"That's different," Cole mumbled, swiveling away. His puppy-dog behavior shamed him. His humiliation more acute because Brett and Letty were aware of it.

Letty sniffed and then dabbed at her eyes with the damp paper towel before saying, "You still love her."

Cole shifted to stare out the window, deep into the darkness outside. His first instinct was to deny it, but after what she'd confessed, to do so would be unfair. "Yeah, I still love her."

"Maybe someday you won't anymore. But you weren't able to stop, either. Like me."

In a slow rotation, he faced Letty. "No, I haven't been able to stop loving her."

Letty sank back into the pillows, her abused eyes weighted and blinking slow. She blew her nose into the soggy paper towel. "Love sucks."

Cole smiled at the flippancy of her statement. He had no idea why he laughed. She was right. Love did suck.

The ring of the telephone traveled down the hall. He cast a glance toward the open door, even though he couldn't see anything. The only phone upstairs was in his bedroom. When he turned back, Letty was sound asleep.

The phone continued to ring. Cole continued to ignore it. It occurred to him this was the first time in two years he had not hurried to answer the phone. Most times he got to it before the first ring ended, in case it was Danielle. He was a disgrace to his gender.

The phone stopped ringing. Cole settled Letty to a comfortable position and tucked the blanket around her. He stood over her for a moment and then half-pivoted away before an impulse grabbed hold of him and wouldn't let go. In an act flowing naturally, he bent over and placed a kiss on the top of Letty's head, the way he used to for Brett to keep the bad dreams away. That was back before his son told him he was too old for his father to be tucking him into bed at night.

He and Danielle were both already forty when Brett was born. By the time she'd gotten pregnant, they'd accepted they weren't going to have any children. Brett was a true blessing. After his son's birth, Cole thought a lot about siblings for his son. A daughter would have been nice. It wouldn't happen now, of course. Even if Danielle returned home tomorrow, her childbearing years were over.

Beholding the young girl asleep before him, the loss of not having a daughter of his own burrowed deep into his chest. He loved Brett with all his heart, would die for his boy. The last two years would have done him in for good had it not been for Brett. At times, like the night he sat at the kitchen table drinking whiskey all alone, Brett was the only thing keeping the relentless, pounding waves of his pain from washing him away.

Having a son was the best. It's what every man wanted, a boy to teach how to throw and to catch, to work on a car together, to pass on his land, and to carry on his name. Those things he could certainly do with a girl, and would, as girls were entitled to all the same knowledge and advantages as boys. But he presumed a deeper connection with a daughter. He imagined a ligature of emotions and open compassion, the sharing of feelings gone easy on his masculinity.

Wandering over to the bedroom window, Cole gazed out into the night. Somewhere out there in the world was the man who had fathered this girl. Albeit by scientific means, he was her blood. Did the man ever think about what had come of his seed? Did he ever think about the children he'd sired? Had he ever considered the possibility of such a catastrophic occurrence? Probably not.

Chances were, he'd been some young guy who didn't think very far beyond making a few dollars. Maybe he did now that he was older. Maybe he felt the connection, felt he was missing out on his children, because he was.

Cole pivoted back toward the girl with a singing voice so arresting she could silence a riot. The girl had heart, and it encompassed her entire being. The house was different since she'd been in it. Smiles had made their way back into their home, even laughter. It wasn't so much her giving what his family needed. It was more like Letty *was* what he and Brett needed.

When she was with Brett, Letty had been relaxed and playful. Something his son must have been craving for a long time. With Teresa, she'd been a young woman, sharing and laughing together in the way only women can. Letty thought she was some kind of a freak who couldn't belong anywhere, when the truth was, she'd blessed his small family ten times over with the wonder of her innate gifts.

Whoever 003421 was, he had helped create someone very, very special. The man had no idea. Cole felt sorry for him.

The phone rang again. Cole turned off the light in his guest room and, in a quiet motion, closed the door behind him.

****

"Hello," Cole said when he picked up the phone in his bedroom.

He didn't own a cell phone, had no interest in getting one. Most of the time he was right here on his farm if anyone needed to get hold of him. One landline upstairs, one downstairs, was enough. Danielle had convinced him to get a cordless phone up here. The one on the kitchen wall, though, with a long, curling cord and push buttons, he kept the way it had been since he was a kid.

"...Hello...I...is Letty there?" a woman asked.

The unexpected query gave Cole pause. "Who is this?" Without thinking about it, he curved around until his back was to the doorway in a shielding manner.

The woman's tone leapt from uncertainty to anger in a flash. "Connie Norris. I'm her mother. She called me from this number a little while ago. Put my daughter on the phone."

Letty made a phone call? Maybe that's what pushed her into the bottle. "Letty's asleep right now. I can take a message."

"No, you can't take a message. Wake her up. I want to talk to my daughter, *now*."

Cole shot a glance through his bedroom door into the quiet hallway. After a short thought process, he figured it was best to be honest with her. It's what he would want.

"I'll have her call you in the morning. Letty had

too much to drink tonight. She's out cold, and I don't think I can wake her." Cole winced. That was probably a little too blunt. His suspicion was confirmed when the edge to the woman's voice sharpened.

"Letty doesn't get drunk. What have you done to her?"

"What have... Are you kidding me, lady? Look, she's going to feel like crap in the morning, but other than that Letty is fine," Cole said, riled at her insinuation. Annoyance had him add, "She's a hell of a lot better than she was when I found her."

"What do you mean?" Concern mingled with uncertainty, but anger still ruled. "How was she when you found her?"

"Trying to throw herself off a cliff, that's how she was."

"Oh my God," she said, her words more breath than voice.

Cole scrubbed his face with a slow hand. He really needed to polish his subtlety skills. "Look, she's doing well and getting better. But she needs more time to heal. I think she's going to come to terms with Danny being her brother."

"Letty told you Danny is her...? She hasn't told anybody, not even her closest friends."

Cole paced about his room, for once not paying any attention to the white and royal blue décor he so hated, or the mountain of useless, lacy throw pillows he still kept on the bed, or the voluminous blue curtains with a pox of little daisies.

"Yeah, well, she was drunk at the time. Otherwise I don't think she would have told me."

Her sharpness slashed at him again. "I still don't

understand how my daughter got drunk."

"She found a bottle in the cupboard, opened it, poured, and drank, that's how. The girl's bright enough to figure out how those things work."

"Don't tell me about my own daughter!"

Cole took a breath. "Look, give her some time," he told her in a voice striving for calm. The woman was cresting toward hysterics, and she was, after all, Letty's mother. "Your daughter is doing well here."

"Doing so well she tried to take her own life and then went on a bender? Yeah, sounds like you've got everything under control. Listen, Mr…"

"Holloway. Cole Holloway. And she's being well cared for."

"Where do you live, Mr. Holloway?"

Cole considered her question for a moment before answering. He didn't know if Letty wanted to see her mother. Besides, everything would be better if the girl stayed a while longer. She wasn't yet strong enough to face her life back home. The result of a single phone call to her roots was proof.

"If Letty wants you to know where she is, she can tell you."

"You can't keep my daughter from me. That's kidnapping."

Cole almost laughed. Letty had made the same accusation. "Look, Mrs. Norris…"

"That's Miss."

"Miss Norris. I haven't kidnapped her. Letty can leave anytime she wants. She can tell you where she is tomorrow, if she wants you to know. She's a grown woman and can make her own decisions."

"Like jumping off a cliff?"

"I'm keeping a close eye on her."

"Who else is in the house?"

"I live here with my son. He's twelve."

"No wife?"

"…No, I don't have a wife."

Connie's voice twisted with foul suspicion. "What exactly is your interest in Letty?"

"Don't make me out to be some kind of pervert." He bristled at the accusation. "She's staying here as my guest, nothing more."

"…Cole—"

"Mr. Holloway."

"Mr. Holloway." Her reply was tight, but then emotion crept into her voice. "My daughter is my world. Please try to understand."

Cole exhaled long and sank down onto his bed, on what he still considered his side even though both sides were his now. For once, he paid little notice to the flourish of red roses on the white comforter that annoyed him every time he looked at it. The damned thing made every day look like Valentine's Day.

"I'm a parent, too," he said. "I understand this must be very difficult for you."

"Yet you still won't tell me where she is."

"It's not for me to say. Everything I told you is true. Except for tonight, she's been doing well. Letty's been resting and eating, getting stronger. She and my son have become friends. They talk and laugh and joke around with each other. She really is doing well. I promise to do my best to get her to call you in the morning. In case I can't convince her, give me your phone number, and I'll call you myself tomorrow night. You have my word."

After a moment, she said, "Fine."

He wrote down her phone number and again promised she would receive a call the next day, either from her daughter or from him. Letty's mother hung up without saying goodbye.

Chapter 7

Cole stood in his kitchen wearing his standard jeans, work boots, and flannel shirt with a white T-shirt underneath, morning light warming him in window-heated sunshine that belied the truth. Outside, the temperature was in the low fifties. It wouldn't be long before the nip in the air became a bite. For the time being, though, it was still pleasant enough to work outside.

Most of his crops had already been harvested, the barley, the rye. The potatoes could wait a little longer, but not too much. He still had to take up an acre or two of oats. The oats were going to be his chore for the day, as soon as he took Brett to school and ran a couple of errands. First, though, he'd have another cup of coffee to bolster his fortitude and warm his blood.

Holding the delicate teacup steady in his big hands, Cole refilled it at the counter before taking it back to set on the matching, ladylike saucer mocking him from the kitchen table.

He didn't sit. He stood there and stared down at the ridiculous cup. The feminine yellow daffodils painted around the outside emphasized its fragility. It didn't hold more than a gulp and a half, and the finger loop was too small for him to use with any kind of comfort.

"A man needs a mug, not a cup," he said to Danielle, who of course wasn't there to give him her standard response of, "But a mug won't match the set, Cole."

Scotty, the small brown-and-white speckled mutt who lay against the wall near the heating vent lifted his head to hold his human in a long, questioning glance. After a moment, he lay back down, huffing once through his flews before closing his eyes again. The golden, Burt, who lay beside Scotty, didn't bother. He knew Cole well enough by now.

"So why don't you buy a mug?" Letty asked from the doorway.

Her voice was raspy, like it had been buffed with some low to midgrade sandpaper. She entered the kitchen in slow motion. Her movements were more compact than usual, as if her body was conserving energy, or had little to expend. She took two bowls from the cupboard and set them on the table. The sluggish motion of her limbs could make one believe she was working in water.

She'd showered and dressed in jeans, a clean, lavender T-shirt, and a thin, coal-gray hoodie. Her hair was free of its braid and still damp. Beneath all of the freshening up, though, she was still on the wilted side of well.

Cole curved away from Letty, embarrassed at having been caught talking to a teacup. Why *didn't* he buy a mug? He closed his eyes for a moment, struggling to breathe through the crushing darkness always hunting him down like a hungry beast stalking a wounded animal. He knew why he didn't buy a mug. Damn it, he knew.

Switching thoughts before they could further emasculate him, Cole asked Letty, "How are you feeling today?"

It was something else he already knew, but he still had to ask. Even if he hadn't seen her last night, the gravel in her voice, the octogenarian movements, and the pale-greenish tint to her face were a dead giveaway.

Letty glanced toward him, just short of direct. "A little bit of a headache is all," she answered.

Cole doubted it was little, but she had her pride, too. He opened one of the cupboards and took out a bottle of aspirin. He popped open the top, tipped the bottle, and then handed two tablets to Letty. "Here, these will help."

"Thanks."

Letty filled a glass with water and swallowed the aspirin. With slow movements, she set the glass in the sink before making a sluggish rotation to lean back against the counter. He suspected she was waiting to see if he was going to say anything more about last night.

Cole maintained silence. He wasn't angry at her; he was worried. But after the conversation with Letty's mother last night, he was afraid if he spoke, he would more like as not say the wrong thing. Less than a minute passed before she continued going about her business.

After taking out a box of corn flakes, she opened it and poured cereal into the two bowls.

"Getting Brett's breakfast for him now?" Cole asked, going back to the table.

"He's running a little late. I'm just setting him up to save time. Do you want a bowl? I'm going to slice up a couple of apples, if you want some fruit. I'm making toast, too."

"I'll have something later, thanks."

Letty retrieved the cutting board and then two apples from the refrigerator.

"You feel like eating?" he asked.

"Surprisingly, I am a little hungry," she said, setting the jam on the counter.

Cole grinned. "Yeah, I'm guessing your stomach is pretty well emptied out by now."

Her small blush of embarrassment told him he was right. He grinned wider and hoped she'd gotten something useful from the experience. He had learned his lesson with alcohol in his youth and could never understand people who didn't catch on after a solid hangover or two. The foggy pleasure wasn't worth sacrificing a day of his life to inertness.

"Cole," Letty said, rotating with slow caution, as though she might lose her balance if she turned too fast. She leaned back against the counter again. "I'm sorry about last night, you know, about the drinking. I really never do that. Honest."

Cole sat down at the table and drank some of his coffee before answering her. "We'll put it in the past. But don't let it happen again."

"It won't," she told him. "Look, about what I told you last night, if you tell me to leave, I understand. I wouldn't want someone like me in my home, around my son."

While Letty spoke, Cole had glanced back at the dozing golden retriever he'd found wandering around a couple of miles outside of town almost three years ago. The poor thing had been starving. After a visit to the vet, Cole learned the dog had suffered abuse over a good stretch of time. He didn't have a collar or a chip, not that it mattered. Whomever he'd belonged to didn't deserve him, and they weren't getting him back.

The golden he named Burt was well into his years of life then, though the vet wasn't sure of his exact age. Up until recently, Burt still had some play left in him, tumbling around the yard with Scotty, the little dog they'd taken in two years later when his owner passed away. Now Burt spent most of his days in a relaxed state, deciding if it was time to eat or time to sleep. Sometimes Cole envied him.

Cole shifted his attention from the dogs to Letty. Her head hung low, and her hands clasped each other in a tight grip before her. He fought off a similar stance every time someone saw him drinking from one of those ridiculous little teacups. Shame kept busy hovering around this house, he mused, in search of its next victim.

"I'm surprised you remember last night's conversation," Cole told her.

In a small voice, Letty said, "I wish I didn't."

She wasn't looking at him, but Cole still gave her a sad smile and nodded. "You don't have to talk about it if you'd rather not."

"Good, because I'm not talking about it. I just…" Letty released her hands and crossed her arms in front of her. She raised her head some but didn't meet his eyes. "Do you want me to leave or not?"

"No, you don't have to leave, as long as you stay out of the liquor." Not that it would be a problem now. He'd poured the whiskey down the drain, and there wasn't another bottle anywhere in the house.

"Don't worry," Letty said. "Not drinking will be an easy promise to keep."

Cole didn't miss how Letty sagged with relief when she learned she could stay. It was hard for him to imagine wishing to be away from home. In times of trouble, this was where he most wanted to be. Even when Danielle left, with her touch everywhere, and her taunting scent still clinging to the very air he breathed, he had not the slightest desire to be anywhere else.

Cole shifted his gaze around to take in the décor he didn't like, the abstract picture he hated, the garish yellow paint on the walls, and the teacups not designed for any man to hold. In a superficial sort of way, yet no less disquieting, without the woman who had bound him to these things, the home that was no longer Danielle's wasn't all the way his, either.

"For what it's worth, Letty," Cole said. "I think you're being way too hard on yourself."

She lifted her head to look at him, and her need was obvious and raw. The longing gripped him again, the wanting to make things right for this girl. If she was his daughter, he would go to her right now. He would hold her, and he would smother her with so much love and care it would dilute her pain. But he wasn't her father, and to do such a thing could be misinterpreted. Her mother had already insinuated as much last night. So Cole stayed where he was, sipping coffee from a cup and not a mug.

"But…I told you, Danny is my…" Letty stopped talking and shot a quick glance toward the window, where she squinted into the sunlight.

"I know. It's all right. You don't have to say it."

"Something is seriously wrong with me," Letty said, crossing her arms and squeezing around her middle while her chin lowered until it almost rested on her chest.

Seeing her like this, one could believe she was literally trying to hold herself together. "Let me ask you something," Cole said from his seat at the table. "If you'd have known about your relationship to Danny on the day you met him, would you still have dated him?"

Her head snapped up. Her appalled expression alone was an answer. "No, of course not," Letty said.

Cole let her response hang in the air while he lifted his cup for another sip of coffee. It was empty, of course. He'd already had his gulp and a half. After setting the delicate teacup back on the matching saucer, he stared at the vacancy within it. Maybe he would buy a new mug, maybe next week, or the week after. If Danielle didn't come home by Christmas, maybe he would make that a gift to himself.

Cole lifted his attention back to Letty. Her eyes were downcast, but her head no longer hung low. The fingers of each hand dug into the other in little pulses.

"But I still feel...I have feelings I shouldn't have," she said, her voice quieter than it had been a moment before, her words a painful struggle.

Cole stared down into that damn teacup before giving her a quiet response. "I do, too." From the corner of his eye, he caught Letty staring his way.

"I know why," she told him. When he gave her his full attention, she said, "Letting go even a little bit is the first step in letting go. And if you're not ready for the big change, it's too hard to start on a little one."

Cole nodded. The girl had a fair amount of wisdom for someone so young. She was right. Sooner or later, they were both going to have to take that first step. She wasn't ready yet. Neither was he. So he changed the subject. "You called your mother last night."

Letty gaped at him, her brows drawing together over hardened eyes, a sure warning of the anger to come. "Were you listening in on my phone call?"

"No, and calm down before you get yourself all worked up again. You're in no condition for a fit." She had the decency to look chastened. "Either you forgot about caller ID, or you forgot to block the number when you called her from my house phone. She called here last night after you...fell asleep."

"You talked to my mom?"

"I did."

Wariness diluted her anger. "What did you tell her?"

"Not much," Cole said, sitting back. "I let her know you were doing pretty well here. A parent has a right to know their kid is okay."

"Did you tell her where I am?"

"No. That's your business."

"...Thank you."

"She's worried about you."

"I imagine she is," Letty said, but the sarcasm in her tone said her mother deserved to worry.

As Cole got up to refill his stupid little cup, he said, "I told her I'd try to get you to call her this morning."

"You can't make me call her," Letty said, shoving away from the counter, away from Cole.

"Will you relax? I'm not making you do anything. I said I'd try. The decision is yours. You need to find an outlet for all your anger." Cole poured his coffee and pivoted to face her, holding the cup in both hands to keep it stable. "Don't you have a hobby or something?"

Letty took in a long breath and then huffed it out.

"I used to play guitar," she said wryly.

They looked at each other, and in the span of two heartbeats, the tense moment split. Laughter bubbled up from the tear. It arose suddenly, without warning or reason, and it grew fast. Letty wiped moisture from her eyes that for the first time in weeks, was not summoned by pain. When their mirth should have waned and settled, it flourished, drawing the curious attention of both dogs.

In a bark of laughter, the teacup slipped from Cole's hands and hit the off-white tile floor, breaking into three pieces and spilling the half gulp left. Letty gasped. She grabbed the dishtowel and squatted down to clean up the mess. While she examined the broken pieces of the cup, she said, "Maybe it can be glued."

"No," Cole said.

Letty raised her head toward Cole. He stared down at her, his grin tugging back his whole face.

"One down," he said. And their laughter erupted once again.

When Brett walked into the kitchen wearing jeans and a long-sleeved red T-shirt, he stopped as if he'd walked into somebody else's house by mistake. Letty was laughing, which wasn't too weird, Cole mused. But seeing his father laughing so must be quite a shock.

"Hi, Brett," Letty said, sucking air and expelling giggles. "Your cereal is already poured." She dropped the broken pieces into the trash bin and finished wiping up the spilled coffee. She washed her hands and took out a fresh towel from the drawer. "I was about to cut some apple slices."

"Thanks," Brett answered. He stayed where he was though, staring at his father and his friend. "What's so funny?"

The two adults exchanged glances bursting with mirth. How could they put the ridiculousness of their laughter into words? "Well, Son," Cole said as he took another cup from the cupboard and filled it with coffee. "Apparently, even grown-ups can sometimes be silly for no good reason."

It wasn't much of an answer, but it was enough to satisfy his son. Brett opened the refrigerator for the carton of almond milk Cole had picked up on Letty's request and then got him to try. Brett must have liked it enough to want to have it again. Maybe Cole would give it a try later. This day had an open feel to it. Maybe he should expand on that.

****

"Do you mind if I go with you when you take Brett to school?" Letty asked Cole. She put the bowls and spoons from their breakfast into the dishwasher while Brett trotted upstairs to get his backpack. "I'd like to pick up a few things. If you're not in too big of a hurry."

Cole paused for a moment. He had work to do, and the days were getting shorter, giving him less time in which to get it all done. "I'm not in too much of a hurry today," he told Letty. "Go get your jacket. It's chilly out."

"Yes, sir," she said with a smile. "I'm almost done here."

She held out her hand for Cole's empty cup. He gave it to her, both of them grinning at the cautious exchange, and then added it to the dishwasher.

"I'm ready," Brett said, bounding into the kitchen and shoving back his wayward lock of hair. He wore a fleece-lined, dark blue hoodie over his T-shirt. His backpack hung from his right shoulder.

"I won't be but a minute or so," Letty said as she flew through the door. Her footfalls carried into the kitchen as she ran up the steps, then down the upstairs hallway.

"Letty's coming with us?" Brett asked, his eyes glancing up at the ceiling as if he could see Letty moving about her room.

"Yeah, she wants to pick up a few things in town."

"What kind of things?"

"Who knows?" Cole answered, leaning out the door into the connecting mudroom to lift his jacket off of the peg. "Women always need things."

"Did Mom always need things?" Brett stared at his father with the innocence of a child, no doubt thinking it was nothing more than a simple question.

Cole paused with his well-worn jacket clutched in hand, his chest shifting into an all-too-familiar constriction.

During the first month or two after Danielle had left them, Brett asked about his mother, mentioned her, often. It pierced Cole's heart every time. He gave his son vague answers, not telling him much. What could he say, your mother got tired of us? She doesn't want us anymore? Besides, he'd been so sure Danielle would come back, he figured he'd just let her handle it when she returned. She was better at that kind of stuff than he was. After a while, Brett stopped asking.

Those moments when he had to look into his son's questioning face were the only moments Danielle's departure angered him. The feeling was foreign but never truer. It was one thing to leave your husband, but to run out on your child was cruel beyond any manner of comprehension.

Often times Cole strained to fasten his thoughts and his heart to that anger. Anger was so much easier to handle. No matter how hard he tried, though, the pain and longing were always strong enough to smother the anger before it could get a good hold on him.

Cole couldn't say when Brett had stopped asking about his mother. Thinking about it, quite a while. He wasn't sure what to make of it now. Was Brett feeling a resurgence of bereavement? Or was he finally coming to terms with his loss, able to look at his mother's desertion in retrospect rather than grief?

Shrugging into his jacket, Cole gave some thought to his son's question before answering. "Yes, Brett. Your mother needed things, too."

****

Vibrant spatters of oranges, reds, yellows, and gold, bright as a sun-kissed morn on a cloudless day, were flagging the trees into fall.

Some leaves already lay finished on the ground. A few sailed on the cool breeze, passing before the windshield of the truck, even floating upward again as if to extend the ride. Most, however, still shone lively from up in the trees. This was their season to show.

On the ride down the mountain, Brett and Letty talked about school, about living with snow, and a few other things Cole half heard. The simplistic sentence he'd spoken to his son before they left the house kept running through his head. Yes, Danielle had needed things.

Cole always believed he was a good provider. He thought his wife had everything she needed and everything she wanted. It was what made her leaving so hard to understand. The possibility swamped him now; how maybe Danielle's needs extended beyond what he was able to supply. The idea had often sought to burrow into him during the past two years. Up until today, however, Cole had been able to turn his back on it before it could twist another knot in his gut.

For the first time, Cole looked at his loss from a different angle.

Maybe his wife wasn't so much running away from her husband and son, as she was running to something else. But what? What could she want that wasn't already in her possession? She had a terrific son who loved her, a husband who adored her, a nice home, good land, stability, financial security, and a future which promised a continuation of it all. No, it didn't make any sense then, and it still didn't.

There hadn't been another man. Cole was sure of it. Even if he had not so trusted her, the two of them were either physically together, or close to, almost all of the time. Danielle hadn't the opportunity to carry on an affair.

That terrible day, Cole had asked her the question anyway. Since he couldn't come up with any viable reason for her to leave them, he'd peered into the blackness that was closing in on him with alarming precision, searching for something he could grab hold of and repair. After all, he was the man of the family. He should be able to fix what was broken.

That late autumn day was still as sharp in Cole's head as the ache in his heart. The morning had been so blissfully normal. Even now, he couldn't distinguish it from any other. They'd all eaten breakfast together. The conversation was as usual, the morning beginning the same as all the others, mundane in the very best sense of the word.

Danielle had driven Brett to school. Not even a hint of what his wife had been thinking wafted through their routine, warning them the bottom was about to drop out of their lives.

It was close to noon, and Cole had come in from the pole barn where he'd been tinkering with the engine on his tractor. His stomach was growling, and he was ready for lunch. He remembered going into the first-floor bathroom to wash his hands. As he dried them, it struck him how quiet the house was. The silence should have tipped him off how something wasn't right.

Danielle always played the radio. She liked listening to classic rock music. Cole preferred country, but he was working outside most days, so they didn't compromise on the choice of music in the house. It was all hers. After draping the hand towel back over the bar, he went looking for her.

He'd found his wife in their bedroom. She was packing a suitcase.

As clear as if it had happened this morning, Cole remembered the sight outside the bedroom window, even as his shock had turned to frustration, and in a hasty decline, was degraded to anguish.

The season was further along than today. The leaves had finished changing color and were falling *en masse*, letting go of their branches and floating to the ground in soft, gliding waves. The tranquility outside their bedroom window was a deep contrast to the tumult taking place on the inside of the glass.

Every detail of every second of what happened

next had replayed in Cole's mind often enough to create a permanent stamp.

As Danielle breezed about their bedroom adding things to her suitcase laid out on the bed, Cole spoke to his wife. His words and movements were frantic as he paced their room, grasping for any reason she would leave, and anything he could say or do to make her stay. It shamed him still, the level to which he'd sunk in his efforts to convince her not to leave them.

In anything else, Cole would suffer the direst of consequences before he'd stoop to begging. But desperation had crumpled his pride in its mighty fist and tossed it out into the chilling day without so much as a speck of human compassion.

Danielle had sworn it had nothing to do with another man, having one or wanting one. He remembered her saying those words while she tucked her beige, low-heeled church shoes into her suitcase. He could still see the scrapes and the scuffs around the toes and recalled thinking to tell her it was time to buy some new ones. Even then, he knew it was an odd thought to have at such a time. Yet there he was, living his future even as his wife packed it away.

Danielle had made a few vague references to a lost youth, as they had married young. Then something about having a life that was hers. She wouldn't be clear, though, not on anything. By then she was packing toiletries. Cole remembered seeing her favorite perfume go into a smaller case. The bottle was close to full, as he had given it to her for her birthday a month before.

As her body went about her preparations for a new life, Danielle engaged in a verbal tango, gliding from one reason to another, gathering them in a cluster because none of them had the strength to stand on their own. But she couldn't give Cole one single specific reason for her leaving, and to this day it gnawed him right down to the bone.

When he demanded a clear explanation, the best his wife could give was to say she wasn't happy anymore. She told Cole it had nothing to do with him, said he had been a good husband, but there were things in this life she wanted to do before it was too late.

"Travel?" he'd asked, grasping at this point because her suitcase was almost full. "You want to travel? We could take some vacations, if that's what you need to be happy. Tell me where you'd like to go. I'll arrange it today."

A very small shake of her head was the only indication she'd even heard his offer. As she continued her packing, Danielle said how they'd made a good boy together. It was the one moment she'd shown any emotion, her voice hinting at a break. She said she was leaving while Brett was in school because she couldn't bear to say goodbye to him, and asked Cole to tell their son she loved him.

Not a day passed where the scene in their bedroom didn't run through Cole's head, as well as the preceding days and weeks, looking for clues as to why.

In the months before her departure, Danielle had begun wearing makeup on a regular basis. Not a lot, but since most of the time she didn't wear any, even a little bit was noticeable. She'd started dieting, too, changing what she ate and downsizing her portions. She purchased some exercise videos and used them almost every day. His wife had gone and lost at least fifteen pounds. Cole didn't like it. It was one of the few times he'd criticized her. Not that it had any effect. She'd gone and lost another five.

He thought about that now, again. At some point he'd come to see the ways his wife had begun living her new life right under his nose.

Danielle had told him straight out not to look for her, said she would hate him forever if he did. At the time, Cole figured she needed some space, some time away from everything she had so she could appreciate it. He respected her need and her wish and did not search for her.

The very day she left was when he'd started his evening vigil, sitting on the porch swing, watching his land, waiting with labored breath for his wife to come home. He was so sure she would.

Three weeks after Danielle left, a manilla envelope arrived from a law office in Jacksonville, Florida. It contained a letter from Danielle and divorce papers.

She didn't want anything, land, property, nothing more than her two-year-old car and the five thousand dollars she'd withdrawn from their bank on her way out of town.

She signed over full custody of Brett. They could work out some kind of child support if he wanted it. He didn't. Cole was more than financially able to support Brett. He had a good income. He owned the house and land outright. He was, however, concerned about turning their son into a bargaining chip, and was afraid he was hurt enough to try if they got into it. So he left it alone.

Other than those few things, she hadn't much to say. Danielle wanted out, period. Her letter was simple and succinct. She offered no further explanation for her leaving. She left no phone number or address except for her attorney's, who refused to give Cole even a scrap of information to lay over the bleeding wound of his heart.

After staring at the divorce papers for more hours than his pride would allow him to count, Cole signed his name to them because he didn't know what else to do. With a few signatures, Cole had released his wife from all parental and marital responsibilities. That was the night he'd driven down the mountain to buy the bottle of whiskey.

How he wished he could say it was the day he was able to say goodbye to his wife and let go. He wished it almost as much as he wished she would come home.

"Dad, you passed my school," Brett said, twisting back to watch his school disappear behind them.

Cole blinked and berated his good sense for becoming distracted while driving. He turned around at the next street.

"Have a good day, Son," he said as Brett climbed out of the truck. "I'll be here when you get out."

"Bye, Dad," he said. Then he smiled up at Letty who was scooting across the bench seat of the truck from the middle to the passenger side. "See you later. I can't wait for dinner tonight."

"Good," she said. "So don't fill up on a bunch of junk when you get home."

"I won't, I won't."

They stayed until Brett was through the gate of the school, blending into the crowd made up of kids from a variety of surrounding towns that weren't big enough to support a school of their own. Cole put the truck in gear, and they made their slow way out of the school zone.

"What did he mean he's looking forward to dinner?" Cole asked.

"I'm cooking tonight."

Cole cringed. "Good God."

"What? I know how to cook."

"You've had one cooking lesson from a woman who has boiled the life out of every vegetable she ever met and thinks chickens need a grease Jacuzzi."

Letty laughed. "Hey, you liked my green beans and potatoes."

"I did," he had to admit. Letty had steamed the green beans just right, and her roasted potatoes had been delicious.

"And be nice to Teresa. She cooks with love."

"She should cook with a cookbook. Look, I can handle dinner tonight."

Letty swung around to gape at him and said, "You turn everything into jerky, including potatoes. How do you even do that?"

Cole managed to rein in the smile her insult inspired. He'd have been irritated if her words weren't so true. "You ate those potatoes."

"You ate Teresa's cooking."

"*Touché.* All right, the kitchen is all yours tonight. What are you going to make?"

"Vegan lasagna. Do you like Italian?"

He liked about anything he didn't have to cook or chase with a handful of antacid. "Italian is fine," he said. "Vegan? As in, no meat?"

"And no cow cheese."

Cole's slanted an incredulous look her way.

"Give it a chance. It's delicious, you'll see. Your mouth will like it, it's healthy, so your body will like it, and it's cruelty free, so your soul will like it."

Cole chuckled. "Well let's hear it for my soul."

"So I need to go to a grocery store for a few things."

"All right."

Cole drove into the parking lot of Elvin's Grocery and stopped in front of the doors. "I have a couple places to go. I'll meet you back here in what, about forty-five minutes or so; is that enough time?"

"Sounds good," Letty answered before getting out of the truck and closing the door.

Cole hit the button to roll down the passenger window. "Hold on a minute," he called to Letty. When she'd walked back to the truck, he had his wallet out.

"No, no, I've got this," she said.

He was well aware of what groceries cost and, having gone through her things that first day, knew the state of her finances. "I don't expect you to buy dinner," he told her, sliding several twenties out of his wallet.

"I want to do this."

"Letty, there's no reason for you to spend your money on our meal. Here, take it," he said, holding out the bills.

"No, really, Cole. It's my way of saying thank you for…well, for everything. You've done more than I could ever thank you for."

Letty's voice quieted, and her body stilled, as if everything about her was focused on remembrances she'd prefer to avoid. Cole let his hand full of money drift to the seat.

A breeze blew some of her long hair in front of her face, and Letty swept it back. The physical movement must have been the tug her words needed. "If it wasn't for you, I…I wouldn't…"

Her voice caught on a swell of emotion so large it laid pressure against his heart. He waited, debating as to whether or not he should tell her to get back into the truck, or wait right there for him while he parked. In a sudden strike, he didn't want Letty to go off by herself where he couldn't keep an eye on her. He gave her a minute or so. Cole watched her, though, watched close, and waited.

****

Letty tipped her chin down some, embarrassed and even frightened, thinking about what would have happened to her had it not been for Cole. Where her life would go from here, she didn't know, and it still hurt too much to think more than a day or two in front of her. That was progress.

Less than a week ago, she couldn't think more than an hour into the future. Sometimes it was no more than keeping a fingerhold on life for a few more minutes, of forcing another breath into her lungs, and willing her pained heart to beat yet another pulse. Everything, even what was natural, had been a grinding effort.

Today, good fortune, maybe nature, was making an effort to ease her back into place. She was still treading turbulent waters, still struggling to keep her head above it, but now she had hope that maybe someday life would be tolerable. And if she could be so bold as to wish a daydream in the direction of reality, maybe at some point, life might even be pleasant.

Letty raised her head to meet Cole again, eye to eye. A light sheen threatened to lead her to another good cry, but she was able to blink back the tears before they gathered enough weight to fall.

A frown creased Cole's face, and he sat still and stiff behind the steering wheel. He couldn't hide his concern if he tried. Letty smiled at the big teddy bear of a man so he would know she wasn't upset. In the few days Letty had known him, she'd learned his concern often riled his surliness.

Letty said, her voice brighter than before, "Making dinner for you and Brett is the least I can do. I want to, Cole. It would make me feel good." She smiled wider and wheeled away before he could say anything else.

****

Her deep gratitude made him uncomfortable, but it was good to see her smile. Still, he didn't want the girl spending what little money she had on their meal. But it was too late. The automatic doors of the store had already opened for her, and he still couldn't think of what he should say.

Letty crossed the threshold of the store with a slight bounce in her step. That was an expression Cole had always found ridiculous and never connected it to anyone he'd ever known who was over nine years old. It fit Letty today, even with her hangover. It fit her well, and he liked knowing he'd been able to provide a safe haven for her to begin working out her problems, and he liked thinking maybe he'd given her some comfort.

The sensation of being less weighted, a little less burdened, settled on him for the second time today, and with it, came a wonderful idea.

He forgot all about the errands he had to run. Cole steered the truck in the opposite direction of the hardware store, his heart beating a tempo of enthusiasm for a change.

Chapter 8

Connie Norris steered the rented SUV off the vacant, two-lane road, her foot easing down on the brake as she rolled onto the rocky shoulder. While the car was still in motion, her hand rose to cover her mouth against a giant yawn. They were coming so close together now, her mouth barely closed before yet another yawn pried it open.

The car slowed to a crawl. Her tires crunched over the scattered gravel until at last she stopped. The yellow SUV she had rented in Billings kicked up a brief flurry of dust, flecking her view. The dull accumulation of dirt swirled forward before dissipating into the bright, clear air around her.

Weariness slogged through every single muscle. Fatigue weighted her mind and taxed her body. She had to go on. Her motherly instincts required it. But these past weeks had depleted her energies to dribs. A few minutes of rest. It's all she would need. Then she'd hit the road again, a little faster to make up for lost time.

After shifting into park, Connie shut off the engine. The GPS screen darkened, and the soft rock music playing low on the radio died in the middle of a chorus. Silence surrounded the car and leaned against the windows.

She took a slow gaze around. The sensation of being the last person on earth unsettled her readiness to sleep.

Not a single car, truck, or motorcycle traveled in either direction for as far as she could see. Connie couldn't remember the last time she saw another vehicle. It had been many a mile since she'd seen so much as a house out in this desolation, and she couldn't say for sure if the last house she'd passed was inhabited.

Grades of green hills surrounded her, boxed her in, and appeared to go on forever, as if nature had dropped a mass of fresh land over the entirety of civilization and somehow missed her. The only sign mankind existed at all was the paved, two-lane road on which she now sat.

Connie shook her head. "If there ever was a place that could be called the middle of nowhere, this has got to be it."

She yawned and rubbed her temples. Sleep, she just needed a little bit of sleep. Then she could be on her way. She blinked once, slowly. Her eyelids so heavy it took effort to lift them again. A vague glance around her through the dark tint of her sunglasses reaffirmed her first impression was right. She couldn't be more alone.

She still had hours to drive and was more anxious than ever to get where she was going, but she'd been nodding off at regular intervals, and if she didn't close her eyes for a little while, chances were good she'd be in an accident before arriving at her destination.

How she wished she could have taken a direct flight into Pine Bluff. But apparently, the town was in the same boat as many other towns out here which she never heard of before, too small to have a commercial airport. Well, Connie supposed she was lucky to have gotten here at all. If it hadn't been for all the connections she'd made in her years of catering parties for plenty of big wigs in Vegas, she'd still be waiting around for a phone call that might never come.

Letty hadn't called in the morning. Mr. Cole Holloway had said he'd call her some time tonight, but Connie couldn't wait around and see if he would stick to his word. She had to see her daughter. She had to see with her own eyes that Letty was all right. Spending another day wallowing in anxious wait was unthinkable. So she'd made a call to a client/friend, and within minutes of giving him the phone number from which Letty had called, she had an address.

Her fingers fumbled along the side of the seat until she found the recliner button. She eased the seat back and let her eyelids fall down to cover her burning eyes. It had been weeks since she'd had a good night's sleep, and in the days since Letty had taken off, she'd had little more than restless, intermittent naps. As exhausted as she was, Connie should have been asleep in an instant. Closing her eyes, however, did nothing but leave her tired in the dark.

The image of her daughter jumping off of a cliff haunted her vision in a dozen different ways, each more horrible than the last. She made a feeble effort to believe it wasn't true. But Connie was a realist and had to admit it was the fear of Letty contemplating suicide that had been prowling around the recesses of her mind for the last couple of weeks.

Adding to that, she now had new fears for her daughter.

The man said he was keeping a close eye on her. The images sparking in her mind from what he considered an assurance weren't any good either. Letty was young and pretty. She was smart, but she was gullible in the way young girls tended to be. Topping it off, at this challenging patch of her daughter's life, she was vulnerable to an extreme.

How hard would it be for a grown man to win Letty's confidence enough to take advantage of her? Not very hard at all was the answer to that question.

In an effort to get more comfortable, Connie removed the hairclip from the back of her head, tossed it on the passenger seat, and shifted a bit. However, it wasn't her body's positioning causing her such discomfort as to keep her from sleep.

She switched the channels in her mind, striving for something bland to which she could drift off for a little while. Every scenario led back to Letty. Sleep called to her, pleaded with her, but her mind refused to give in to what her body needed, even for a few minutes. Not when her daughter could be in real danger.

Connie was an adult. She knew the way of things. Sure, plenty of good men existed out there in the world. She'd known a lot of them over the years. But the bad ones were in no short supply, and she didn't know Cole Holloway from a hole in the ground. The man could be seducing her daughter at this very moment. Maybe he was getting her drunk again, letting it become a routine she was comfortable with before he made his move.

Her daughter was in no condition to handle any kind of situation alone. If he abused Letty, the girl would sink even deeper into her depression, maybe so far down she might never surface again.

Connie had a sudden urge to kill Cole Holloway.

Opening her eyes, she stared at the nondescript

ceiling of the rental car. Letty needed to be with her mother. She needed to be home, where she could be guided in the proper direction. Not within easy grasp of a man who might well have nefarious intentions.

Connie raised the seat back and at the same time started the car. Seven minutes had passed since she'd parked the rented SUV.

Chapter 9

The day had warmed a little, as the few wispy clouds floating by hadn't the capacity or the will to discourage the sun.

Cole unzipped his jacked halfway. He was leaning back against his truck, parked in the first slot next to the empty handicap space in front of the grocery store. He sniffed in a deep breath. The fresh air had a cool scent to it. Yes, cool had a scent. It was of the changing seasons, the burgeon of a new beginning, winter's fresh, baby's breath as it woke in uneven increments.

He was waiting for Letty to come out of the store. Too enthused to stand still any longer, Cole shoved away from his truck and paced a short while before going back to his place to lean again. He made every effort to appear casual, but the childish excitement buzzing through him made it near to impossible.

A smile kept toying with his mouth. He fought it. Every now and then, he'd pivot so his back was to the store, and let it come. Just for a moment, though, so he wouldn't let on.

The glass doors of the store slid open, and it took all Cole had to keep his casual, stone-faced pose. An elderly couple short-stepped out, the man pushing a rattling cart full of reusable bags while the woman dug through her purse and got out the car keys. The Pressers, Hal and Lynette, both retired teachers, still active in the community.

The couple wore matching gray hoodies, beige pants, and white sneakers that were clean, but not new. Cole waved. They waved back. The doors slid closed. Cole resumed his pacing and trying his best not to smile.

"Mornin', Cole."

The voice came from behind him, but Cole didn't have to look to see who it was. He'd known and fought with that glib speaker since the third grade. As it was, the cut on the inside of his mouth hadn't all the way healed from their last confrontation. Cole pivoted to face his longtime foe, Darrell Clayton, walking toward him with a phony half-smile on his mocking face.

Like Cole, Darrell was dressed in a flannel shirt, jeans, and a jacket. They were close to the same size, though Darrell was fairer, with lighter hair cut neat, always styled rather than just combed, and a beard and mustache the man spent way too much time grooming.

"Darrell." Cole growled and said nothing more.

Cole's good mood soured the moment he'd heard the man speak, but it sweetened again at the sight of Darrell's face. The man still bore some of the black eye Cole's fist had delivered the other day on the mountain.

Darrell wore a baseball cap, tugged down low in the front. Early on it became a tradition when one of them sported a shiner dealt by the other. In the old days, the cap was an effort to keep the bruises from their parents' notice, then their wives'. Now it was in hopes *no one* would notice, as they were way too old to be blackening each other's eyes.

"Do any good poaching lately?" Cole asked through a smirk.

Darrell's half-smile stretched into a sneer. "I wasn't more than a hair off of my land. And besides, I wasn't poaching. I was hiking," he said, dragging out the K a little. Darrell's stutter wasn't much more than remnants now, occasional reminders of the halting his words used to suffer when he was a kid. D's, K's, and S's sometimes still tripped him.

"Yeah, right. You were hiking, and you just so happened to have a rifle on you."

"It's dangerous out in those woods. There are bears out there. You know that as well as I do." Another brief pause on the last D.

"Yeah, I can see one of those furry beasts left you with quite a shiner," Cole said, now wearing the half-smile only one of them at a time could possess.

****

Darrell Clayton scowled at the obstinate man before him. Cole had always been kind of easy for him to rile, but since Danielle had left him, he'd been a real ogre. Darrell almost laughed. A grouchy old beast had, in fact, given him a black eye.

It was far from the first time they'd come to blows, though at this stage of life's game, Darrell was hoping it was the last. The wish was a wistful one. Their habits had been set in stone on an elementary school playground long, long ago, and apparently were more binding than a marriage contract. Also, Darrell mused, more painful.

Though he was a few pounds leaner than Cole and an inch or so shorter, Darrell was confident he'd gotten at least one good slug in. It was aggravating how Cole didn't show any of the bruises. Next time he'd try to aim better. Visual victories always made his own

114

injuries much easier to tolerate.

Darrell gave an inaudible sigh. As sure as the sun would come up tomorrow, there would be a next time.

"How's your boy?" Darrell changed the subject from whose land he'd been on the other day before they came to blows again right there in the parking lot of the grocery store.

****

"Brett is fine." Cole put extra emphasis on his next words. "He's doing well in school. Exceptionally well, in fact."

Except for math. Brett needed some help there. He was a little weak in science, too, but he was improving. That reminded Cole of something else. Brett had forgotten to take the clothes out of the dryer and fold them yesterday like he was supposed to. Everything sat in there and ended up wrinkled all to hell. He'd have to get on him about his chores, again.

"And Brett keeps up with his chores around the house, too," Cole said in a voice a little louder than need be so as to make sure Darrell heard. "He doesn't even have to be told. The boy has initiative. He surely does. How's Sandy?"

****

Sandy was Darrell's ten-year-old daughter by his second marriage. Darrell had just come from the school. They'd called him in because Sandy had gotten into a fistfight with another girl out in the schoolyard. It had happened almost as soon as he'd dropped her off.

According to the teacher, his daughter had started the trouble. The woman used the word "bully" to describe his kid. By the looks of Sandy's knuckles, she'd inherited her father's right hook. The fight was going to cost the girl a week in detention.

"Sandy's a peach." Darrell smiled broad enough to conceal the fib. "I think she'll make the honor roll this year," he said, even though school had just started a month before. In truth, he'd be thrilled if she stayed out of trouble and passed her classes. "She's trying out for the Christmas play, too, already practicing her songs. The girl has the voice of an angel and the disposition of a saint."

****

Unfortunately for Sandy, the girl had her father's penchant for a good fight. Word was, Darrell had been called to the school more than once over some sort of trouble.

"Brett is going to play football this year," Cole said. He puffed out his chest as he bragged to Darrell. Cole had done no more than suggest trying out for football to his son, who wasn't even a little bit receptive to the idea.

Darrell crossed his arms. "So is Sandy." The S in Sandy slowed him a tad.

Sandy playing football wasn't hard to believe. Darrell's daughter was tougher than most boys. Fine. Darrell could have that battle, but not the war. Cole leaned in, hands on his hips. "Brett is so advanced in his lessons he's already deciding what he wants to major in when he goes to college."

Darrell stretched his neck until less than a couple of feet separated their hardened faces, and shoved out three of his fingers. "Sandy's already been contacted by three college recruiters."

"She's ten years old!"

"That's right. See how bright she is!"

"Oh, the hell you say!"

"The hell I don't! You calling me a liar, Cole Holloway?"

"I call 'em like I see 'em."

"You son of a—"

"Hi, boys," Teresa said, shaking her head and laughing as she approached. "Are you two at it again?"

Cole and Darrell dragged their glares from each other and toward Teresa, walking toward them with her arms full of groceries and her eyes full of mirth. She was dressed in jeans, a powder blue blouse, and a dark blue sweater. Her hair was tied back in a high ponytail, like the kind she used to wear when they were all kids.

"Sometimes I think you two need to sit in a corner for a real long time-out." She laughed again and shook her head. Her ponytail swayed in a cute, girlish sort of way.

Cole couldn't let go of his scowl, but an effortless smile softened and lifted Darrell's face in an instant. Such a transition had always come naturally to Darrell whenever a female was around. Yet another thing about the man that grated on Cole.

"Hello Teresa." Darrell touched the bill of his hat and tipped his head to show respect. When he raised his head, he gave her a quick, admiring assessment before his smile grew wider. "Well, you look ever so lovely today. That pretty shade of blue in your blouse brings out the heavenly blue in your eyes."

Good God. Cole let loose a snort before rolling his eyes in the direction of the celestial reference.

Teresa cast a brief, albeit narrow-eyed glance toward Cole and his rude, animalistic grunt before giving her attention back to Darrell. "Why thank you,

Darrell," she said, all sweet and playful. "How you do flatter a woman."

Darrell nodded once and tipped his head in a motion of humble admiration. "Only the pretty ones."

Cole rolled his eyes again before he could catch it and stop. Oh, Teresa was pretty, all right. Prettier than most. He hadn't meant to imply she wasn't. But Darrell wouldn't hesitate to give the same exact compliment to an ogress with green warts if it got him somewhere. And that chucklehead was gazing at Teresa as if he had somewhere in mind.

After raising his head, Darrell gave Teresa one of his flirting winks, and Cole's stomach lurched. Cole slid his glance back to her again. Darrell was right. The blue color of her blouse and sweater really did look good on her. He couldn't say so now, though, not after Darrell had already made the comment.

A hint of blush crawled up Teresa's face as she laughed at Darrell's compliment. He'd never seen her blush before. It did make her look kind of precious. The slight color tint faded away, and Cole had a small but distinct notion he'd like to see her blush again sometime.

The sunlight flattered her, gave her an angelic glow. It suited, as she was a generous, decent woman. Cole tipped his head sideways a little. Teresa had nice skin. It looked soft, the way a woman's skin should. He'd bet it felt soft, too, and resisted the urge to lift his finger to her cheek. He liked the crinkles at the corners of her eyes. They spoke of a lifetime of heartfelt smiles. They deepened when she laughed, and it gave him a funny feeling beneath his skin.

Teresa slid a brief gaze toward him, and it struck

Cole how it wasn't her blouse making her eyes so pretty. It was how she looked out here in the morning sunshine, with the magnificence of the blue Montana sky as a background. It was as if nature chose to share its best shade of blue with Teresa's eyes.

Cole's mind wandered back to when Teresa's womanhood was on the cusp of blossoming. She was sweet and thoughtful even when she wasn't more than a kid. He would never forget how she'd used her babysitting money to buy him a birthday present. It still touched him. She was too young for him back then, of course. Then time swept them all down different roads. Maybe if he'd made other choices...

It occurred to him that since her husband died, he'd only seen Teresa indoors, or at night when he walked her out to her car. She always looked fine then. In the morning light, well, he couldn't deny the woman took on a certain kind of radiance. Cole gave a mental shake at the silly ramblings of his thoughts. They continued to drift, however, to a place far less defined by words than by feelings.

Teresa's laughter snapped him back to the moment. He returned with a fair degree of reluctance, as the sensations tingling through his veins were not at all unpleasant.

Darrell must have said something else to tickle her. Teresa was blushing again. Why had she never reacted to him in such a way? *Why did he care?*

The playful tone the two of them were using on each other scratched aggravation up his back to his neck, though Cole couldn't say why, other than Teresa was a friend and Darrell was an ass. What Cole did know, but could only explain as not wanting to be bested by his old foe, was he had a powerful desire to top Darrell's compliment.

Without planning his words first, Cole blurted out, "Yeah, you look…just fine, Teresa."

Cole scrambled through his head to think of something more to say, something better. Relying on his own wit with the ladies, Cole opened his mouth to wing it. What came out was, "Your hair looks okay like that." He hadn't even managed to work up a smile to go along with the lame comment. What was worse, he hadn't meant it.

The ponytail was kind of cute, but Cole preferred her hair down so the rich, brown curls would bounce around her shoulders. But commenting on her ponytail had been all he could think of to say. It wasn't much of a topper, but he was out of practice, and it didn't matter anyway. He didn't care about flirting with Teresa. He just didn't like Darrell doing anything better than he did.

****

Teresa shifted her attention away from Darrell. "Thank you, Cole."

Cole's sweet talk left much to be desired, but since it was so rare, she was pleased he made the effort. His attempt at flattery supported her notion he had feelings for her. Darrell, on the other hand, had flirted with every female whose path he'd ever crossed. He'd been married and divorced three times, and no one familiar with him doubted sooner or later there would be a fourth Mrs. Clayton. Someday, maybe a fifth.

Oh, Darrell married with good intentions, forever love, commitment to the end, the whole thing. He never set out to hurt anyone. It wasn't his nature. Quite the opposite. He enjoyed making women happy. Whatever woman had his attention truly did have his heart. Darrell's love was real. But it wasn't lasting.

He was too much of a hound dog, always sniffing around to see what else was out there. The man was drawn to new love like a puppy to a belly rub. Teresa didn't hold it against him. Nor would she ever be so foolish as to think she was any more special to him than those who'd come before her.

Darrell had always been attractive and...magnetic. Still was, with thick hair, light brown mingled with a few distinguished grays, and expressive caramel eyes that charmed a woman even if his words didn't. He had a friendly smile he wasn't shy about sharing. And he could soft soap. Lord, Teresa figured the man could smooth talk the wind if he had the notion.

Teresa glanced back and forth at the two men before her. Darrell, with his charm and good looks, had worked his way into many a woman's bed and three "I do's" and counting. Cole was better looking, in a rough, outdoors sort of way she preferred, but the scowl he so often wore detracted from his appearance. It was far more than looks, however, that drew her to Cole Holloway.

Someone meeting Cole today would not meet the man she knew him to be. This Cole was hard to talk to and moody. His expression alone could turn people away. That was now. Until two years ago, when Danielle had up and run out on him, he'd been a different man.

Teresa had known Cole since she was twelve and he was fifteen. He'd always been so full of life that in his presence one couldn't help but catch his love of this land and his appreciation for the gift of living upon it. Even all those years ago, Cole had seemed very grown up to her, already rather set in his ways.

It hadn't been such a stubborn quality back then. It was more like he was rooted in honor, had a direct kinship to the right way of things. Cole had always exuded a sense of stability, of concrete values and ironclad reliability. Those qualities, along with his rugged good looks had made Cole utterly irresistible to the young girl Teresa had been.

When she was a kid, she'd had a monster of a crush on him. He was a good friend of her older brother, Randy, and it gave her more access to him than the other girls who were always vying for his attention. Almost from the time she met Cole, Teresa followed him around like a lost puppy. It annoyed her brother to no end, but Cole was always patient, always nice to her, saving a minute or two to converse with her even when Randy had been anxious to get on to their next adventure.

When for his eighteenth birthday she'd given Cole a stupid snow globe with a log cabin on a mountaintop inside, he'd thanked her as if he had received something he'd long wanted. Teresa had almost fainted when after opening the gift, he'd given her a hug. Oh, that was so very long ago.

Time passed in all the meandering ways it did. Her brother, Randy, had gone off to attend UCLA, decided he liked the warmer weather of California, and stayed. After the connection of her brother was gone, their paths crossed less often. But Cole remained in a secret alcove of her heart, undisturbed by reality.

In difficult times, Teresa would indulge an

occasional daydream or two about a life with him, but by then Cole had settled into the role of her friend. Then he'd started dating Danielle and not long after, Teddy had come along to sweep her off her feet.

During the thirty years Cole had been with Danielle, he'd been fun and friendly, a calmer expansion of his younger days. The four of them became friends, getting together during community activities and events, having dinner together every now and then.

When Teddy died, Danielle and Cole had been there for her, folding her into their lives and helping to keep back the torrents of loneliness that grabbed and squeezed and then got worse when her son returned to college less than a week after the funeral.

Then Danielle left.

Up until that time, Cole had been an active part of the community, serving on boards, chairing a couple, attending every town meeting without fail. For two years now, with the exception of their Sunday dinners, he hadn't socialized at all, not with anyone. Teresa suspected he was ashamed, though he had no reason to be. Cole hadn't done anything wrong.

Danielle had become restless, even panicked at the speed with which the years were passing. She'd married young and was haunted with the worry she had missed out on something, some essential part of life, but she could never put her finger on what "it" was.

"Life's clock is always ticking away our options," she'd said to Teresa once during a town picnic. The ominous comment was spoken in something like a trance, Teresa remembered, as if Danielle was already halfway gone. Another time, Cole's wife had confided to Teresa that she felt as if she had spent her life in the care of men, first her father, then her husband. She loved her son, but Danielle gave the impression Brett was yet another male to keep her on a chain.

It had been two years since the Cole Holloway Teresa had known most of her life had sequestered himself. He was still there, beneath all the stoic suffering. She was certain. Sometimes she could swear his heart cried out to her from behind his wall. The fact remained, even though Cole and Danielle were divorced, Cole was still too married to Danielle to accept he wasn't.

Oh, Cole flirted with her in the roundabout manner some men do such things. Well, men other than Darrell Clayton. Like when Cole scooted over to make room for her on the porch swing. Like how he changed when the two of them were alone at the end of their Sunday dinner visits.

The hour would be inching toward late for an early bird like her, and she was ready to say good night. She could count on it happening then. The arrogance of Cole's shell would crack, a little. But it was enough for her to glimpse the fragility he kept smothered under a mountain of masculine pride.

By that time, she always ran out of things to say and was exhausted from trying so hard the past hours. It was the one time she could count on Cole to actively converse with her. Every Sunday night, standing beside her car, the man latched on to any topic. Sometimes they would stand out there longer than they'd sat at the dinner table. His surliness would fade to nothing as he continued to initiate conversation, to bring up new topics, keeping her there a little while longer. She knew why, even if he didn't.

Brett would be in his room doing his homework, and Cole didn't want to be alone with the ghost of a woman he had to know wasn't coming back.

Lately, however, there'd been more.

It started a few months back. Cole looked at her differently when they were standing alone next to her car, like maybe he was thinking about kissing her. At first she thought it was her imagination. Then one night he was staring at her lips, and he bent. So small a bit it was almost imperceptible. She saw it. He caught it, got embarrassed, and said good night. It set her suspicion that his gruffness had more to do with his feelings of being unfaithful to Danielle than lack of them for her.

****

"What are you two little boys ready to fight about now?" Teresa asked, making no attempt to subdue her chuckles. Cole hoped he wasn't suffering the blush of embarrassment at being caught near to fisticuffs with Darrell, yet again.

"We weren't fighting," Darrell said, a calming tone to his voice, as if setting to rest a misunderstanding on her part.

It'd be nice if she bought it, but Cole didn't think she would. She'd known them both far too long.

Teresa touched Darrell's chin, tipping his face so she could get a better look at the fading bruise stamped beneath his eye.

"Good," she said. "You should at least wait until you heal up from your last fight."

Darrell peered at her with a humbled grin and laid his fingertips against the back of her hand in a gentle, too-familiar kind of way.

125

The manner with which Teresa put her fingers on Darrell's face, so tender, so caring, had Cole's hackles raised. When Darrell touched Teresa's hand, Cole was struck with an intense urge to blacken the scoundrel's other eye. The man had no business messing around with her. Teresa deserved better. On her worst day she could *do* better, too. Way better than a smooth-talking ladies' man like Darrell Clayton. Not that Cole cared, of course.

"Here, let me get those bags for you." Darrell took the groceries from Teresa. The stutter-pause on the S was scarce noticeable. The man always managed to pull it together better when he was putting the moves on a woman.

Cole glared as Darrell got much closer to Teresa than he had to in order to take the grocery bags from her. Then, when they were touching, Darrell paused. He sure did! He sure the hell did!

It was one of Darrell's old tricks, pausing when he got close to a woman. He'd developed the sleazy move back in high school. He was wheedling intimacy, the louse. Couldn't Teresa see he was up to his shenanigans? She was smarter than to allow such behavior. What was wrong with the woman?

"Well, thank you, Darrell." Teresa stepped back and put an appropriate amount of space between them. "I'm parked right over there."

"Oh," Darrell said. Disappointment dragged down his words. "I was hoping you'd walked today so I could walk beside you all the way back to your house."

And work yourself an invitation inside. Good God, the man was shameless. Then Darrell sniffed her way, not unlike a dog who catches a whiff of a tasty treat, the mangy hound.

Darrell caught Cole's glare, grinned at how his attentions toward Teresa annoyed him. So of course, Darrell leaned closer to Teresa and sniffed again. "What *is* that perfume you wear?" he said to her. He shot a quick glimpse toward Cole. "It's a wonder you don't have every man in the store out here competing to carry your groceries for you."

Teresa laughed again, less shy this time. Cole liked the sound of her laughter when she was relaxed this way. Why couldn't she be like this around him? He was far less of a threat to her decency than this guy. The urge to punch Darrell returned in full force.

"I'll see you later, Cole," Teresa said. "Say hi to Letty and Brett for me."

Cole gave her a stiff nod. As they walked away, Darrell glanced back over his shoulder and sent Cole a smirk. The guy was asking for it in a big way. But, as Darrell well knew, Cole wouldn't take any action in such a public place. All Cole could do was stand there and take it. Smiling wider at Cole, Darrell touched the bill of his cap before brushing his fingers outward in a mock salute. He then returned his attentions to Teresa.

A low growl hummed in the back of Cole's throat.

"Hi, Cole. Have you been waiting long?" Letty asked as she rolled a cart up to the truck.

Cole scarce paid her a glance, waiting a few ticks before he broke from his stance. He couldn't take his eyes off of Teresa, and off Darrell who was walking way too close to her for common respectability. He was damn glad Darrell was just walking her to her car, and not to her house.

"No, I haven't been waiting long," Cole answered,

still staring at Teresa and Darrell. "A couple of minutes."

"Is that Teresa?" Letty asked as she loaded a bag into the back of the truck.

"Yes," Cole said. He dragged his gaze away and took the other bag from the cart.

"Who's the guy walking with her?"

"Darrell Clayton," he grumbled. He set the bag in the truck bed and glanced down the row of cars again. Teresa and Darrell disappeared behind a truck, heading toward the next row over where Teresa must have parked. He craned his neck but couldn't see either one of them anymore.

"What are you so happy about?" Cole asked when he caught sight of Letty's grin.

"Um…they had tomatoes on special."

Chapter 10

Letty stopped and stood right where she was, in the middle of a field of wildflowers. She had to. It was as if she was rooted in the ground the same as all the nature surrounding her, as if she found her place, and it was as pleased as she.

Overwhelmed, like stumbling from a long trek through hell and landing in a heaven you didn't believe existed, her attention was captured by the scene. It dabbed at her with a loving touch, absorbing some of the sorrow flowing from her wounds. Her surroundings comforted her by including her in its tender fold.

The magnificence laid out in every direction was so freeing, it had the opposite effect. She could not take a step or even twitch a muscle. Nor did she have any inclination to do so. Now Letty understood why Cole, no matter the pain he'd suffered here, would never leave this place.

She plucked a lavender flower from the ground. Except for the color, it could be a daisy. Did daisies come in colors other than white? Maybe it was a different kind of flower altogether. She knew roses. She knew tulips, and she knew daisies. That was about it. She'd never given flowers much thought before, other than they were pretty.

She held it to her nose for a sniff, earthy, with a rich, raw perfume. A tranquil breeze swept across the field in which she stood, unhurried yet persistent. Letty tightened her hold on the stem as the soft petals, along with the other wildflowers, swayed with perfect grace in nature's tangible rhythm.

The autumn air carried a chill, and she hadn't worn her jacket. The sun, however, nudged away the cluster of downy, white clouds, and shone with such radiance that for the time being the illusion of warmth was enough.

The gentle current picked up a bit, lifting her unbound hair and floating it back from her face with an artful stroke. Her T-shirt fluttered. The scents of flora, of earth, and of clean, clean air embraced her, as did the simple peace of it all.

Letty closed her eyes and willed herself to be a part of it. In a way, it worked, too, as she was treated to sounds gone unnoticed a moment before. Fallen leaves, dried, chattering against each other as they rode an unsullied gust. Birds twittered in their variety of dialects, chirping in harmonious chorus with a continuous succession of solos and crescendos. The sweet music made her remember her own.

Letty thought of her guitar, and with scarce being aware of it, her thumbs rubbed against her fingertips. She'd earned every one of the small calluses she bore, with each press, pluck, and strum of the nylon strings over all her years of practice. Almost as tangible was the worn smoothness of the Sitka spruce from which her guitar had been made, the consolation of it resting against her body, the curved weight of it on her lap. And of course, the music she coaxed from it every day.

Playing her beloved instrument used to be a ritual. It had been no less a part of her day than brushing her teeth and combing her hair. Now her guitar lay broken apart in strewn pieces, the same as her life.

Opening her eyes, Letty drew in a cool, deep breath. She rotated her head, inviting the sights around her to overlay the memories.

Grand old trees bordered the field in layers deeper than she could see. Some were pines, like Christmas trees. Maybe those big ones were oaks. Other trees mixed in, too, but she hadn't a clue as to what kind they were, any more than she could identify what kind of flower she held. She recognized the white-petaled daisies lingering into this next season, but not the others.

Having lived her entire life in a city in the desert, she knew so little about this kind of world. Which trees stayed green all year? What kind of leaves turned which colors? What were the names of all these flowers?

Letty stood in center of the field. Wildflowers dawdled in sporadic clusters all around her, flexible in the dark soil which smelled of the richness of earth and nature. Yellows and oranges flecked many of the bordering trees, in the process of putting out their fall decorations. Sunlight glinted off the colors, some of them so much so, they glowed in the afternoon light. How beautiful it must be when in full color.

The only time she'd seen such a popping of floral and autumn colors were in pictures or on TV. Those mediums could never capture this. For a canvas would always lack the feel of a clean breeze against skin, the frenetic tousling of dried leaves sailing by, and the sweet scent of a field of wildflowers in their end of season fragrance.

Letty worked her imagination, wondering what all

those trees would look like covered in snow. Would the landscape appear gray and ominous, or pristine, like in a fairy tale? She'd never seen snow before, at least not up close. It snowed on Mount Charleston, back home, but she'd never made it up there for a visit. It would be nice if she could stay until winter and experience the season.

She gazed long at the landscape.

The giant mass of trees surrounding the field and the house seemed a sentry of sorts, protecting what they encompassed by the simple virtue of their brawn and longevity. It was as if these huge trees were the soldiers of the land, and it was their sworn, eternal duty. It occurred to her how she was standing within their watch. Letty smiled and lowered her gaze to what was close.

From the kitchen window, she'd been able to see the expansive field at the end of the side lawn. The smattering of daisies had her engrossed, their white blossoms broken at intermittent spaces with what was left of the pink and yellow flowers she couldn't name. Deep lavender flowers with yellow and orange centers, like the one she held, made for a nice contrast. They were the heartiest and most prevalent of the crowd.

A sudden desire to stand with those flowers, to see all of them up close, to touch their petals, had ushered her with haste out the back door.

The very moment she stepped outside, Letty became infused with a need to rush, as if they all might disappear before she got there. Faster and faster across the well-tended lawn. By the time she'd entered the field of wildflowers, she was at a run.

Once she was amongst them, she stepped with

caution so as to not crush even one of the delicate beauties. Many of the flowers had already succumbed to the season, leaving tiny stumps and a few shriveled blossoms. A large number still clung to life. The lavender flowers, like the one in her hand, were quite robust, thumbing their slender petals at the encroaching season.

Letty set out to pick some for the dinner table, but as she wandered through the field, the penetrating splendor of the land overcame her. It soothed her every sense. In its own way, the land spoke to her in reassuring tones. It tugged in the sharp facts of her life, pointed side down deep into the malleable soil, allowing fresh perspective its due.

So there she stood. Facing the soft wind, breathing in this world, and letting it hold her in ethereal arms.

It occurred to Letty how Nature's earth was an immense sundry and quite enduring when left in Her competent hands. It looked after itself, picked up after itself, without neglecting or overthinking the ways of days. All seasons served a purpose.

Even now, when the flowers of summer were fading, and the leaves were falling from the trees to their deaths, and all seemed hopeless and headed into permanent desolation, the land understood it was nothing more than a hiatus. It didn't fear the transformation. It didn't struggle against what it couldn't change, but rather flowed with comfort from one stage of life to the next, knowing by instinct spring would come again.

Letty gazed around again before kneeling beside a broad patch of the lavender, daisy-like flowers. She picked a good handful, careful to spread out her trimmings and leave enough so the field would look undisturbed by a human hand.

Chapter 11

What had begun as an unpleasant tremble, a cumulative eruption of goose bumps beneath Connie's thin jacket and thinner blouse, had amplified into a full-blown, bone-rattling shiver. Involuntary movement seized every part of her. If Connie failed to exert enough constant effort to keep her jaw clamped, her teeth chattered until she worried about causing them damage.

Although she was already near to frozen stiff, Connie left the window rolled down. With night moving in fast, the air went from chilly to cold as it gusted loud and erratic through the rental car. Having always lived in the warmth of the desert southwest, she couldn't imagine what January was like in a place like this. It must be hell.

It didn't matter in the least what the weather would be like here in the winter. She'd be long gone by then. Home, in the wonderfully warm desert, with Letty close by.

Connie leaned toward the open window and let the cold wind slap her awake. Her revved up fears were powerful but still losing their ability to overcome her lack of sleep. Even with the bracing air striking her face, it was difficult to keep alert. Connie fought hard against the drag. Thoughts of her daughter, vulnerable, all alone with some strange man, were what kept her going.

Before sitting up straight again, she took in a deep lungful of the sharp air. She'd been doing this at regular intervals, sucking it in as if it were a drug, for a brief time gaining what she sought, holding on to the boost in ever-diminishing increments. That she was pushing herself too far was not a news flash. Even a mother's love suffered human limitations, and it was becoming reckless to the point of dangerous to ignore her dwindling resources.

The rented SUV scaled the mountain road quite well. As it climbed higher, the temperature dropped even farther. Connie concentrated, she focused, she shivered, and she drove.

She glanced at her watch. Hours had passed since she'd pulled over and tried napping on the side of the road. Since then, the stiffness in her body had worsened. Her head ached, her neck hurt, her eyes bore the grit of exhaustion, and the cold wind assaulting her through the car window did nothing but increase her discomfort.

Even as her body screamed for warmth and for sleep, Connie continued to ignore everything but her goal. She glanced at the dashboard. According to the GPS, she was getting close. A few more miles and she could see her daughter.

The sun dropped below the mountainous horizon. Moments ago, the orange glow of sunset had been blinding her. Now, it was fading fast into deep, dusky shadows. Enough light remained so she could see darker shades against the encroaching night. They were trees, of course. Hordes of the damned things blocked her view in every direction.

Connie removed her sunglasses and slid them into their case. She tossed the case into her open purse sitting on the passenger seat, zipped it shut, and then twisted the lever to turn on the headlights.

A lock of hair escaped from her clip. The wind whipped it across her face, so she let go of the steering wheel with one hand and tucked it behind her ear. When she placed her hand back on the wheel, she had trouble keeping a firm hold, as her fingers were so stiff and numb from the cold.

Her efforts to stay awake might in actuality be putting her in more danger. So Connie pressed the rocker button in the door panel to roll up the window and switched on the heater. It would be for no more than a few minutes. Just long enough for her hands to thaw out and keep her grip.

It was a few minutes too long.

Connie awoke to a sudden, violent bouncing of the car.

Her left shoulder slammed into the driver's side door, and her head pounded against the window. For the first few seconds, she was too stunned to act. Then she made a desperate attempt to gather her senses as she stared through the windshield in horrified wonder.

Shrubs popped into view seconds before the car mowed them down and left them to screech against the undercarriage. Branches of all sizes produced horrendous tones, clawing the car as it made a wild descent. Rocks the size of ottomans struck the SUV, pounded from underneath and on both sides as the vehicle bounced and jagged. None of it slowed the car. If anything, she was picking up speed.

Connie slammed her foot on the brake. It had little

effect, as the tires were airborne almost as much as they were on land. When the car did crash to earth, the tires skidded before losing touch with the ground again, and flew for another two or three seconds.

She firmed her grip, but the steering wheel worked no better than the brakes. It jerked hard one way and then the other, as if an invisible, muscular entity had taken control of the SUV. Trees and boulders tore by in flashes of the chaotic veer of her headlights as she careened downhill.

Terror filled the car as it sped through the darkness. No matter her efforts, Connie's fate was not in her hands.

In a sudden, stomach-dropping shift, the front of the SUV tipped, and her downward pace gained speed.

She caught a glimpse of a mountainous boulder through the driver's side window as it gouged the door panel, ringing from the car a hideous, high-pitched shriek. Connie screamed. If the car had been but a few inches to the left, she would have crashed head on into the boulder.

The headlights pounced in erratic fashion, like small spotlights gone mad. More shrubs and a tiny tree popped into view. Her car plowed over all of it without hesitation. All Connie could do was sit strapped to her seat, screaming into the darkness.

Then the land gave the impression of leveling some. She slowed a little bit, but the car was still speeding downhill at a frightening pace. Connie stomped on the brake pedal. The SUV skidded and then shifted into a sideways angle. The turn was notable and added a new level of terror.

Afraid of flipping and rolling, Connie let up on the

brake. The car straightened but picked up speed again.

The right front fender of the car scraped against a grouping of boulders. Metal shrieked. The car pitched to the left, jarring her bones. Another scream burst unnoticed as she applied pressure on the brake pedal, restraining the powerful urge to slam down her foot.

The last thing to pop into her view before the crash was an enormous tree trunk, illuminated in all its steadfast girth in the dusty glow of her headlights.

Chapter 12

Although Letty had given the kitchen a thorough cleaning after they'd finished dinner, the blended aromas of garlic, spiced tomatoes, and whatever else she'd used still lingered throughout the house. It was an essence of culinary wonders reminding them of what had been.

Cole drew in another deep sniff. Even that was a treat.

Brett had remarked how it smelled like an Italian restaurant, and his son was right, except it was better than any place they'd ever been. Cole would love it if one of the restaurants in town served food like what they'd eaten tonight. He and Brett would be regulars there for sure. A lot of other people would, too.

The girl wasn't kidding when she said she could cook. Letty had served him one of the best meals he'd ever had in his life, the kind that sooner or later he would look back on with a vicious craving. His guess was sooner.

The lasagna noodles had been layered with tender vegetables and one or two other things he couldn't identify, but they were not the traditional meat and cheese. He knew this only because Letty had told him. It was different from what he'd had in the past. But damn, the meal was delicious, especially after the aroma tempted and teased him all day long.

For hours, her homemade sauce simmered on the stovetop as Letty stirred and added ingredients with the precision of a scientist with well-honed skills and a critical undertaking. The wonderful aroma, having been far too grand to be confined to the house, had wafted outside, wrapped around him, and gave him a hard tug.

For a minute or so after he'd parked his tractor and cut the motor, Cole sat as motionless as his machine, thinking his sense of smell had developed a fabulous imagination. He sniffed a couple of times before his nose led him toward the house. Could it be Letty's cooking? The question prodded his hope as he hopped from his tractor seat. Another deep inhale through his nose, and his stomach sounded a growl while his watering mouth begged for a taste of what his sense of smell was already enjoying.

The aroma led Cole into the kitchen as if he had no will of his own. He'd stumbled through the door nose first only to have Letty laugh and tell him dinner was still a couple hours away. His stomach could have wept for want of it.

When at last they sat down to eat, when he placed the first bite on his tongue with a reverence to which it proved entitled, Cole could believe he had departed this life and gone straight to food heaven. A glance at Brett's look of euphoria told him his son felt the same.

She'd placed a basket of fresh-baked garlic bread slices on the table, a small towel tucked over it to keep in the warmth. Letty had also served fresh asparagus with the meal. She'd steamed the spears with pimientos, she said, to make the vegetable aesthetically pleasing as well as tasty. Green and red colors—a perfect dish to place on the table with Christmas dinner.

Later, as he rocked on his porch swing, little Scotty and big Burt positioned on the top step keeping their dog's watch over the yard, Cole wished Letty would stay through the holidays. For more reasons than her fabulous cooking.

Change had been weaving through the anguished debris of his life. Cole couldn't help but catch dribs of optimism where a few days ago nothing existed but perpetual gloom. Today's purchase, for example, made for no other reason than to see Letty smile, had already given him more pleasure than he could put into words. And he hadn't even given it to her yet.

Once more, Cole likened himself to his land, but with a slight, albeit significant difference, as now he viewed the elements with a more human mix to his perspective. The feeling was akin to an awakening. Stirring to life after lying dormant through the bitterness of an extended winter, breaking through icy crusts once too formidable to be anything less than permanent. But it was not permanent.

Stiff and age-old, yes, but able and willing to give a tentative stretch and take a breath of a new season. From this standpoint, it also occurred to him it was not necessary to always be unyielding. It was all right if every now and then he flinched.

Cole's memory rewound a few hours, to when he'd stepped out of the pole barn wiping his hands on a rag and looking toward the sky. Clouds were deciding whether to gather, and he was wondering if they'd have rain later. Then his attention sank down to the land, toward the field of wildflowers where dots of color still flashed here and there.

Letty was picking flowers out in the field between

the lawn and the woods. Her head tipped down. She was wandering, turning, searching through the last remains of the daisies and buttercups, the violets, the heather, the few geraniums, and the annual autumn blast of asters.

If he had to choose one flower, Cole would say the asters were his favorite. This was their time of year. While the other blossoms were shutting down in the chill of the coming season, the asters, with their lavender, daisy-like petals, delicate, yet defiant against what aimed to thwart them, were in full bloom.

She crouched down in the center of the field. Her hand sought one of the asters. Her fingers curled around the stem, and she plucked it. She stood. The breeze lifted her hair in a mid-float while she held the flower in her delicate hand, petals close to her nose. The sky shifted. Through a scalloped break in the clouds, light poured over Letty in a gauzy gold sun-fall. Then, as if even time needed longer to take in the enchanting sight, everything paused.

The gilded scene could hang in a gallery, the work of an artist who possessed enough talent to bestow tranquility onto a canvas. *Girl in a Field of Wildflowers*, it could be titled. The image would forever be both sweet and present in Cole's heart and in his mind. For in that one perfect picture, Letty had given him a presentation of such utter peace, it almost overwhelmed him.

Hours later, after the meal had been eaten, the kitchen cleaned by all three of them, and praise and gratitude bestowed, Cole sat alone on his porch swing.

A flock of snow geese passed overhead, their nasal honks echoing and then fading as they crossed his property. The sun dipped into the horizon, casting late-day gold across the landscape. It was the kind of evening both settling and unsettling. The peace of the land, the disturbances upon it.

As the chill of dusk crept along in the swelling shadows, Cole acknowledged a profound wish that he had been the one who'd fathered Letty.

If he had been so fortunate, he could keep her here on the mountain along with Brett, keep them both safe and protected. He could provide for her, make sure she put on some more weight, and serve scalding looks to the boys who came to call but weren't good enough. And if any young man were a threat to her happiness, Cole would be a threat to them.

These whipped up thoughts of her Danny, the man she almost married. Cole had a powerful urge to hunt down the guy and shake him until his teeth rattled, until he understood this wasn't Letty's fault, and how he was making an innocent girl suffer by refusing to speak with her. Cole had a potent hankering to do it for her anyway.

While he was raising Brett to be a man, Letty would always be a girl to him, no matter her age. Sweet, sometimes temperamental, a humane counterbalance within the boundaries of his home to the inhumane realities outside of it. Maybe that was a gift only women could give. It could be all these thoughts lacked the gender correctness of the modern world. Cole didn't know, nor did he care. Honesty of the heart deserved some slack.

Cole shook off the foolishness of allowing such thoughts to seep into his head. He wasn't Letty's father, of course, nor would he ever be. Still, the unbidden sentiment loitered in his mind, like the aroma of her sauce and the simple yet gripping image of her crouched in autumn's sunlight, picking wildflowers in his field.

Scotty's little triangle ears perked up, and the dog stood, woofing once, drawing Cole's attention back toward the dirt road. At Scotty's second bark, Burt lifted his tired old head and stared toward the driveway. After a minute or so, the dogs lay back down. Cole scanned the land for the telltale rise of dust following a car to his driveway, and found not a speck. No one was coming.

He glanced down at the little dog. Scotty directed his gaze at the floor of the land, toward the tree line at the end of the yard. The dog must have spotted a squirrel or some other woodland animal. Scotty's small body stiffened, and he held still as a stone. The dog didn't leap from the steps, meaning the little guy had lost sight whatever it was that had captured his attention.

He could have caught a glimpse of Spencer, the golden tabby they'd taken in after Darrell's daughter became allergic. If so, that would explain why Scotty didn't bother him. He'd learned his lesson the first day they had the cat, and all it took was one moderate scratch to the nose. Scotty was a rambunctious little tumbler, but he wasn't stupid.

The dog lay down again, and Cole's thoughts drifted back to Letty. He should tell her how her laugh was contagious and how he enjoyed her wry humor. She needed to know she brought color back into their drab lives. He should tell her how her gifts were many and she was not flawed. Someone should tell her she

was special. She was valuable. The world needed
people like her. Letty deserved to know all of these
things. She deserved to hear them from somebody.

A flashback of earlier in the day struck him. His
lame compliment to Teresa. Hell, he'd more likely
insulted the woman than said something nice. If he tried
telling Letty his florid thoughts, he would no doubt
make a muck of it. The girl was already kind of
sensitive.

A small, self-deprecating chuckle escaped Cole as
he recalled the glare Teresa had given him in the
parking lot of the grocery store. Yeah, he'd best keep
his mouth shut. He'd already put one foot in there
today.

His smile faded in the hungry haunting of his ex-
wife's words.

On several occasions, Danielle had told him she
needed to hear things from him. Silly, needless things,
Cole believed, like how he still thought she was pretty,
and how much he still loved her. At those times, he
remembered thinking his wife was just having one of
her moods. It meant nothing and would soon pass.

When he touched her, when he made love to her,
she had to know he still found her attractive. And how
could she not know how much he loved her? He
married her; he provided for her and their son. Even
though he didn't share Danielle's taste, he hadn't made
too much of a fuss over the way she decorated the
house, because it made her happy. He showed her in a
million different ways how much he loved her. Why did
he have to come out and say it?

Cole gazed out over his land, yet he could have
been staring at a blank wall. Was that the reason

Danielle left? Women were so different. He could never understand why all the proof in the world needed to be backed up with words. Then it occurred to him, maybe he didn't have to understand the why. Maybe all he had to understand was the need.

The porch swing had ceased its motion. Cole didn't notice until the hoot of an owl nudged him from his pond of ponder and back into the present. Then another sound caught his attention.

Cole tilted his head back and stared at the neat row of boards over his head. Brett's bedroom window was just above the covered porch. Muffled laughter coming from his son's room was loud enough to make its way through the window and down to Cole's ears. They were loud, belly laughs, the likes of which had been absent for so long they were foreign and exotic, yet at the same time, rang of home.

After dinner, Brett had helped clean up without anyone asking him to, and he'd done so with a smile. Cole wondered if Letty had a trick for gaining such cooperation. He'd pay a hefty fee to acquire such knowledge. Oh, Brett usually did what he was told to do, but never with anything close to enthusiasm, or with such worthy consideration to detail.

With a temperate press of his feet, Cole sent the porch swing into motion as his mind sank back into habit. The position of the sun told him he had another fifteen or twenty minutes of light. His eyes roved across the land, slower in the direction of the dirt road, though tonight it had more of a ritualistic feel than one of irrational obsession.

The front door wasn't so thick it blocked the patter-pound of four feet bounding down the stairs. It drew

Cole's attention from the diminishing daylight.

Letty had been up in Brett's room helping him with his homework. She was good at arithmetic, she'd said, and would be happy to assist Brett climb his latest mathematical mountain. Cole liked the way his son had become a little brother, even a little boy, at times. Letty's presence had rejuvenated a part of the past, a part that was good, and, he was overjoyed to know, not lost.

The front door opened about a foot, and Brett's head poked outside. His face bore a wide, wonderfully dopey smile, making him appear younger than his twelve years. Cole couldn't help but smile back at his boy.

"Come on, Dad." Brett bounced with excitement as he waved his father into the house with two swift scoops of his hand. "Letty's cutting the pie."

When Cole had seen Letty rolling out a piecrust on the kitchen counter, he'd been more than impressed and pleased. It ushered back one of his fondest childhood memories. He hadn't seen anyone rolling out a homemade piecrust since his sweet grandmother, and she had done so in the exact same spot.

"I'll be right there," Cole told his son. Scotty, wheeling toward sounds from the kitchen and not willing to wait for a chance at a treat, jumped up, scampered across the porch, and ran inside the house. Burt followed. Brett held the door until the old dog walked through at his slow and steady pace.

After the door shut, Cole stared outward again, scanning the dirt road one more time and wishing he wasn't.

He was still sitting there a few seconds later when

Brett poked his head out the door again. "Dad," the boy said, anticipation sparkling in the clear blue of his son's eyes, Danielle's eyes, the way they were at the beginning of their story. For the life of him, he couldn't remember when she'd lost her sparkle of delight. "I almost forgot. Letty told me to ask if you want coffee with your pie."

"I'd love some."

"That's what she thought you'd say." Cole still sat there staring at his son. "Come on, Dad," Brett said with impatience, though without any rancor.

Cole smiled as his hands lifted high over his head, and he arched his spine in a stretch. "I'm coming, Son. Give these old bones a chance to get moving."

"Dad, you're not old, just older."

With those words, Brett's spry feet thumped through the house toward the kitchen, toward the pie holding his focus. Cole got up and headed toward the door. The sun had scarce dipped below the horizon. What little was left of the day glowed soft tangerine on the polished red cedar of the front door.

For the first time in two years, Cole did not stay on the porch swing until the day was good and over, waiting, always waiting, and dreading the darkness sure to come. Cole did not even look back toward the setting sun, to what he knew it would show him. Danielle's car hadn't driven up to the house in two years, and he had no good reason to think it would be any different today.

Still, he stood there a moment longer, fighting the temptation to drop his pride and glance back toward the road.

Finally, with the flat of his hand, he opened the door Brett had left ajar. The house exhaled the aromas of dinner, of home, of vibrant, existing life. Brett laughed at something in the kitchen, followed by the unmistakable sound of a single piece of silverware clattering on the tile floor. Letty and Brett laughed together. Still, Cole stood in place, just outside the threshold. It was as if he was abandoning his post, slipping out behind the boss's back.

So what's the worst that can happen? I fire myself for leaving early and not watching for my wife? My ex-wife, he corrected.

Cole stepped inside his home.

Laughter erupted from the kitchen again. Brett shouted something, and Letty screeched. More giggles followed. Cole smiled again. He closed the door against the coming night but did not lock it. Then he curved around toward the interior of his home and put one foot in front of the other.

When he entered the kitchen, Cole's smile faltered. Not because he was displeased, quite the opposite. Emotion surged through him, curious, really, for such a small thing. But that small thing represented a great deal more than he cared to admit, and it touched him in ways he wouldn't have imagined possible.

Brett sat at the table, his hands clasped in his lap and his eyes on the fat slice of blueberry pie before him. A glass of almond milk sat beside his plate. Letty slid into the seat across from him, a glass of water beside her smaller slice of pie. The empty seat between them was Cole's. At his place was another generous slice of pie and a cup of coffee beside it.

No, it wasn't a cup. It wasn't a fancy, delicately swirled, crappy, ladylike teacup. Next to his slice of pie was a mug.

The mug was a plain ceramic white with a bright yellow smiley face, and no elegance whatsoever. Steam billowed from the top. It was full of hot coffee, and it held way more than a gulp and a half.

"I saw it at the grocery store," Letty said when she caught his line of vision. "I couldn't resist. I wish they would have had something nicer, but…" She shrugged her small shoulders as a finish to her sentence.

They were both staring at him. Brett eager for him to sit down already so he could eat his pie. Letty should know she'd done a wonderful thing for him, something he appreciated. He had to say something. But for the moment, Cole was mute and immobilized. Because what sat beside his plate wasn't merely a silly, grocery-store mug.

No, it was far more than a mug. It was a step.

Cole imagined Danielle staring at the mug, lips pursed together in a forced smile so she wouldn't offend the guest, already planning which cupboard she would stuff it into later so it wouldn't upset her fancy dishes with its crassness.

"If you don't like it, I can take it back," Letty said.

"No, no, of course I like it." Cole crossed the kitchen and took his seat at the table. He cleared his throat of the roughness in his voice. "I love it. The mug is perfect. It's just what I needed. Thank you, Letty."

As soon as Cole sat down, Brett dug into his pie. "Mmm." He hummed with all the sincerity his blissful taste buds could express. Before he even swallowed, Brett said, "Letty, this is the best pie I've ever had."

"Thanks," Letty replied, taking a small bite. She glanced over at Cole. He hadn't tried the pie yet. He was drinking from his mug.

"What other kind of pie can you make?" Brett asked.

"I can make any kind of pie you want."

"What about apple, can you make apple pie? Oh, no, chocolate! I love chocolate pie."

Letty chuckled. "Well, you think about it. The next pie is your choice."

Brett's eyebrows rose, and he beamed, given such power. He stared at his plate for a moment, thinking. Then his forehead scrunched in concentration. "I have to give this some serious thought. It's a big decision."

Letty laughed some more. "Take your time."

"Wow," Cole said after swallowing his first bite of the pie. "When my son is right, he's right. This is the best blueberry pie I've ever had. Your crust could rival my grandmother's, and until now, I've never known anyone who could do that. And this coffee, it's fantastic. I don't think I've ever had this brand before. What is it?"

"It's my own special mix. I'm glad you like it."

"I love it."

****

"Thanks," Letty said, relishing the compliment. With the catering business, the compliments came, but they were fleeting, and the only real way to know they were genuine was when she and her mother got a call to cater their next party.

Oh, sometimes the guests strolled into the kitchen as they were cleaning up at the end of an event, tipsy or flat out drunk. They'd rave about the food...and then about the host, the music, the company, the rugs on the floor, the moon in the sky, the latest gossip about people Letty and her mother didn't know, and any other bits of nonsense floating through their pickled minds.

It was different cooking for a family. This mattered more.

Today was the first time she put together a whole meal since the terrible day when she and Danny had discovered their shared roots and lost their future to a past that was none of their doing. She had spent most of her time since then crumpled on her old bed at her mother's house, soaking her pillow with impotent tears.

She had always loved cooking, but she loved even more cooking for Danny. Sometimes he would sit in the kitchen, and they'd talk while she chopped and sautéed. He had once told her he found watching her cook sensuous. Letty looked forward to cooking for the children they'd planned on having. Two, they had agreed, one of each. But if they ended up with two of the same, that would be good, too.

Letty's chest tightened, and she had to force air into her lungs. She suffered a moment of panic at the realization she could fall into one of her wretched bouts right there in front of everyone. Little more than a bare thought of Danny left her teetering on the brink. But Letty was able to close off the horrid road on which her thoughts were traveling before the ground disappeared beneath her again.

She blinked. She breathed. She put a small bite of pic on her fork, but she did not lift it to her mouth.

****

His son shoveled another forkful of dessert into his mouth. "Why didn't you tell Teresa you knew how to cook?"

Cole glanced at Letty. She gazed back at him. How could they explain to Brett why Teresa would not want another woman to overshadow her in the kitchen without making the woman out to be shallow? Since he didn't know, he looked to his son and said, "Brett, don't talk with your mouth full."

The question was forgotten, as Brett went back to focusing on his pie, and his attention span didn't stretch any further. Cole needed to explain some of the intricacies of a woman's mind and pride. He'd like to give it some thought first, especially since he'd not all the way unraveled the tangle. He glanced back at Letty and received a smile for his effective distraction. She understood.

Cole had a second cup of coffee while Brett and Letty cleaned up the small mess in the kitchen. "Brett, this is unusual," Cole said.

"What do you mean?" his son asked.

"Most of the time you're pretty lax about cleaning the day before Tracy comes."

Brett stopped what he was doing, a crumb-laden plate in his hand, and glanced back from the sink at his dad. From his expression, brows raised, mouth forming an O, it was obvious he remembered what day of the week it was.

"Oh, I forgot she was coming tomorrow." That said, Brett spun back to the sink to finish rinsing the dishes.

"Who's Tracy?" Letty asked.

Brett answered as he handed her a rinsed plate to put in the dishwasher. "She's our housekeeper. She comes in twice a month to give the place a good cleaning."

Not long after Danielle left, his and Brett's lack of tidiness degenerated their home to a real mess. His mother would have thrown a royal fit. It surprised him, how fast it all fell apart. It also made him very aware of how much Danielle did for them. Should he have thanked her for all her efforts, at least acknowledged her work? Maybe hearing his appreciation was one of the things she'd needed.

He had made an effort to keep the place clean, enlisting Brett's help, which sometimes turned out to be more hindrance than help. One day he even got out the vacuum. After wasting half an hour trying to figure out what all the attachments were for, he searched the phone book, yes, he still used a phone book, and found Tracy.

She was young, starting a business of her own, but she already had some fine references. He hired her on the spot. The house had been clean ever since, but still not the same. Danielle nurtured their home. The housekeeper did what Cole paid her to do.

"Here, Brett," Letty said. Cole glanced over as she handed his son his glass. "There's still a swallow of almond milk in there. You want to grow big and strong like your dad, don't you?"

Brett smiled before taking the glass and tipping the last of the milk down his throat. He then puffed up and lifted one of his skinny arms, making a muscle one could see, if one strained hard enough and used some imagination. Letty laid her hand upon his laboring bicep and gave it a squeeze.

"Ooh," she said. "It's working already." Brett nodded in a "see I told you so" kind of way. The boy then rinsed his glass and handed it to Letty.

After the amusing exchange, Cole shifted his attention back to his mug, with a handle fitting his grip and plenty of coffee still inside. He couldn't help but grin at the mug. It smiled back.

"Why is a zebra striped?" Cole asked from his seat at the table.

Brett and Letty glanced at each other. Quiet, a little confused, but mirth brimmed in their eyes as they both swiveled to stare his way.

His son asked the question. "I don't know. Why?"

"Because it doesn't want to be spotted," Cole said.

Letty laughed, slight giggles at first, but her merriment gained momentum. Brett hadn't understood the joke. Cole waited while his son puzzled through it.

Brett said, "I don't get it."

Letty laughed and gave him a gentle shove to the shoulder before saying, "Brett, think. Spotted could be like with polka-dots. Or spotted, as in, it doesn't want to be seen. Two meanings."

Brett got it then, laughing at the silly old joke as if it was the funniest thing he'd ever heard. At least it's what Cole believed until his son caught his breath and said, "Dad, that joke is so stupid." However, the insult lost all meaning when Brett fell back into another hearty fit of laughter.

Cole chuckled, deep and from the heart, seeing his son with the sillies. Better still was knowing he'd been able to make his boy laugh. It reintroduced some of the best of the past, the way things were before their lives were razed by a cruel, unnatural disaster.

"That might even be the stupidest joke I ever heard," Brett said as his gulps of laughter eased and then started up again when Letty's did. Whether she was laughing at Brett or the joke, Cole couldn't say, nor did it matter.

Cole's smile rivaled the ones on both sides of his mug. "Yes, I suppose it lacks the sophistication of a good knock-knock joke."

Brett laughed some more before saying, "*Spotted,* oh please. That's so *stupid,*" he repeated. Then Brett obliterated his insult by saying, "Dad, do you know any more?"

His son's question accelerated Cole and Letty's laughter until it was up to speed with Brett's.

When his laughter settled a bit, Cole said, "No, Son. I wish I did."

Cole got up and carried his empty mug to the sink. Brett rinsed it and handed it to Letty who put it in the dishwasher. Brett added the soap. "Thanks for the mug, Letty. It's the best mug I've ever had, and that's a fact."

Letty smiled as she closed the door to the dishwasher and touched the start button. "You're welcome."

"Quite a coincidence," Cole said as he headed for the back door.

"What do you mean?" Letty asked. She and Brett were both staring at Cole again. Brett was hoping for another joke, Cole was sure. He'd make it a point to learn some.

"I picked up something for you today, too."

"Really? What?" The corners of her lips rose along with her eyebrows.

"Why don't you two go into the living room, and I'll go get it. It's still in the truck."

The two kids stared at each other, like siblings asking the same question without words, both answering with an I-don't-know shrug and a smile of anticipation. They left the kitchen together, giggling between their whispers.

A few minutes later when Cole entered the living room through the kitchen, Brett and Letty were sitting on the floral-patterned couch together. Surprise lifted both their faces at the sight of the guitar case in his hand.

"Dad, you bought a guitar," Brett said, as if his father hadn't realized what he'd purchased.

"Oh, Cole," Letty said in a quiet voice, coming to her feet. "You shouldn't have."

"It's no big deal," he said as he handed her the case.

Letty took his gift with reverence before sitting down again to unclasp the case. She raised the lid and sucked in her breath. "Oh, Cole, this is too much. It had to cost a fortune."

"Not really. It's used, so I got a deal." The deal was he paid a thousand dollars for it, and he got to take it home. It was worth it, though, to see Letty inspecting the guitar, running her fingers along the smooth wood with awe and reverence.

Then she took it out of the case, set the case on the floor, and laid the guitar flat on her lap. She stared down at the instrument, inspecting every little bit of it.

Cole dug a slip of paper from his pocket and read aloud. "It's quality tone-woods and a solid top, dovetail neck joint, solid mahogany, top, back, sides, and neck. Morado fingerboard and bridge material, with a satin finish. And a customized rosette."

When Cole looked up from the piece of paper where he'd written his notes, Letty was grinning.

Cole returned a sheepish smile. "I wrote down what the guy at the music store said. I hope I got it right."

"You got it right. Cole, I…"

"Come on, Letty," he said. "Play something for us."

"All right. I have to tune it first."

"Take your time." Cole got up and set a match to the stone fireplace he'd readied earlier, while she plucked out notes and made her adjustments.

"You know how to play guitar?" Brett asked.

"Yes. I've been playing since I was about your age."

Brett turned to his father. "How did you know that, Dad?"

Letty stopped what she was doing and shifted her gaze up and toward Cole.

He caught her meaning. She didn't need to worry about him telling any part of her secrets. "It came up once in a conversation," Cole said. He sat down beside the fire in an easy chair he swiveled toward the couch.

Letty finished her tuning, and then she was playing. Her fingers danced on the stings with effortless grace. The music was touching, something soft and ample, layered with varying depths of emotion. Cole recognized it as a classical piece, though he couldn't name it.

"Wow, you're really good," Brett said, wide-eyed, impressed. He leaned toward the guitar. "Do you think you could teach me how to play?"

"Sure," Letty said. Her words had a disconnected air, an automatic response from the polite teachings of her upbringing. Her music held the bulk of her awareness.

"Later, Brett," Cole said in a soft aside. "Let her

enjoy it right now."

Letty glanced at Brett and gave him a few seconds of her attention. "Tomorrow I'll teach you some cords."

Brett smiled, his bright eyes watching her right hand and then her left hand and then back again. "Do you know any rock songs?"

"Of course. I don't usually perform for anyone. It's…strange to have an audience."

"Oh, please," Brett begged. "Do you sing, too?"

Cole kept his grin from showing. *Yes, she sings, with a voice to make the heavens weep with envy.*

"I sing a little," Letty said. "All right. What would you like to hear?"

"Um, how about some Green Day?"

Cole's insides cringed, but he said nothing. Green Day. It was probably some of that noise Brett loved and Cole hated.

"I know a few of theirs," Letty said, casting a quick glance toward Cole. "I even know one your father might like."

Her fingers paused. In the anticipatory silence, they hovered over the strings as mind and body switched gears. From the first notes, it was obvious this tune was altogether different from the previous piece. But it wasn't erratic or annoying, as Cole had expected. The mellow glide caught his interest right away.

His son nodded and smiled his approval as he recognized the song. "Dad, this is called 'Good Riddance (Time of Your Life).' It's a great song."

Then Letty sang, and Cole figured he liked Green Day after all.

Her voice, the voice from an impossible dream he'd first heard streaming through his land, washed over him like a hot shower after a strenuous day.

The lyrics spoke about life's changes, about making the best of what you have. From his seat beside the fire, Cole slid a leisured scan from the joy on his son's face to their surroundings. Cole loved this house where he grew up, where, in truth, the good memories outweighed the bad by several tons. The house his father and grandfather built sat upon land which Cole loved even more. Looking at the whole of his life, it was indeed good. Better than good. It was blissful.

Letty played and she sang. The music overlaid the sore spots of their lives, enriched the house and all the needy hearts beating within it. When the song was over, the silence did not summon the void Cole awaited, naturally, because for the last two years that's what followed every flicker of joy.

The end of the song held not the teeming bereavement of something precious once had but now lost. It was more of a chapter ending, the tones fading not with finality, but with tidings of enjoyments yet to come.

Loitering aromas made room for pearls of delight. Tonight, long-standing sorrows, despite their fervent efforts to grow roots, were wrenched from this home and carried off on a sweet bay of music. It was so, at least for the time being. Cole glanced out the window. Darkness had come, but on this night, it stayed outside where it belonged.

He returned his attention to Letty. Her fingers rested on the strings. A cascade of her golden hair draped the body of the guitar. Her eyes were closed, and a small but sated smile eased her downturned face.

When the last note faded, Brett revved up and

applauded. Cole did the same. A light blush colored her cheeks. "Aren't you used to this?" Cole asked. "You must get this kind of praise all the time."

"Like I said, I don't perform for audiences. Almost no one has ever even heard me. Most of the time I...I just play for myself."

The flicker of pain in her eyes told him she'd played for her Danny, and Cole wished he'd have thought ahead before he said anything.

"Any requests?" Letty asked Cole, prying him from his regret.

Cole ran the fingers and thumb of his right hand down either side of his jaw, turning choices in his head before saying, "I don't suppose you know any country songs."

"*Country songs!*" Brett shouted. His face blared the expression of a boy appalled at the very notion of such a musical travesty.

Letty grinned. "I know one you might like, but it's an older piece."

"That's okay." Cole settled back. "So am I."

Letty laughed. Brett gave in to a smile as he leaned his shoulder against the backrest of the couch and stared at Letty.

"Let's see if this one sounds familiar to you." Her fingers returned to the strings.

Cole recognized the song after a couple of notes. He was more than a little surprised and a whole lot pleased a girl as young as her even knew the classic. With a satisfied grin, he rested his head back and enjoyed.

"Who's she playing, Dad?"

"Patsy Cline."

"Never heard of her," Brett said.

"For shame. Hush now, Son. This one is called 'Crazy.' It's timeless."

As Letty sang, Cole, except for the raise of a small, contented grin, fell into perfect stillness. He could say in all honesty her singing rivaled that of the great Ms. Cline. Of course, he'd known ahead of time she had it in her. But when something was as pure and affecting as Letty's voice, it's easy to wonder if his imagination had dabbled with embellishment.

The country station Cole listened to on the radio out in the pole barn sometimes played the old song. While he'd heard it many times before, this was the first time he'd listened to it with such attentiveness. By the time she sang the last words, he had to wonder if Letty's choice of songs had not been so random, bemoaning love's lack of sanity.

The last notes were still a gift to their ears when his son started clapping, even though it was for a country song. Cole joined him with full, enthusiastic applause before putting two fingers to his lips and giving a loud whistle. Letty smiled at her audience, her discomfort in performing for them emptied of most of her shyness.

"Play another one," Brett said. And then he screamed in terror.

Tucked into the corner of the couch, Brett faced the front window. Cole swung his head to look toward the pane of glass where Brett's wide eyes were staring. The sight almost made him scream, too. Letty swung around. She did yell, at the ghostly, blood-streaked woman who stood on the other side of the glass like a scene from a horror movie.

Letty shouted, "Mom!"

Chapter 13

Connie's lower lip stiffened at the sight before her.

After her rental car met a violent death against the trunk of a girthy tree, she'd spent a good fifteen minutes panting shaky breaths in the sudden quiet. At first, giving assurance she was still alive, and then assessing her personal damage while the blessed airbags deflated like knifed balloons.

The headlights must have broken in the crash, as the only light was the pasty flush of the moon trickling in patches through a mass of trees. She took a slow glance around at what little she could see. The clutter of crowding woods, a few leaves floating in the dirt haze she'd created, and the tree she'd hit, close enough to her face to tell her the SUV's front end was good and crumpled.

She tested each limb with small, tentative movements. No broken bones that she could tell, but she was going to be plenty sore. The twinges tugging at various parts of her body were for the time being little more than bubbles of discomfort; however, they were already swelling.

With curious trepidation, Connie pressed the button for the inside light and twisted the rearview mirror toward her. Her partial image appeared jagged and offset due to a diagonal crack near the center of the mirror. It made the horror looking back at her even worse.

Her eyes stared back, unnaturally wide, her expression wild. The accident had taken her clip and styled her loose hair into a tempestuous display extending well beyond the boundaries of the broken mirror. Connie angled her head to the left. The right side of her face appeared to be fine, ashen, but unscathed. Then she turned the other way, leaning to the right a little for a better view.

A small cut high above the end of her brow expelled a surprising amount of blood. A glistening, crimson stream circled the outside of her left eye and flowed down her face. Connie was unaware of the cut until she'd seen it. After seeing it, however, the pain of the injury overtook all of the others.

A moment of panic seized her at the sight of all the blood, already running a narrow river down her throat and into her shirt. While wondering how much blood she could lose from such a small wound, Connie grabbed for her purse, but it was no longer on the passenger seat.

She unbuckled her seatbelt and felt around the dim foot wells. Nothing. Twisting to check the back roused some dormant pains, but she did it anyway to search for her purse in the back seat and foot wells back there. A few drops of blood made small, wet plops on the console.

No purse in the back. *Think, think.* She felt around the spaces of the front seats and found her purse wedged between the passenger door and the passenger seat. Connie rummaged through her purse until she found the mini package of tissues. She plucked every one of them out of the pack and wadded them tight against the cut. After a couple calming breaths, her mind turned the page.

She had to get out of the car. Maybe gas was leaking and a fire might start, trapping her in the car. The car might even explode. She hadn't a clue if such a thing were possible, but it happened in movies all the time, and she wasn't about to wait around to see if it was Hollywood hyperbole.

With usual effort at first, then with growing frustration, she worked the driver's side lever that should have opened her door. It wouldn't budge.

The accident had crushed the driver's side door into place, and she hadn't the strength to force it open. As bad a condition as the SUV must be in, she figured it would take some sort of machinery to pry off the door. With cautious movements, she managed to maneuver over the console and tried the passenger door. It opened as if nothing had happened.

All the interior lights popped on, and their glow poured out of the rental car. It was inordinately bright against the desolate night and more blinding than illuminating. Connie leaned over, found the button, and shut off the interior lights, as well as the smaller one she'd used. Darkness encased her.

A minute or so later, her eyes adjusted to the ghostly light of the moon. Her one piece of luck tonight, the moon was full. Hanging high and white in the night sky the way it was, it reminded her of the lights she and Letty had put in their closets a few years ago. It was an odd thought popping out of nowhere. Then again, maybe not so much. Letty was nearby, maybe gazing up at the moon, too, and having the same odd thought.

That is, if Mr. Cole Holloway didn't have her locked in his basement, chained to a wall. Or a bed. Connie shoved the car door all the way open.

Crawling outside with slow, careful movements, Connie eased her body weight onto her feet in experimental increments. Soreness invaded her left hip. She was sure it was already darkening to an awful bruise. At least her legs, although wobbly, would be able to carry her. Her left shoulder ached where she'd slammed into the door, and she hurt across her body where the seatbelt had kept her from flying through the windshield.

Well, she didn't need her shoulder to walk. Connie closed the door and stepped away from the SUV.

Movement caught her eye, and she peered toward the front of the car. Something was covering the hood. No, not a thing, they were things. Connie gazed at the strange sight as leaves the size of pancakes floated down from the tree she had hit, and landed on the car. Maple leaves, maybe? The colorful leaves of gold, yellow, and deep red reflected the moonlight in their autumn hues, giving off an almost gilded appearance in the mystic light. It was plain eerie.

The leaves continued to fall in a dry, placid rain, but the pace was slowing. A few steps to the front and bright pale shades of the tree's exposed interior shouted the destruction she had caused. She leaned forward a bit for a closer look. The light beneath the tree was too meager to determine the extent of the damage.

A leaf landed on Connie's head and startled her from her observations. She flicked it away with her right hand, recoiling from the resulting friction of movement of her left hand against her head wound.

Wetness seeped from beneath the wad of tissues, so after blotting the blood from her eye, Connie flipped the wad around to the other side. She winced from the pressure she had to apply. More blood oozed through her fingers and down her hand, a macabre spill of warmth against the cold.

The cut on her head hurt and was going to be a nuisance. It wasn't much wider than the length of her thumbnail, but the damn thing was bleeding enough to have already saturated the clump of tissues. Rifling through the shock and forcing sensible thought, Connie remembered the small travel bag she'd packed for the trip.

She opened the back door on the passenger side and retrieved her bag from the far side of the seat, sliding it close. She unzipped it and felt around until she found a sock. After rolling it into a ball, she used it to apply pressure against the cut on her head. Then she hooked the long strap of her purse over her good shoulder, took her travel bag out of the battered car, and closed the door.

She stepped back again and gave the car a cursory scan.

The front window, while still encased within its frame, was shattered into nests of webbing. At least two of the tires were flat. She could confirm by personal experience the frame had taken a good beating. In the glow of the moonlight, fractured by overhead branches, her rented SUV huddled against the tree trunk, scraped, crumpled, and awaiting the formal sentence declaring she had totaled it.

Connie shoved the dismal condition of the vehicle behind her more immediate concerns. She couldn't do anything about the car right now anyway. Still, however, was the matter of her daughter. As much as her head and body were rattled, the accident had not steered her from her focus, had not diminished her worry.

She gave the car her back and stared up the incline she'd descended at a harrowing pace. At first, it appeared to Connie as if she had dropped into a sloped hole, so steep was the rise. Which was about how it felt when she was racing down. If she lived to be a thousand years old, she'd never forget the powerlessness of careening downhill, the brutal slams against trees and boulders, the pounding to the undercarriage, or the all-encompassing terror.

The accident replayed in her head, in front of her eyes, through her battered body. A shiver racked her hard. Connie was well aware of how lucky she'd been. Not only was she still alive, but she'd be able to walk away from this accident with nothing more than cuts and bruises. It could have turned out so very differently.

Though the trauma of the most recent minutes of her life made it difficult, she was able to calm her breathing and her pounding heart and clear a path. Later she would think more about her close call with death. It couldn't be helped. But she had no time for such contemplations now. Her daughter was in danger.

The trembling of her limbs surprised her, though it shouldn't. Just because her mind had chosen to closet the accident for the time being, didn't mean her body would go along with the plan. She could ignore her body's callings, at least for a while. Then, as if to blight her defiance, the ache in her head took a vigorous march through her skull.

Will and determination warred with the growing statements of her injuries. She believed they were superficial, but they were vivid enough to harass her. Connie took a couple of breaths and closed her eyes for a minute. While she'd like to claim a soothing numbness to her pains, she was willing to settle for the slight decrease her mind was able to muster. It was as if her body understood its need to persevere in order to survive.

Connie then ranked in place the next order of business. Still concerned over an explosion, she dragged her travel bag several yards away. She rummaged through her purse until she found her cell phone.

Without even taking it out to see if she had service in this uncivilized corner of the world, Connie opened her chilled fingers and let the phone drop back into her purse. It would take hours to handle this accident the proper way, and she wasn't about to wait around. Not after coming so far and being so close. The car wasn't going anywhere. She, however, was.

A brief study in the direction toward which the car was pointed told Connie she was partway down a valley. The world down there appeared silvery in the strange glow of the full moon, as if it were not actual landscape, but rather a stark and grim rendition of a world gone by, a barbaric world better left in the past.

Oh, it wasn't like she couldn't appreciate nature's scenery. She could. Say, on a day trip. Or better still, on canvas or video. She preferred an actual floor beneath her feet, a solid roof over her head, and breathing air run through a conditioning system of some sort, maybe scented with her cooking, or a nice candle.

All Connie could smell out here was dirt with hints of pine and some other earthy aromas she couldn't name and didn't care to know about anyway.

With eyes now well focused in the night, she rotated in a full circle, figuring the best way out of this situation.

Beyond the weeping maple tree where the car sat in forlorn uselessness, the land sloped down much farther than where she had stopped. Maybe half a mile or so, and the incline was steep. In several places the ground dropped off, where, had she kept going, she could have descended into a freefall. The monstrous tree that had jarred her and totaled the SUV might well have saved her life.

All she could see for forever was a downslope of ruffled treetops with some vacant patches of land in between, many of them darkened by the screen of the trees or rocky overhangs. Those shadowy areas appeared to be hungry holes in the ground, the ill-tempered, earthbound sisters to the mysterious gapes in outer space.

The drop-offs, those darker pits in the night, were going to haunt her. The chain of possible events already unfolded in her mind. If she'd have plunged into one of those, in this wild and overgrown terrain, it was a real possibility she might not ever have been found. She would have disappeared forever into the grave of this beastly, infinite wilderness, never to be seen again.

Nausea rolled through her stomach, and dizziness swirled her head. With nothing manmade in sight, the living bulge of growth surrounding her closed in, overwhelming her with the foreign lay of this world.

It had chased her all day, the feeling of

encroaching encasement, a hopeful fiend determined to claim the interloper. Even as she had passed through the occasional small town, grateful for the sight of human life, Connie couldn't escape the dread of what awaited her on the other side. More miles of nothing but raw land, land she was all but certain elongated as she drove through. The wide-open spaces were like a living beast, closing in on all sides while distracting her with its views.

At one point, her imagination saw fingers of desolation working behind her, pinching closed in her wake the civilized world, sealing her in its realm like diced berries in a raw piecrust.

Suddenly, the aggressive belligerence of fear, worry, pain, as well as the weariness, suctioned itself to her innards, loosened Connie's formidable grip, and left her teetering on the precipice of near insanity.

An unfamiliar vulnerability swooped in and clamped on with powerful jaws. Tears gathered in her eyes. Her shoulders slumped, and her knees turned gelatinous. A childish fear washed over Connie. All that was left in its ebb was the want of her home, to be safe in the warmth and cleanliness of her convenience-laden house with her daughter by her side.

Letty.

Her precious daughter, the heart of her life. Letty was suffering, quite possibly in danger from some strange man who had her under his control, and no one else in the world was going to save her little girl. The image of her daughter, of this man taking advantage of her, straightened Connie's spine and dried her tears.

From the broad and tender hole in her heart, cleaved when Letty left town, burst the same resolve that had given her a daughter in the first place.

Grit and determination could get anything done. She'd started her catering business with little money and no experience other than what she had learned in her mother's kitchen. She'd made a success of it, too. And when she wanted to have a baby, but not a man, she found a way to do it without resorting to reckless sex or entrapping herself or some hapless male.

With her usual efficiency, Connie gathered and categorized her ideas. She laid out her options and arranged them according to viability. Like sitting before a blank piece of paper to write out a catering itinerary in accordance with a client's likes and dislikes, Connie put everything in order and tackled her next move.

As nothing even close to civilization lay in any direction but up the incline down which she'd come, her only reasonable option was to make it back to the road. Fortunately, enough moonlight streamed down so she'd be able to see her way to climb. The incline was steep and rocky, and she'd have to use extra caution, which would be even more challenging since she still had to apply pressure to the cut on her head. But it was the single logical move available.

First, Connie returned to the SUV, as of yet not aflame, and slid into the passenger seat. Leaning over, she turned the key enough so the GPS brightened to life. She had to squint at the sudden illumination, as her eyes had already adjusted to the night. The first relief from anguish she'd had in a long time skimmed across her when the GPS told her she was less than a mile from Cole Holloway's house.

After turning off the key and closing the door, she looped the strap of her purse over her head and let the weight hang from her good shoulder, raised the handle of her travel bag so she could drag it behind her, and began her uphill trek.

Most of the climb wasn't as bad as she had expected. Her movements were slow and methodical, testing each step before relying on it. A good part of the ground was hard and steady and not quite as steep as she'd first thought, thank goodness, as she was dragging her small travel bag along with her.

Once, in a careless moment of distraction, she put her weight on a patch of loose dirt without assessing it first and slid back down a few feet before catching grip again. Dust rose over her crouched form and then settled upon her. Connie coughed, rubbed her eyes, and took a minute to rest and catch her breath before resuming her climb.

When at last she got to the road, she sat on the blacktop to rest. She was safe doing so, as not another car was in sight. At night, with the full moon shedding its strange light on the endless wilds, the sensation of being alone in the world once again crept under her skin.

It took some force to expel those thoughts. Her injuries, lack of sleep, and worry had taken a toll on her mind's strength. This creepy environment didn't help. Shadows swarmed like ghosts on the prowl, and sounds from the woods flicked all around her. Who knew what kind of creatures lurked out in this land searching for a meal? Bears? Yes, there must be bears out there.

Focus, Connie. Focus.

While she was stretching some of the tension from her neck, Connie happened to look upward. Stars cluttered the whole of the sky in a way they never could above the glorious lights of Las Vegas. It did have a certain beauty, in a backwoods kind of way. However, at the moment it was plain disturbing. For the sight of so many stars glaring down on her without the buffering of electric lights emphasized her isolation.

Breaking away from the sights in the sky, Connie worked to shut out the fears creeping up on her. A fat drop of blood drew attention to the cold by way of its damp warmth as it glided down her face. Cautiously, she lifted the sock from her head and turned a clean patch against the cut.

This land around her was far too vacant of civilization, the same as it had been all day. Only now, she didn't even have the radio to dilute the sense of being the last living soul on the planet. Nor did she have the security of the car to protect to her from whatever might be lurking out in the grim concealment of the woods.

Connie longed for her city, with all the varied restaurants, shops, and services, with people everywhere. It couldn't be too soon for her to be back to her tasteful house, where neighbors were close by and she could see the city lights from anywhere. This untamed world full of trees and bears, and who knew what all, was pitted with far too many dangers.

Before she could go home, though, Connie had to rescue her daughter. With an artlessness to which she was not accustomed, she got to her feet, catching her balance when a wave of dizziness tipped her. She zipped her thin jacket up to her throat in an effort to keep out the growing cold, before taking the handle of her travel bag and rolling it behind her as she headed east.

Along the paved road, the light of the moon was different than it had been down by the wrecked car. It took her a minute to figure out it was because this was where streetlights should be guiding her, not the moon.

The lack of electric light, the weird lunar glow, and the crush of woods capped by a crazy litter of stars all worked to create a sinister ambiance. The unsettling light, broken by far, far too many trees, would have to do. Not a single streetlight was visible in either direction for as far as she could see.

Before her, the trees, plenty of pines, maples, and some other skinny tree with a whitish bark, crowded along the side of the road and formed almost a full canopy. It blocked out a good portion of the moonlight. Gazing at the road ahead of her, Letty feared she was about to head into a forbidding, black tube-sock of a tunnel. With no hope for better, she pushed onward, upward, ascending the road's incline which made her trek even more challenging.

She continued to apply pressure to the cut on her head. Maybe it was her injuries making it seem like the cold was getting worse, but she didn't think so. She shivered inside her jacket. The thin garment was designed more for fashion than for protection against weather. Connie vowed she would never again take for granted the warmth of the desert.

Nor would she take for granted the sounds, the lights, the colors of her town, and the ever-present conveniences. Back home, at night, the Las Vegas strip was a beacon wherever she was. This strange world through which she walked was creepy, quiet, and claustrophobic, banding her in with all these damn trees.

When she was sure her situation couldn't get any eerier, a sudden, long wail, a ghoulish howling of some wild creature, sliced through the darkness. Her scalp tightened.

Connie stopped to listen. She glanced around, but it was too dark to see very far into the woods. A wolf, probably. Were wolves aggressive? Were they afraid of people, or did they eat them? She had no idea.

It howled again. And then again, one howl not quite faded before another frightening plaint breached the night. Was there an echo, or was there more than one of those wild animals yowling in the woods? It was impossible to tell from what direction the cries came. She couldn't even estimate how close it was. It, or they.

Then all was quiet again.

Despair used fear to toy with her. But anger soon took over. Anger at this godforsaken land, anger at the man who was keeping her daughter from her, even anger at Letty for running off and putting her in this situation.

She kept a steady pace and shook it off, all of it. Later, once she had her daughter, once they were home, she'd vent her wrath then and make sure Letty had a clear understanding of all the trouble she'd caused.

At times, as Connie walked the road surrounded by too many shadows, she half expected some mangy, hunched werewolf-like beast with bared teeth and readied claws to vault from the all-encompassing night and pounce on her. She walked on, though, a little slower so as to lessen the sound of her footsteps and the wheels of her travel bag, while attempting to judge the distance between her vulnerable body and those gothic howls.

The tunnel of trees opened, the leafy roof retreating back to the woods after she'd rounded a wide curve in the road. A minute or so later, Connie stumbled at the abrupt, albeit short, drop-off. The paved road became a dirt road. No warning. No reason. The single piece civilization in this primitive land, and it just stopped. It was as if the road workers had run out of asphalt, or maybe motivation, to go any farther into this awful place.

It wasn't as if the road branched off left or right. Relentless woods still surrounded her along both sides. As far as she could tell, the road kept going, only now it was unpaved. So Connie shook her head and dragged her travel bag onto the damned dirt road, hoping her GPS had not been mistaken when it sent her this way.

A surge of eagerness rushed through her when she stumbled upon a mailbox staked on a thick wooden post on the right side of the road. The name painted on the side in white, block letters read *Clayton*. Disappointment made her pause and groan. Squinting in the direction she was headed showed nothing but more woods, bisected by more dirt road. Maybe this was what people here considered a neighborhood.

Onward.

About fifteen minutes later, another mailbox appeared on the same side of the road. This one was nicer, in the shape of a log cabin, mounted on a chest-high tree stump. Connie could have wept with relief when from the side of the mailbox she read the name *Holloway* in stenciled, white letters.

No sign of a house from where she stood, as the driveway wound through yet more woods. But it was there. Connie could almost feel her daughter's presence nearby. She hiked with renewed vigor up this last leg of her long and arduous journey.

Half a minute later, she stumbled and almost fell as she crossed onto the slight rise of a paved driveway. Paved road, dirt road, paved driveway, did the people here have no sense of continuity? It didn't matter enough for her to care. Soon she and Letty would be away from this backwoods hellhole.

The driveway was longer than the street she lived on back in Vegas. The shadowy trees along the paving were as bad as they'd been along the road, blocking her in on all sides, cloaking untold dangers, giving all manner of creatures endless hiding places. What kind of person would live in such a place? A person who didn't want anyone to know what they were up to, was her guess.

When she walked around a bend which opened to a broad clearing, Connie's heart picked up speed.

A porch light beside the front door cast a buttery glow. The door to Mr. Cole Holloway's house, where he was keeping her daughter.

The house, although it was a log cabin style, had a grand stature about it. Two stories, a log-railed porch running along the entire front. To the left of the door beneath a picture window sat some potted plants and several Adirondack chairs in some sort of pale-colored natural wood. To the right, a porch swing facing front hung from two thick chains. A smaller window behind it.

The house was larger than what she'd expected. Cleaner, too, as she'd pictured it with a front yard full of overgrown weeds, broken-down cars, and other miscellaneous junk. From what she could see, the place was tidy and well-tended.

The most promising sign yet, lights! She could have cheered aloud seeing something, anything, running on electricity. But desperation to get to her daughter smothered all thoughts of the primeval conditions through which she had traveled to get here.

Yellow light from the large window spilled across the porch, past the railing, and onto the mown lawn. Her daughter was in that house. It's where she'd been these last days, where she might be in serious trouble at this very moment. How in the hell Letty ended up way out here was a question she would get answered, later.

She left the driveway and rushed across the yard as fast as her battered body would take her, letting go of her travel bag before she flew up the steps.

As her fist raised to pound on the front door, the music of a guitar flowed onto the porch, as did the unmistakable sound of her daughter's sweet voice. Connie limped over and stared through the big front window.

On the other side of the glass was a neat living room, decorated with a fair amount of taste, albeit a bit overdone and more suited to a Georgian-style mini-mansion than a log cabin. Royal blue carpeting, a tasseled rug, and tasseled throw pillows in bright hues of gold and red. The river rock fireplace wavering with flames was somewhat out of place in the upper-crust setting but cast a pleasant warmth to the scene.

Letty sat on a couch across from the lit fireplace, playing a guitar. A man and a boy, she assumed it was Cole Holloway and son, sat watching her. The boy was on the couch near Letty. The man was leaning back in a chair with a clear expression of ecstasy as he gazed at her daughter.

A surge of red-hot rage shot through Connie.

Her own expression contorted to match her ugly mood. Her hand, now wet all around with blood from the saturated sock, dropped to her midsection and fisted. Blood dripped from the sock through her fingers and made small plops on the wooden planks.

Everything fuzzed out, except the bliss on Cole Holloway's face. The man looked too relaxed and far too...too satisfied. What had he done? What had he done to her daughter? Then Connie's glare shifted back to Letty.

She could hardly believe her eyes.

Letty didn't look afraid. She didn't look abused or suicidal. She didn't appear to be in any kind of distress. In fact, she looked better than she had in weeks. Connie's eyes widened a bit at the sight of Letty smiling. Smiling!

Her daughter's color was good. If Connie wasn't mistaken, Letty had put on some much-needed weight. She hadn't played guitar or sung a note since the night she and Danny discovered their history, but here she was, playing and singing and looking as happy as she ever had. Of all the damn things she imagined finding, well, this sure as hell wasn't one of them.

Though it wasn't at all logical, Connie had a powerful urge to snap up her daughter and shake her. Every horrible image that had tormented her over these last days leapt back to mock her. She'd been sick with worry, had gone without food and sleep. She'd totaled a car and damaged her own body in her panicked haste to get to Letty and rescue her.

She'd trudged up this horrid mountain, plagued

with injuries and stalked by howling beasts. She could have died out in the woods, or been attacked and eaten by some wild creature. And there sat her daughter, warm and safe, having a good ole time!

No, Connie could not believe her narrowed eyes.

Then she couldn't believe her ears.

Somebody screamed, a terrified, high-pitched peal. Something one might hear in a horror movie at the first sight of a monster. The scream had come from the boy, who was gaping at her as if she was said monster. Letty and that man had jerked from their relaxed states and come to attention. They were staring at her, too.

Then Letty hollered, "Mom!"

Chapter 14

Within seconds of Brett's terrified scream, Letty flung open the front door. An instant after that, she had her mother's upper arms in her grip while she gave her a panicked, visual scan.

Her mom's face was ashen with copious tiers of dirt covering her from head to toe. In the yellow glow of the porch light, her mother had a vaporous appearance. The only things on her looking alive was the wild fury in her eyes and the glistening crimson of her mother's blood. It seeped from the left side of her forehead and oozed through the filth in a gruesome trek down her face. No wonder Brett had been frightened enough to scream.

The sight before her sent Letty's words scrambling around each other, muting her as they could not make a coherent connection. She needed to help her mother, but all she could manage to do was to stare.

Then Cole was beside her, taking charge and making sense.

"Let's get her inside," he said. The strength of his voice and authoritarian instructions set everyone in motion. "Brett, get some clean wash cloths and wet most of them," he told his son without looking away from her mom.

He helped Letty get her mother inside and straight to the couch. Letty sat beside her, staring as if the woman before her might be an alien replica.

"Mom, what are you doing here? What happened to you?" she asked the second she regained her ability to speak. Worry elevated the pitch of her voice.

Connie shifted her position and gave Letty an inspection of her own. "You look so healthy and...happy."

"Mom, I'm fine. But how—"

Her mother's brows drew together. "I half expected you to be shackled to a wall, or locked in a basement. Instead, I find you fresh and clean, and apparently quite free."

She should have stopped the chuckle before it escaped, but Letty couldn't help it, so absurd was her mother's anger. "So you're mad because I'm not beaten and bound?"

Her mother's jaw tightened, but not so much as to restrain her wrath. "Do you have any idea what I've been through since you left? Or what's happened to me trying to get to you, to save you? I totaled a rental car!"

Brett's footsteps pounded down the stairs. His arms were full of clean, damp cloths, and at his father's nod he set them on the coffee table. Cole sat on the other side of Connie.

"Mom—" Letty said, but her mother cut off her sentence with her usual sharp efficiency.

"I've been frantic," Connie continued. Her eyes widened, grew wilder, angrier. "Every day has been a goddamned living nightmare, full of every horrible possibility."

Cole picked up one of the cloths and used care as he washed the dirt and blood from Letty's mother's face. If she was aware of his ministrations, she didn't show it. The woman was well off on one of her tangents.

Connie continued to rail at Letty, her voice escalating near to yelling. "I've been literally sick with worry! And here you are, having a nice relaxing vacation for yourself. Ow!"

"Sorry," Cole said, though he didn't stop. "Brett, go and get the first aid kit out of the kitchen."

Brett sprinted from the room. Letty suspected it had more to do with putting some distance between him and her mother's angry rant than his father's order.

"Damn it, Letty," her mother said, resuming her rant after a pause scarce long enough to take a breath. "You leave the house, leave town without even taking your cell phone! I don't hear from you for days, and when I do, you won't tell me where you are. I hear all this anguish in your voice, and then you hang up on me! Do you have any idea what your selfish behavior did to me?"

Brett hurried back into the room, carrying by the handle a red box with a white cross on it. He set the box on the glossy coffee table beside the cloths. Brett stepped back then, but kept his eyes on the wild, seething woman on the couch. Although he now knew Connie was her mother, the fright he'd suffered when he'd first seen her through the window looking like a zombie straight from the grave would probably stay with the poor kid for a long time. Maybe forever.

With calm efficiency, Cole flipped opened the lid to the kit and searched through it, removing the things he needed and setting them on the coffee table. At her mother's accusatory remark, his lips parted, but he closed them again. Letty was grateful for his restraint.

When her mother got like this, it was best to stay low and take cover.

"Brett," Cole said. "Go get Miss Norris a glass of water."

Brett hurried back to the kitchen.

"Then," her mother said, gestures broadening, eyes widened enough to see white all around the turbulent sea-green of her irises, "I called you back to talk some sense into you, and some *man* answers." Her mother raged on, uncaring that the man she referred to with such scorn was right beside her, tending to her wounds. "I hear from a perfect stranger how you tried to throw yourself off of a cliff!"

Letty pitched forward to see past her mother. "Cole!"

Cole gave a quick glance toward the kitchen door, then to her. "The conversation got a little heated, and it came out."

"Why did it get heated?" Letty asked, not that it mattered. Even though it was true, he never should have told her mother such a thing. But Cole didn't have a chance to answer. The storm that was her mother continued to blow.

"And then this man, who I know nothing about, tells me you're at his house. I have no idea where, he won't tell me, then he says I can't talk to you because you're passed out drunk!"

"Cole!" Letty shouted at him, leaning forward so he would catch the full force of her outrage. What had he been thinking, saying such things to her mother?

"Um, sorry," Cole said, more sheepish this time. She caught he was somewhat sorry, but still…

Brett came back with the glass of water, giving

Cole a valid excuse to not answer further. It didn't need to be said—how neither of them wanted the boy to hear about her attempt at suicide, or her bout with drunkenness. Brett set the glass on a coaster beside the towels and stepped back.

They'd gotten lucky, with Brett being out of the room during that last bit. If her mother should decide to revisit either of those two topics, Letty would stop her. She'd take the hit to protect the boy.

"He knows I'm your mother, and I'm worried sick, and he still refuses to tell me where this house is," her mom said, talking with more hand movements as her emotions outgrew verbal expression. "And then you don't have enough decency to call me back."

A finger of guilt poked at Letty. Not calling her mother had been deliberate, in an oblique sort of way. She had been feeling so good all day, her mind had draped off anything with the potential to spoil the peace, like talking to her mom. Of late, emotional comforts had been very few, their strength feeble. Most days, nonexistence was the norm.

It had been a month since even a meager stir of joy had touched her life, and the mercy she'd found here had been too precious to put at risk.

Still, it wasn't right for her to have left her mother hanging. "I meant to call you, Mom, but I forgot." The excuse was weak, and not altogether true, but she had to offer something. Her mother, most times an emotional rock, was teetering on the verge of complete hysterics.

From the look on her mother's face, the explanation was a lengthy distance from the one she'd expected. All the lousy excuse did was rile her even more. The woman's squally demeanor swelled to a full-blown tempest as a second blustery wind infused her sails.

"Oh, you forgot, well, no big deal, Letty. I almost killed myself trying to get here in time to save you!"

"Save me from what?"

"From him." Connie stabbed a thumb toward Cole, who was applying some antibiotic cream to the cut on her head.

"From me!" Cole said, hands jerking away from his work, leaning back as if her thumb was a knife, and it was aiming for his heart.

Connie spun around, spitting her wrath on Cole. Dust sprayed from her wild hair. Her shoulders tensed. Letty raised her hands a few inches, ready to restrain her mother if she launched a physical attack on Cole. Letty had been a witness to this side of her before, but never on such a grand scale.

When riled, her mom had a temper fierce enough to keep her employees in line, her vendors from trying any shenanigans, and her daughter from straying too far from her control. It didn't flare to the wild often, but it could be explosive. While her mother had never been violent, Letty had not ever seen her this crazed, had never before seen her bunch her fists into little cannon balls like they were now.

Connie continued her tirade, now aiming for Cole.

"Yes, you! Unlike my young, vulnerable daughter, I've lived long enough in this world to know you could very well be some sort of pervert, a serial killer, or any one of a wide range of unsavory types of men."

"Good God," Cole said in harshness as he wiped his hands on one of the damp cloths and threw it down on the coffee table. He then snatched up a bandage and peeled open the little pack with more vigor than was necessary.

Cole's entire face had tightened at her mother's vicious allegation. Bless his kind heart, he was holding on to his patience for Letty's benefit. She owed him yet another great big thank you. Especially since her mother's accusations were outrageous, false, and insulting to a man like Cole, who was ingrained with a solid moral standard.

Connie had turned her body so she could better face Cole and glare her daggers his way. Her temper sharpened. Though, she had nothing to back her suspicions, quite the opposite, in fact, as Letty was proof before her eyes. But her present state of mind was only dexterous enough to maintain balance on one side. To her mother's way of thinking, the side she chose would always be to the ill.

"What have you been doing with my daughter in this house anyway?" Connie asked. Her accusatory tone biting enough to prickle the spine of anyone in the vicinity.

It was enough. Her mother had gone too far, and then some. Letty couldn't let her do this to Cole. Nor would she have Brett listen to things he shouldn't have to hear. If it meant poking her head up and into the line of fire, then that was what she would have to do.

"Mom, stop it! Cole has been nothing but good to me. I swear to you; he's done *nothing* inappropriate."

Swinging back again, her mother said, "How do you know what he did and didn't do, Letty? You were passed out drunk!"

Letty glanced at Brett. The boy took a step closer toward his father, his lean body straightening to full height, lifting his chin, gathering courage. Letty was proud of him, as the boy was not there seeking protection, but ready to dole it out should the need arise. With her mother on such a feral tangent, the need might be real.

"Look," Cole said to her mother, his words and composure roughened with agitation. "I haven't done anything to Letty but befriend her."

Connie tore into him with her foul sarcasm, grazing the boundaries of viciousness. Letty had always hated her mother's sarcasm more than her anger. Those lashes always left scars.

"Oh, is that what they're calling it these days, befriending?" her mother said, directing the malicious comment to Cole.

"Mom, stop it," Letty said, doing her best to make it sound like an order. "You don't know what you're talking about."

Her mother didn't stop. She didn't even slow. As expected, she spun back to Letty to spew her rage.

"No, Letty, *you* don't understand. This situation is shady, and you're too young, rash, and inexperienced to know it. Men don't take in young girls just to be nice. It doesn't happen. There is always a payback expected, an ulterior motive. I tried teaching you so you wouldn't be taken in by someone like him. All you had to do was *listen* to me. But no, you were too thickheaded to make use of the wisdom I handed you for free."

Having beaten Letty with her words, Connie wheeled around to strike Cole with some more. "And you. You just pick up a pretty, young girl off the street and take her home with you, and I'm supposed to think you're a good guy with saint-like intentions? Give me a break."

Cole slanted a short glance at Brett before he addressed her mother, his voice shedding mercy like an overtaxed cloud expelling what it could no longer hold. Letty couldn't blame him for his evaporating patience. The ugliness of her mother's accusations was bad enough, but to spew them while his son was standing right there went too far.

"First of all, I did not pick her up off the street."

In hopes of extending his restraint a little bit more so maybe her mother would get her wrath out of her system and calm down, Letty said, "She's in a bad way right now, Cole. Please, be tolerant with her."

"Tolerance may well be a virtue," Cole said. "But it shares a border with gutlessness. I won't sit here in my own house and put up with these filthy accusations. I'll not set such an example for my son."

Her mother either didn't notice or didn't care she had pushed this man as far as he would go, as her tirade climbed another peak. "I don't know anything about you other than you're a man who takes girls into your home and offers them alcohol."

"I did not offer her—"

"So it's not a mental challenge to guess what your intentions were toward my little girl."

"Little girl?" Letty said. Her agitation at the way her mother was talking to Cole coarsened in a new way. The man had saved her life. He'd taken her in, a complete stranger. He had taken good care of her when she needed it most. Never for one second had Cole been even the slightest bit inappropriate. Besides all that, she was not a "little girl." She was a grown woman. For a reason she couldn't at present discern, having her mother refer to her as a child irritated her most of all.

Letty looked her mother straight in the eye. "I've been living on my own for three years now."

"So what?"

"I've been partners with you in the business for even longer."

Her mother flicked a backhanded wave. "Doesn't matter. You're still a child. You're not old enough to know it."

"I am not a child. I'm a grown woman."

"You're a baby."

"I was practically married!"

The back and forth screeched to an awful halt as the breadth of the sentence spoken in haste threw a blockade against any further dialogue.

Letty swung her head away from her mother, away from the argument, speared once again through the heart with anguish for which the respite had been far too brief. Her mother had come to save her from harm, she claimed. What she had done was bring back the worst pain of her life.

For a short while, Letty had been able to behave as if her troubles lay on the other side of a chasm. Narrow, yes, but at last with enough distance to hint her future might not be a misery forever.

Now, beneath the profound weight of its truth, the solidity of everything she lost collapsed upon her head to crush her all over again.

****

Connie sat in frustration, and a small measure of regret, as the terrible pain of these past weeks reclaimed her daughter. If she could shove the clock back a few minutes, she would handle it in a different manner. She had spent a great deal of the past month wishing she could go back in time. Regrets, something she'd almost never abided, held a steadfast place in this instance.

She should have done the research right off, long before Letty and Danny had gotten serious with each other. She should have looked into the matter as soon as she learned how Danny was conceived. It was a reflection she'd had on a regular basis since that terrible night when they all learned the truth of their biological connection. If only.

Letty had learned about Danny's conception early in their relationship. They'd all laughed at the coincidence. No one even considered the chance both mothers had used the same donor, not with so many possible choices. There'd been such a great abundance of catalogs, each one huge, and dozens of facilities throughout the country. The donors must have numbered well into the thousands, maybe tens of thousands.

She was the mother, the person responsible. She should have checked. But the possibility they'd used the same donor had been miniscule, close to nonexistent, really.

Still, she should have looked into it right away. It would have been as simple as a brief conversation with Danny's mother. She could have saved Letty from all the suffering she'd had to endure, and all still yet to come. But who in a million years could have guessed something like this would happen? The odds against it made it seem so impossible, she hadn't even considered a chance Letty and Danny had the same father. None of them had.

But Letty had taken the attitude the heartbreak she

suffered was something her mother had inflicted upon her, as if she'd done it on purpose. It was the pain talking. She couldn't mean it. Letty needed to throw blame, and Connie was the natural target. But no matter how she put it to Letty, her daughter could not see her side.

More than anything Connie had ever wanted, top of the list, was to be a mother, and no amount of humility could keep her from knowing she'd done well by Letty. The girl was intelligent; she was moral. She understood the value of sincerity and honor.

Her daughter could be trusted with anything—money, the business, all the responsibilities that went with it. Connie never for one second doubted her ability to be a good mother. Maybe it was arrogant to have such a thought, but it was still the truth. Letty was a good girl. No one could say she'd been raised by anything less than a great parent.

She had provided for her daughter, taught her, guided her. She'd raised her so well, even Letty's teenage years had had very few difficulties. Especially when compared to what some of her friends had gone through with their teenagers. Letty didn't take good for granted, and she'd never found bad to be insurmountable.

At least, not until Danny. It was a heartbreak no one could have predicted.

Connie had never seen anyone so distraught, so inconsolable. The mass of Letty's depression could find no floor on which to crash. How could her daughter ever pick herself up if she just continued to fall? Letty's bright spirit had plunged so far into darkness, she had become little more than a ghost, an apparition with similar characteristics. The further Letty fell, the more Connie's fears for her daughter ascended. What was worse, the more she tried helping, the harder Letty pushed her away.

Most of the time, her daughter was fair-minded about things. She could see a situation from the other person's point of view. But not about this. No matter how Connie phrased it to her, Letty could not see things as they were, as they had been, and would someday be again.

Adding to Connie's frustration, her daughter refused to put any effort into progressing even a tiny bit. No amount of encouragement helped, not urging, not even threats. So her little girl was stuck on a continuous loop of despair, unable to gain a fresh perspective.

The fact that Letty was so very wanted before she was even born didn't soften her daughter's anger. Connie pushed more, staying in her face, doing and saying anything she could think of to make her understand. She kept her daughter under constant watch for fear of what might happen if she was out of her sight for a single minute.

If Letty was in the living room, then so was she. If Letty was in her bedroom, she insisted her daughter leave the door open. If Letty was in the shower, then Connie parked outside the bathroom door until she came out. If she was in there too long, or if the silence stretched more than it should, the door knocking began.

Her daughter was able to pull it together enough to work the catering business with her. However, Connie wouldn't let her run any errands by herself, not even short ones. She had to stay by her mother's side the whole time. Besides, the way Letty looked lately, pale, drawn skin, red, swollen eyes, down to skin and bones, it was best if she stayed in the kitchen where the customers and the guests couldn't see her.

As Letty hadn't been able to get there on her own, Connie had made the decision to force her daughter into the healing process. As a good, caring mother, she had to use her might because Letty was too weak to find the path on her own. It was her job as a mother to lead her in the right direction. But none of her efforts had worked.

Connie had ushered her in every constructive direction. To take Letty's mind from her troubles, she'd printed out some online brochures for classes in a variety of subjects and activities. Her daughter refused every one. Connie had gone so far as to give her permission go out with her friends for an evening, not mentioning she would be in a car nearby, watching.

In her efforts to convince her of this, she told Letty she should go out and meet someone new. The last suggestion was met with a spark, but not the good kind. Letty had glared at her as if she'd said something outrageous and cruel.

Nothing worked. She'd exhausted every reasonable possibility, until she had to wonder, to suspect, even, Letty might be taking some sort of revenge, doing what she could to make her own mother feel powerless. Well, not since she moved away from her bully of a father had Connie been in a relationship where she was rendered powerless. She wasn't about to crawl under somebody's bootheel now. Certainly not her own daughter's.

Finally, beyond frustrated with Letty's refusal to be

fair, with her cold shoulders and colder glares, Connie demanded her daughter get professional help. She did some research, made the appointment for Letty, and then told her what time to be ready to go.

Connie didn't even consider taking Letty's single word response of "no" for an answer. She told Letty enough was enough, and the appointment stood, period. If she wasn't dressed and ready to go in proper fashion, then she would go in her pajamas.

Less than an hour later, her precious daughter was gone.

Sitting beside her now, as Letty sank back into the depths of her sadness, Connie couldn't help but wonder if her daughter would ever come around and see her side of things. Could they get back to normal, or had the life they'd known been cursed into memory?

No, no, she would not allow such a thing to happen. She wouldn't stand for it. She would pound away until Letty understood, and then her daughter would recover. Connie was sure of it. All she would admit to was pounding too hard too soon. Letty hadn't been ready. She would be, though, and before long. All she had to do was reestablish her control, allow her daughter to wallow a bit more in her self-pity, and then she could force the pieces of their lives back into place.

Connie took in her daughter's face and, no matter the want, was unable to deny the obvious. Such suffering would hurt anyone who laid eyes upon Letty right now. For a mother, it was torture. Connie was too pragmatic to ignore what was right in front of her.

In the brief time since her daughter had escorted her into this house, Letty had become smaller, shrinking from the inside. Yet the spark of rebellion in her eyes had diminished no more than a single click. A paralyzing thought burrowed into Connie's head. What if their troubles extended beyond her long-ago choice of becoming impregnated by a donor? What if Letty was growing away from her mother's control?

Maybe the sight of her mother would always cause Letty pain. Would it become too much for her little girl? Would she go so far as to want her mother out of her life? After all, Connie was a constant reminder of her heredity and all the grief it had caused.

No. Connie would not allow it. This was *her* daughter.

She'd studied the paperwork of so very many donors before choosing, then carried Letty for nine months, changed her diapers, taught her everything, loved her. She would not lose her, no matter what she had to do. The first and most important thing necessary right now was to get Letty away from this place and back home where she belonged. Then…then what? She would formulate a plan, something to put her little girl in a more amenable state of mind.

Maybe Letty wanted an apology. Well that wasn't going to happen. She would not apologize for anything because she hadn't done anything wrong.

She had empathy for the pain her daughter was suffering. But she couldn't be sorry for causing it because to do so would be to regret having been impregnated without obligations to another adult, having carried the baby with the utmost care, having given birth to her precious baby girl. Those were things for which Connie could never be sorry.

"I'll drive the truck around to the front," Cole said, breaking through Connie's thoughts. "Letty, maybe you should stay here with Brett while I take your mother to the hospital."

Though seeing a doctor was probably a good idea, as she was battered and bloodied, she hadn't come all this way to have some man she didn't know or like whisk her away from her daughter within minutes of finding her. She would make a few phone calls, settle the matter with the car, and get her daughter home. Once there, she'd make an appointment with her own physician.

"I don't need to go to the hospital," Connie told him.

"You have a head injury. You're going," Cole told her, his tone as clear and straightforward as his words.

Through gritted teeth, Connie said to him, "I told you, I'm fine."

The man was just as defiant, more so. "There's a chance your injuries could be worse than you think. You can go to the hospital in my truck, or strapped to a gurney in an ambulance. Don't doubt I can make that happen."

Connie shot to her feet and punched her fists against her hips. "Who the hell do you think you are, making threats to me?" However, her blast of bluster diffused in an instant when she had to sit back down again, forced to the couch by a tidal wave of dizziness.

Her daughter wrapped an arm around her. "Cole," Letty said, the word penetrating the slow exit of vertigo.

"I'll go get my truck," Cole said, his boots sounding as he walked away.

Chapter 15

"More hot chocolate?" Letty asked.

Brett lifted his head and smiled at her. She was so pretty and nice. Also, kind of magical, the way everything had gotten better since she came to stay with them.

The light in the kitchen drifted down from the forty-watt bulb encased in the yellow and gold-swirled orb over the table, and the dim light tucked up in the range hood. It was all soft, like sunlight when a cluster of puffy clouds floated across the sky. Steam rose from a pot on the stove, giving a sense, if not the actual sensation, of warmth.

"Sure," Brett answered. "You make the best hot chocolate I've ever had in my whole life. It's real chocolaty, not like the powder stuff in the packets my dad always makes. It's so cool how you can make it with almond milk, too."

It was all the truth. He *really* loved having Letty here. Everything she did was great. She made the best food he'd ever eaten. She enjoyed reading books, even some of the same kinds he liked about vampires, or aliens, or adventures about traveling around the world. This afternoon they'd spent more than an hour talking about books. Then they spent another hour talking about movies.

Letty was fun, and beautiful, and just plain nice. It

was hard to believe that terrible woman raised such an awesome person.

Letty smiled as she carried the pot from the stove and ladled more hot chocolate into his teacup with the yellow daffodils painted all around the outside. She liked being here, too, liked him. Brett could tell.

He leaned over his cup, pursed his lips, and blew, tempering the puff with care. His breath skimmed across the top and sent a wave of steaming fog over the opposite rim. He liked watching that almost as much as he liked drinking the hot chocolate. It had the look of a mist out of a fairy tale, the kind where a genie or a good witch would appear and grant a wish to the first person who saw them.

It was a childish thing to do, searching the steam for what didn't exist, but he couldn't help it. Brett had a wish too big to trouble his pride.

With a casual manner, so he wouldn't appear obvious, Brett glanced at Letty as she returned to the seat across from him. Just observing her was a privilege. She kind of reminded him of an egret, slender, graceful, the bird even more beautiful in the warmth of spring after the long, freezing winter. A person couldn't help but watch her.

If he were a grown man, Brett would wish for Letty to be his wife, his princess. It was a private thought, and it would stay private because if his friends found out, it would earn him a boatload of teasing.

Brett toyed with the handle of the teacup. Letty deserved somebody better than him. She deserved the best man possible, not a scrawny boy with a noticeable overbite, ears too big for his head, and a personality not even his own mother had been able to stomach long enough to see him grow up to an adult.

A reappearing ache threatened to hurt his heart again, but Brett glanced over at Letty, and it went away.

He wished Letty would live with him and his dad here in their house forever. She could cook for them because she liked to, and they would laugh with her every day. There would be years of good times, as good or even better than what they'd had this past week. Yes, better, because he wouldn't have to worry about her going away.

Brett took another sip of his hot chocolate.

On her birthday, he and his dad could take her out to dinner. The Lotus Tree was a real nice place in town where they served Chinese food. The restaurant had red, paper-like lanterns with lights in them hanging from the ceiling and fortune cookies at the end of the meal. She'd like it there.

Brett could picture her smiling at them as she walked down the stairs wearing a pretty dress and some of those fancy girl shoes, the kind where her toes would show. They would tell her how beautiful she was, and Letty would smile at them. He wouldn't tease her too much because it was her birthday.

After dinner, they would come home to a cake he and his dad would have baked. The cake wouldn't be very pretty, but it would taste good, and she would love it because they'd made it for her. Then they would give her presents. They would give her everything she wanted, give her anything, because they'd be so happy to have her here.

Except for wanting his mother to come home for the first year or so after she'd left, Brett had never wanted anything so badly in his life than for Letty to stay here with them forever.

He blew a gentle breath across his cup of hot chocolate again. Although, as expected, no magical figure appeared out of the dissipating mist, Brett made the wish anyway. It couldn't hurt.

Brett didn't know the reason Letty had left her home in Las Vegas. All she told him was she needed to get away for a while. But something bad must have happened. Maybe somebody abused her. He hadn't seen any bruises, and he'd looked. All he ever saw bared were her face and her arms, but they appeared well enough. It was a good thing. He would take his fists to anyone who ever dared to hurt her, even if it meant his own destruction.

Maybe her parents were mean to her without hitting her. It was possible. He'd learned from television and from life, people could hurt you in all kinds of ways. Sometimes one person could hurt another without laying a hand on them. Sometimes even without using words. There were many terrible ways to cause someone to hurt.

Brett lifted his cup and took a small sip of his hot chocolate.

Letty liked him just fine. Brett was sure of it, and the knowledge gave him a sense of golden peace. She liked his dad, too. Ever since his mom left, his father wasn't always so easy to like. But his dad had gotten better since Letty had been in their home.

Brett set his cup back onto the saucer. Yes, even his father had rediscovered his smile since Letty had come to stay with them. He still couldn't believe his dad told a joke. Brett tried remembering if his dad used to tell jokes when his mom still lived with them, but he couldn't recall. His life before his mom left was so long ago, parts of it were fading.

It was just as well.

He used to think about his mom all the time, the way she was always happy to see him when he got home from school, how she'd play checkers with him on Saturdays, the way she tucked him into bed every night, kissed him on the forehead, and wished him sweet dreams. He didn't like thinking about her anymore and wished all those memories about his mother would go away and leave him alone. It hurt his heart to remember her.

Letty, however, was too valuable to let go into memory. He was sure she wanted to stay with them as much as he wanted her to stay. She liked it here. He could tell.

Whenever Letty paused and looked out any of their windows toward the fields and the woods, she had the same expression his father always wore, like she was looking at a miracle. It was so obvious she belonged right here with them on this land. She was fun, and sweet, and smart. He could listen to her play guitar and sing all day. And she said she'd teach him how to play! He couldn't wait to learn. It was all so perfect.

But just when everything was settling into place, Letty's mother had to show up and ruin everything. She'd come to take Letty away. Letty was so great. Who wouldn't want to keep her? The way those two got along with each other, though, Brett didn't think Letty would leave them to go back with her. At least, he hoped she wouldn't.

He took another sip of his hot chocolate.

****

Letty stared into her cup, thinking.

It had been more than an hour since Cole had driven away with her mother in his truck. They should have heard something by now. But Brett said the hospital wasn't very close, and Letty understood these things could take forever. Though she was concerned about her mother, Letty took comfort in knowing her mom was in good hands. Even angered, Cole would do his best by her. Still, all she could see right now was her mother covered in dirt with blood dripping from her head.

Letty glanced at the wall clock again.

Maybe she should have gone to the hospital with her mom instead of honoring Cole's request for her to stay at the house. Letty understood his true meaning. Brett would have been fine here alone for a while. Cole had suggested she stay here with his son to give her peace and time to collect her thoughts.

"I'm sure she's fine," Brett said.

"I'm sure she is."

"I got a cut bigger than the one your mom has on my head one time," Brett said. He leaned toward her and separated the waves of his soft, child's hair to expose a section of his scalp. A thin, jagged white scar ran along his hairline behind his ear. It was indeed twice the size of the cut her mom had on her head.

"What happened?"

"Fell out of a tree when I was eight," Brett told her. He sat back up in his chair. "I must have hit a sharp branch on the way down."

"Ouch."

"Yeah." He nodded. "It bled an awful lot. The whole shoulder of my shirt was red. But you know what? I didn't even have to get stitches."

"Your parents must have freaked out when they saw all the blood."

"My dad didn't act freaked out, but I think he was. My mom started crying right away. She couldn't even look at me. All she could do was call for my dad. She didn't want to go to the hospital with us, but she made cookies for me while we were gone."

Why wouldn't a mother go to the hospital with her injured son? She'd once broken her arm roller blading, and her mother wouldn't leave her side, even when the doctor asked her to go to the waiting room. Letty held her tongue. Brett didn't act upset when he talked about his mother, but like with Cole, talk of her summoned shadows to his eyes.

"The next day my mom and dad let me stay on the couch and watch TV and read books all day."

"Cool."

"Yeah, and I missed two days of school."

She smiled. "Double cool."

Brett's brow crinkled a bit. "Yeah, but then Dad said I had to make up the work I missed."

Letty smiled again. Even after these past horrific weeks when she could never find even a tiny moment of joy, she smiled in Brett's presence, a lot. He was thoughtful, and funny, and full of heart. With the sudden jolt of a great idea, she wondered if Cole would let Brett come visit her in Vegas some time. He'd get a kick out of all the sights. Then she thought better of it.

While Cole might agree, she didn't like to think of the man here all alone. Maybe Cole would come for a visit. She almost laughed at the image of the mountain man wandering down the Las Vegas Strip.

Vegas. For the first time since she'd come here, Letty considered going back home. The notion didn't horrify her, but it didn't it please her, either.

She liked it here. She liked the people, at least the ones she'd met so far. And she loved the land. It was so different from the desert, and from the city. The trees were magnificent, varied, and abundant. Brett told her about a nearby lake. She said she wanted to see it, and they'd made a plan to walk to it in the next day or so. He said they kept a little rowboat there and if she'd like, they could go for a ride. Brett thought it was crazy funny when she said she'd never been on a boat before.

It struck Letty again, how she'd like to see everything around here when it was covered in snow, and then in the springtime when nature was in bloom. What would the field of wildflowers look like then? It had to be gorgeous.

But staying here would just delay the inevitable. She had obligations to their catering business. Her mother had been running it alone, as she did before Letty was born, and before she was old enough to help. They'd grown the business since Letty had become a partner and added the vegan aspect to their services. It wasn't right to leave it all on her mom's shoulders.

Three years ago, they'd hired some part-time help, but she and her mom still did most of the work. Letty needed to get back to the business, back to her life. If for no other reason than because it was hers. She was a guest in this escapist life in the mountains, and for all she knew, she had already overstayed her welcome.

As if her mind was transparent enough for Brett to get a peek, the boy said, "You like it here, Letty, don't you?"

"Of course," she said without having to think. She didn't have to think about it because she liked it very much. All the greenery, the serenity, the slow pace of life. Las Vegas was a great town, the best. She loved it there, too. Something was always going on, a concert, or event. For a catering business, you couldn't pick a better town. But something about being here in the mountains, well, it gave her a real sense of peace.

She looked to Brett. "Why do you ask?"

Brett ran a slow forefinger around the rim of his cup. "I was wondering if this was the kind of place women didn't like to stay for too long."

She knew what he meant but asked anyway, opening the door for him to talk. "Because of your mom?"

"Yeah, I suppose," Brett said, keeping his gaze on his hot chocolate.

"People leave all kinds of environments for all kinds of reasons. My mom and I have catered parties where the couples throwing them seem happy, and then we hear later they got a divorce. One of my friends is divorced. I can tell you this, Brett, usually a person leaves for their own reasons, not because of somebody else."

Brett glanced up at her and, after a moment, gave a somber nod. "I don't think I'm ever getting married."

"I don't think I will either," Letty said.

"Why not?" Brett asked, his voice rising in conjunction with his eyebrows. "A woman like you could have anybody you want. Oh, I know the problem."

"You do?"

"I'll bet you have so many boyfriends to choose

from, it gives you a headache trying to decide which one to marry."

Her bark of laughter was loud in the quiet kitchen. Brett hadn't been smiling when he said it, though. He'd been serious in his assumption. God, he was good for her self-esteem.

"No, Brett, that's not the reason," Letty told him. "But I'm flattered you think so."

Brett sipped his hot chocolate. He set his cup down and studied Letty with care. "Are you a lesbian?"

"Brett!" Letty laughed. "No, I'm not a lesbian."

"That's too bad," Brett said earnestly. "I've never known one before. It would have been pretty cool to have a lesbian friend."

"Sorry to disappoint you," Letty answered, with a small, airy laugh.

"That's okay. So why don't you want to get married?"

After a pause, far less brief than full, Letty threw back his question. "Why don't you?"

Brett picked up his cup and took another sip before answering.

"It's not worth the risk," he said.

The thought of someone so young already jaded was disheartening. It occurred to her then, maybe Cole thought the same thing when he looked at her.

"Then again," she said and could not believe what was about to come out of her mouth, "maybe someday when we meet the right people, we'll change our minds."

Another moment passed. Brett picked up his dainty teacup and touched it to hers in a toast.

Chapter 16

Cole had planned on carrying Connie into the house, the same as he had done for her daughter. She'd been breathing soft, deep snores, slumped against the passenger door of his truck for about an hour. The quiet during the ride home from the hospital was a blissful contrast to the ride he'd taken to get there.

The reminders of the hellish journey were Miss Norris's inert form in the darkness beside him, and her endless, offensive wrath still ringing in his ears.

They'd left the hospital after she was patched up and Cole personally got an okay from the doctor she didn't need to stay. He wouldn't take her word for it, which increased her contempt of him. Of course, by then it was already clear the woman was going to hate him no matter what he said or did. One more mark against him didn't make any difference. Her mind was set on him before they'd even met.

Cole soothed his ravaged character with some pride at how well he'd held his tongue. Even though he was doing it for Letty, it had been damn hard. Connie Norris shot insults and accusations like a pro. It didn't matter to the woman so much what she said, as long as she hit her mark; and her aim was good.

Her physical state hadn't worn her down in the least. All the way to the hospital the woman tore into him with the gusto of a person who had a quota to fill, a big one.

More than once during the miserable drive, Cole had been tempted to drop her off at the hospital doors, turn around, and go back home. He didn't, of course. Nor did he fight back beyond an occasional spurt of self-defense. Letting his temper loose on an injured woman would have been vulgar, and by extension, rude to Letty. So, for the most part anyway, he kept his rebuttals behind his teeth. But his temper ached from its restraints, and his dignity was pocked.

Once or twice, the fact she was Letty's mother had been the *only* thing keeping him from defending his character against her vile words with a few choice ones of his own. That, and Letty's plea as they were leaving for the hospital for him to please be patient with her mother. His teeth were near to bursting out from all the effort it had taken to hold back the arguments perched on the tip of his tongue.

For a time, Cole volleyed back rationality. Her daughter had access to a phone, as the woman well knew, because Letty had called her. Letty could have phoned the police if she'd felt she was in any kind of danger. Her daughter had been eating; she'd put on weight, was playing guitar and singing. All solid proof of her well-being. Fat lot of good any of it did him. He might as well have been confessing to every insinuation and outright accusation she flung. The woman's ears were closed to everything but her own voice.

Her common sense, if she even possessed any, either drowned in or fled the colossal deluge of her horrible charges. Nothing was going to set her straight. Good God, she had seen her daughter; they had spoken. She knew good and well the girl was fine, knew he'd treated her well. She'd heard it more than once, and straight from the horse's mouth.

Yet Letty's mother behaved as if Cole had done things warranting prison time, maybe even a TV special. The woman could strain the patience of a Buddhist monk.

Since all the way to the hospital Cole had gotten nothing but hostility on everything under the sun, he'd been braced to hear it again all the way home. But Letty's mother had fallen asleep almost as soon as he'd exited the parking lot. In fact, she'd been so still he'd glanced over a couple of times to make sure she was breathing. She was, of course. A woman like her was too full of spit and vinegar to die.

It amazed him she'd given birth to someone as sweet as Letty. Although, he had seen Letty's temper flare a time or two, so he knew she carried at least some of her mother's workings. Still, the two of them were as different as sun and storm.

While the bristles of Connie's temperament scratched even his thick hide with her abrasiveness, Letty moderated her willful side with a measure of reasonability. She was younger, too, still learning her fit in the world. Her age earned her some flexibility, in his opinion. Her mother, on the other hand, should have developed better behavior by now.

The differences between the two plunged deeper still. Cole wondered if they were part of Letty's paternal genetic mystery, or if other adult influences in her life had softened the girl's edges. It would be a good study in the old nature-versus-nurture debate.

Cole turned off the headlights as his truck rolled to a slow stop in front of the house. The porch light still lit a yellow glow over the chairs, the potted plants, and the porch swing. The windows were dark, except for a dull light flickering and pausing and then flickering again through the picture window downstairs. The television.

Of course, Letty would be waiting up to see if her mother was all right. He could have kicked himself for having been so thoughtless as to not call from the hospital to alleviate her worries. But by the time he learned her mom was going to be all right, all he'd wanted was to get home and close his bedroom door behind him.

It was his guess his son would be waiting right along with her. In fact, he'd lay hard cash on it.

Yesterday, Cole was pleased by the way Brett had become so fond of Letty. His son was laughing again, pouncing around the house like a boy should. The friendship had given quality to his son's life the boy needed and deserved. Now, though, Cole found their closeness troubling. Letty's mom had made it quite clear she'd come to take her daughter home as soon as possible, and he had no doubt the woman would not be swayed or delayed in her mission.

A heavy exhalation passed through Cole's lips as his chin sank to his chest. His son was about to suffer another loss.

Cole unbuckled his seatbelt and shut off the engine. After staring into the darkness for a minute or so, he draped his forearms over the steering wheel and rested his weary head upon them. He was almost as drained as the shrewish woman who was dead to the world in the passenger seat of his truck. His eyelids grew heavy, and he let them close for a moment or two, shutting off at least one of his senses.

The truck's closed windows muffled the rolling squawks of wood frogs. There wouldn't be too many more of their concerts before hibernation. Still, due to the ever-long consistency, the sound gave him comfort. All things should be so, he thought, he believed, he wished; all the while knowing such wasn't the way of the world.

On the other side of the truck, Letty's mother took in and released a deep breath, as if gloating in victory over his fruitless want. He half-believed it was deliberate. In the quiet solitude, Cole opened his eyes and accepted the inevitable, but he didn't like it, on his son's behalf as well as his own; for he was well aware Brett wasn't the only one who was about to suffer a loss.

After taking in a slow and steady breath, Cole sat up again. He glanced over at the bandaged woman who had been responsible for Letty's pain, the same woman who would next be responsible for his and his son's. He damned her decisions, and for an instant, Cole hated her. Then he couldn't. If she hadn't gotten pregnant the way she had, then Letty wouldn't have come into the world, and the world would be a sorrier place without her. His and his son's world certainly would.

Cole opened the truck door, and Miss Norris awoke.

"Are we at your house already?" she asked, her words groggy as she lifted her head and looked around through heavy eyes.

It had been an hour's drive. It had been peaceful, but the depleting toll she'd taken on him earlier made it feel like three.

"Yes," was all Cole said and got out of the truck.

By the time he walked around to the passenger side, Connie was already getting out. He helped her and then put his hand between her shoulder blades to steady her. She, of course, shrugged him off as if he were a drunken barfly with an absurd notion he was about to get lucky. Cole obliged her and stepped away.

They climbed the porch steps at the same time, but not together.

Chapter 17

Careful and quiet, Letty slipped out of the guest bed. She glanced back. Her mother didn't so much as twitch an eyelid.

After Cole had helped her get her mom upstairs the night before, Connie insisted on a shower. At least she allowed Letty to help her and then get her into her nightgown. It was like dressing a child who wasn't all the way awake. Connie was sound asleep before Letty had the pink patchwork quilt laid over her.

As quietly as she could, Letty gathered her things, closed the bedroom door behind her, and crossed the hall to the bathroom. She showered and got dressed before making her way downstairs. At the bottom of the steps, she stopped, surprised to see a woman she didn't know dusting the mantel over the fireplace. Then Letty remembered, the housekeeper.

"Hi. You must be Tracy."

The young woman stopped and turned around, duster in hand. Letty guessed her to be maybe a couple of years older than she, maybe twenty-four or so. She was slender with waves of vivid, auburn hair gathered into a high ponytail. She had stunning blue eyes in a face sprinkled with a few freckles, and an instant smile one couldn't help but return.

"Yes," Tracy said in a pleasant but hushed voice. "Cole told me he had a couple of houseguests. I'm waiting to run the vacuum until you're both awake."

"My mother is so sound asleep I don't think she'd even hear it."

Tracy waved her hand in a dismissive fashion. "Oh, I have some other things to do first anyway."

"Okay, but please don't let us stop you from doing what you have to do," Letty told her. She and her mother both knew from experience how awful it was to try and get your job done while working around the particulars of inconsiderate people.

Every so often the hosts she and her mom had worked for would want them to come back the next day to clean up and collect their things instead of doing it right away. The day after a catering job was, whenever possible, a day off. It was their break before getting ready for the next event, time to take care of their personal business. They were always quick in their cleanup, but sometimes the hosts would be too exhausted from their evening of drink and merriment to wait for them to finish.

"Oh, you don't have to take care of all this right now. Give yourself a break and call it a night. You can come back tomorrow and wrap up," they would say, as if doing them a favor by causing them to work another day.

Her mother would make it clear that wasn't going to happen. Emphasizing her point, her mom wouldn't even pause in their cleaning and packing to discuss it with them. Sometimes Letty worried they would lose a customer, or worse, gain a bad reputation. But the quality of their food and service was so good, people were willing to overlook her mother's brazen inflexibility.

While it wasn't unusual for her mom's conduct to bleed into blatant rudeness, Letty was always pleased her mother wouldn't let the customer add an extra day to the job. Sometimes, though inexplicable stubbornness would never allow her to admit it to her, Letty wished she could be a little more like her mom.

There'd been times when Letty wished she could handle a situation with complete disregard for the judgments of others. In some ways, it would make life easier. But it wasn't her way, and she couldn't force it.

Her mother's constitution was brawny and bold. Her shoulders were strong enough to bear anything. The woman was an emotional powerhouse to be respected and admired and, if good sense prevailed, feared a little. She didn't allow anything to stand in her way.

Rude or not, her mother's embedded might *did* gain results. Her effectiveness motivated Letty's wish to adopt some of her mom's qualities as her own. In the end, her mother almost always got what she wanted.

Too many other factors came into play for Letty. As a rule, she didn't like confrontations, and she couldn't stomach the thought of initiating one, especially since her opponent was sure to come up with some reason she couldn't dispute. Every now and then she tried. On occasion, she even succeeded. Not often, though. Letty couldn't wear any more than remnants of her mother's dauntless garb.

It was just as well. Letty preferred a peaceful setting, even if it required a stockpile of tolerance to deal with her mother/business partner. Though, she had to admit, over the last month or so, the kind of stubborn fortitude her mother possessed would have been a great asset.

She glanced at Cole's housekeeper, kneeling at the coffee table, using a rag to polish the dark wood to a gloss.

Brett had told her how the housekeeping service was Tracy's own business. He said it was doing so well she was going to hire some help. Good for her. And she managed to run her successful business while being polite to her customers. It shone a little pinprick of light on a thought, a dream Letty had always kept in the dark. Maybe later, when she was home, she could give it a closer examination.

"Well, I'll let you get back to work," Letty told Tracy before going into the kitchen.

She found Brett sitting still and bland at the table with his hands in his lap, a bowl of cereal in front of him. He'd set out the carton of almond milk but hadn't poured it yet. He'd put a bowl and a spoon out for her, too. Letty was certain it was for her because Cole just had coffee, and maybe some toast, first thing in the morning. The gesture was small but very sweet and thoughtful. Her heart tugged at how much she was going to miss the boy.

"Good morning," Brett said, scarcely glancing in her direction. The greeting was pleasant, but it lacked the cheerfulness of the day before. Then he leaned over and scooted the empty bowl with the yellow daffodil pattern a little closer to the edge. "I waited for you."

Letty glanced at her watch, which sparked a moment of alarm. "Brett, you're going to be late for school."

"They're having teacher conferences today," he told her, staring at his dry cereal.

"Oh. So you get the day off. Nice."

Brett nodded, his expression flat.

Letty walked toward the table as she spoke. "I can't believe I slept so late."

With the business, she was usually up early. Even on a day off, things still needed to be done. Clean her apartment, do laundry, run errands. In between jobs, they still had work to do. Reorganizing, planning in accordance to their next scheduled event. She was always testing new recipes in her own kitchen, adding to the vegan choices their business would offer. She liked it though, the feeling of sustaining accomplishments.

"Well, it was pretty crazy last night," said Brett. He was still gazing at his bowl, watching the flakes do nothing but sit there.

"Yeah, really," Letty said as she took her seat. She opened the box of cereal and poured some into her bowl.

"How's your mom?" Brett asked Letty, still staring at his cereal.

"Sound asleep. She's going to be sore for a few days, but she'll be all right."

Brett took hold of the almond milk. He held the carton in a loose grip for a moment without lifting it, fingers flexing and curling together in small, silent taps against the side. Then, without pouring his milk, he laid his hands in his lap again.

Sitting back, Brett lifted his head and faced Letty for the first time since she'd come into the kitchen. "You're going to leave, aren't you," he stated more than asked.

Letty sighed, short but deep. "Sooner or later, I

have to go back."

"I thought you liked it here," Brett said, his eyes fixed on her, his voice straining for stability.

"I do like it here, Brett, very much. But I have a life back home, and it's waiting for me."

Brett's brows drew together, and he spoke with a calm conviction very adult for such a young boy. "You must not have liked it much, or else you wouldn't have come here and stayed."

"I…there was a problem."

"Is it gone now?"

Letty's glance dipped. "No, it's not gone."

Candor couldn't resist the addendum in her head, *it might not ever be gone*. But at least she didn't say it out loud. She slid her bowl back, her stomach too full of dread to hold anything else. She was going back to what? Her old room at her mother's house and a city full of sweet memories gone sour.

Letty's head pounded, and the din soon echoed in her ears. It was as if the past were marching back again, flags raised, smug, and victorious in its return. Her eyes closed for a moment. She couldn't shut out the menace, but she did manage to dull it. For how long, though? Would the misery submerge her again once she was home, drown her in hopelessness and unbearable pain? Or could she bargain it down to a tolerable ration?

A whimper echoed against her insides, more out of frustration than surrender. What if the best she could hope for in her life back home would be learning how to live with the grief? No, she would have to become numb, to everything, so the pain couldn't scrape her raw again. The thought weakened the strength she'd found since coming here. She shoved back against the collapse.

Could she spend the rest of her life existing as little more than a hollowed husk, feeling no pain, feeling no pleasure? With such an attitude, she'd never look forward to anything, never experience the thrill of life, the joys a person should know, anticipation. Such an existence would just be a slower death than the one Cole had prevented.

In a flash, the thought of going home sparked a panic, one threatening to grow. Then it struck Letty how sometime during the past week or so, how much life had improved. She must have known it. She just hadn't *known* it. But now she was sliding back. The blessed dullness to the pain she came here with was already wearing off.

Her suffering hadn't faded, but rather, stepped back, waiting for the right time to return. By comparison to how she felt twenty-four hours ago, the dissimilarity was stunning. And terrifying.

Letty couldn't say when her tortuous grief had eased to a more tolerable sorrow, but she knew it had happened here in Montana, up on a beautiful mountain with Cole and Brett Holloway.

What would happen when she returned to her life back home? Might it be even worse, knowing the passage of time hadn't helped, and maybe it never would? Letty didn't know, and the not knowing was torture. One thing she did know, however unsettling, was sooner or later she had to go back home. And later would only prolong her angst about what would happen once she got there.

But she had to go. What else could she do?

Danny didn't want to talk to her, but he was going

to have to, even if it was by text. The two of them needed to discuss some things. Her mom had gone and made the necessary cancellations. They would get some refunds, and part of the money was his. Mostly, though, was the matter of what they were going to tell everyone.

All she'd said to the few friends she'd spoken to was they had broken up and she was too upset to talk about it. Maybe Danny had spilled the details, but she couldn't imagine it. Because of who they were, because of the shame in the relationship they'd had with each other. The fact they hadn't known they were siblings didn't erase it.

The worst of it was, even though Letty knew the feelings she continued to carry for Danny were wrong, she still felt them. Damn it, she still felt them.

The thought of seeing Danny again, of being in the same room and knowing she could never, ever, touch him in the ways she always had because that would make her a sick and demented twist, made her neck tighten and her stomach roil. Knowing her touch would disgust Danny had her close to crumpling into a ball and weeping.

The slight crack in Brett's voice almost undid her. "Don't go, Letty."

He clutched his hands together atop the table, squeezing, as if to contain some measure of dignity and not sound like he was begging. Letty recognized the effort, for so recent was her experience with the same. She'd pleaded with Danny to compare the numbers again, and then again, to keep searching until he found there'd been a mistake. Her dignity had withered to dust, and all for nothing.

While returning back home was going to be tough, she couldn't stay with Cole and Brett forever. They'd been good to her, and they'd been good *for* her, but if she stayed much longer, she would be taking advantage of their generous hospitality. She wasn't Cole's responsibility. This wasn't her life. Danny wasn't her life, either. She was going to have to find a way come to terms with that. She hoped getting there would just be hard, and not impossible.

Fear wound through her, fear of going home and landing in the same unbearable anguish she'd left. Maybe it would be waiting for her, like a monster in the closet, maybe prepared to make up for lost time.

Dread made a grab for her battered heart. The bit of grief she'd been able to shed became disputable as the misery inched forward to wrap itself around her again, squeezing, suffocating, taking what it could like the hungry fiend it was.

She shot a brief glance toward her finger, the one now vacant of the engagement ring Danny had given her. She could still see it, though, feel it, too, as if she still wore its shining weight. A simple white gold band with a half-carat round-cut diamond. He'd saved up to get it for her. It sat in her dresser drawer now, behind her socks. She'd have to make arrangements to return it.

Letty raised her head and spoke, but the words almost strangled on the forming knots of emotions. "I have to go back," she told Brett, hoping against reason the strength she'd gained here on their mountain would come with her, hoping she didn't leave this house in a worse way than she found it.

The thought of causing Brett any pain made her

stomach hurt. He'd already suffered so much in his young life. But what else could she do?

Brett rose from the table and left the kitchen without another word. Letty scooted away her bowl of cereal. She went to the counter and made coffee for Cole and her mom.

****

Cole sat fully dressed on the edge of his unmade bed, staring down at the royal blue carpeting he'd hated since the day Danielle had it installed. Clean, morning sunlight poured through the window and brightened the floral-patterned bedroom, but he couldn't pay the light and the warmth any mind. Storm clouds might as well have darkened the view of his property for all he saw of the new day.

With less than half an effort, because he was certain it would be futile, Cole scanned his gloom for the muse that had danced before him with such merriment last night when Letty was singing. It was gone now. But, oh, it was great while it lasted.

What had started as inklings when she was playing her songs had blossomed into actual ideas. Yes, ideas. They were big, important ideas, and they'd formed in his mind with very little effort. All of them had glorious potential.

Then Letty's mom appeared at the living room window.

By the time he got back from the hospital, he was too tired to think. He'd dragged his tail into his lace and floral bedroom, stood there in a stew amongst dainty pillows, snooty carpeting, and a fancy makeup table with clear light bulbs across the top and a little fluffy pink stool. That's when the ideas made a grand return.

Within minutes, they became plans, solid plans, ready and eager to be enacted. They burst from their cage in a stampede, bringing with them a second wind strong enough to breathe some fresh life into him.

The whys of the timing didn't matter. The rush of momentum, however, did. He worried about losing it, or the ideas, if he waited too long. So after trotting back downstairs, he sat at the kitchen table with a pad and paper making notes. For the first time in two years, he was missing out on sleep over something good.

Now, this morning, all the buoyant plans he'd made might as well have been a dream he'd had; the kind where you solve a complex problem and then wake up and find the answers you had were too grandiose to carry forth into reality.

He'd seen Letty in the hallway this morning. After inquiring about her mom, they stood in silence. Then the words he dreaded hearing stumbled from her mouth. She'd be going back to Las Vegas with her mother.

He should be happy Letty was well enough to face her life again. He *was* happy for her. For Brett, though, and for his own piece of mind, her time here had been way too short. She was the one bonding them back together. He couldn't help but worry they weren't ready to not have her with them anymore, to tread forward from their past, he and Brett alone. But Letty wasn't theirs to keep.

Cole got to his feet. It was an effort.

For a moment, self-scorn disgraced him. No reason in the world he and Brett couldn't still follow through with all his ideas. Well, no good reason. The best he could do to explain his waning motivation was to point to the loss of their catalyst. The plans were there, though, waiting for their chance, and he supposed he should feel grateful. For it put him further ahead than he had been before Letty stepped into their lives.

Such was progress. Better something than nothing.

Cole left his big plans behind him in the bed he didn't make today, vestiges of possibilities in a tangled mess. He then walked out of his bedroom, a room Danielle had copied from a home decorating magazine, a room still looking like a space he shared with a wife.

Chapter 18

Her mother's booming voice marched into Letty's ears seconds before the woman entered the kitchen.

Cole, who had been leaning back against the counter drinking coffee from his smiley face mug, glanced toward the kitchen door. On his face, Letty read resignation. It was tinted with a bit of dread.

Letty glanced down at the bowl of dry cereal Brett had poured for her, and rose from her chair with weighted reluctance. The whirlwind was about to sweep through, and it was better if she faced it standing.

On the one hand, Letty was glad for the normality of her mother, strong and undeterred, back to her old self already. It had been horrible to see her so weak last night. Her mom had always been such a solid support in her life. To see her worn down to someone less than a superwoman had been unsettling.

The vigor of her mother's voice, the power, the self-assuredness, served as a forewarning. Letty couldn't help the small tug of a smile. Most people who'd been through what her mom had would take at least this first day to recover before reclaiming their grip on the steering wheel. How could she not admire such strength?

The volume and power of her mother's voice intensified as her mom approached the kitchen. She was back to normal. Good. The familiarity dimmed the memory of her mom outside the front window last night, filthy and bloodied, looking like a crazed monster from a horror flick.

On the other hand, the one cradling the feelings of others, she hated how the peace of this house was about to be further disturbed. Letty would have to get her mother out of here before it was ruined.

"No, I cannot wait until tomorrow," her mom said with equal parts intensity and indignation into her cell phone as she burst into the kitchen on her heeled boots.

Her clothing and makeup were fresh. The bandage on her head covered the cut that, unlike Brett's injury back when he was eight years old and fell out of a tree, had needed a few stitches. Purple smudged the minor swelling beneath her eye. She had a slight limp, and her multitude of bruises hindered her natural, graceful flow. None of it made a dent in her fortitude. Her vigor covered her physical weaknesses like a good cosmetic.

Cole set his mug in the sink and took two long strides toward the back door. He stopped and glanced over at Letty for a moment before going back to retrieve his mug. He took it to the coffee maker and refilled it. Then he leaned back against the counter again and gave Letty a wink and a half-smile. She smiled back, basking in his subtle protectiveness.

"No, that's too late in the day," Connie said into her phone. The tone of her voice held enough mockery to make the person on the other end feel as if they might be dull-witted, but not so much as to be blatant about it. Her blade was sharp, and she wielded it with precision.

"Are you kidding me?" Connie continued with rising ire, pausing in her awkward pace. "No. I don't want to spend another night in this godforsaken place!"

"Mom!" Letty shouted in a whisper.

Cole was standing right there, had heard the insult to his home. She had to stop her mother before she took this any further. Sometimes when her mom got on one of her rants, the woman had no care for who or what she crushed beneath it. Besides, Letty loved this place and was going to miss it almost as much as the friends she'd made here.

Connie flicked a hand at Letty, outward palm coming to an abrupt halt directed at Letty's face. She always hated when her mom did that. It was dismissive in the very rudest possible way. Today, it bothered her far more than it ever had before. Maybe because Cole was standing right there to witness it. Maybe because he, and this peaceful place on the mountain, didn't deserve to be subjected to such an offense.

"That's impossible!" Connie raved into her cell phone, incredulous at whatever she'd been told. Her voice tightened, as did the muscles around her mouth, pinching her sentences.

"How can you only have one tow truck?… Where is the next closest tow truck?… Are you kidding me? What kind of ass-backward place are you running?" Connie said, continuing her pace of the sunny kitchen.

Her shadow passed across Letty. An eclipse, thwarting the light.

Connie flung her free arm up in outraged acquiesce, wincing at the twinge of pain. She shot an angry glance at her daughter, one bolstered with blame, before focusing again on her call. Letty sank back down in her chair.

"Well, I guess it will have to be this afternoon

then," her mother said into the phone, frowning. "No later than two o'clock, though... No, I'm telling you, two o'clock, at the absolute latest. Good. Yes, I'll meet you there."

Connie stabbed her index finger against the screen of her phone and for a moment, glared at everything and nothing, fuming. Her color had come back and carried a few extra shades with it.

Cole took a sip from his mug. "I take it you were talking to Eddie."

"Well, it was Eddie's Garage, so it could have been. Apparently, it's the only garage in Pine Bluff in possession of a tow truck."

The corner of Cole's lip quirked upward.

"What?" her mom asked.

"Eddie is good with cars, but he's a little slow on everything else. He might be there at two o'clock, or around that time he might remember he was supposed to be somewhere. It would be a good idea to call later and remind him about your appointment."

Connie swung an accusing look at her daughter, hands fisted on her hips, her summation flowing in the manner of a tireless litany.

"I know the car is totaled," Connie said. "The insurance company will pick it up from the garage. Right now, they want all kinds of information, and they need to talk to someone at the garage, which they can't do until he tows it there. Which won't happen until this afternoon because this Eddie has the only working tow truck within fifty miles of this place. They *are* sending another rental car. It'll be here in three hours. I'll meet the guy from the garage at the crash site, and then we can leave from there. I'll be able to take care of the rest of this business when we get home."

"Three hours?" Letty asked.

The suddenness stunned her a little, but it shouldn't. This was her mother, after all. Taking care of business with perfect efficiency was what she did best. While it was an asset in their line of work, the inflexibility of it clashed with the nature of this world on the mountain.

Sometime over these past days, Letty had become acclimated to the unhurried mind-set of this cozy little branch of the country. She wondered if the high altitude laid a relaxed hand on everything. More likely, it was the skirting of progress. Cole's mountaintop lacked the mishmash of development that ate up Mother Nature as if she were nothing more than an appetizer.

Her mother pointed a look her way. "That's right, three hours. Good news, huh?" She continued before Letty could respond, "You shouldn't have much to pack."

"…No. It's just that, well, I…" Letty shifted her attention to Cole. His attention was on her, but she found his expression unreadable. To her mother, she said, "I can be ready. I'll go get my things together."

****

"Coffee?" the bear of a man asked Connie after Letty had gone.

For a quiet flash, Connie glared at Cole. He had some kind of gall, coming between her and her daughter. The crime was unforgivable. At the same time, Letty showed no signs of abuse, didn't appear intimidated or afraid in the man's presence. Quite the opposite. She could almost believe her daughter wasn't ready to leave.

Connie had to admit, though she'd never say so out loud, Letty had done well here. Still, no man could be so good as to take a young girl into his home and not have at least a few impure thoughts. Every man's mind led him in particular directions, city or the country, it didn't matter. Good fortune and grit had brought her here before Holloway could act on his thoughts.

This morning while she was dressing, Connie had searched through her mental card catalog of reasons to hate men. Even with her sparse dating experiences, she'd had more than her fill of their egos, their possessiveness, and their preoccupations with sex. Men were nothing but a bother. All she'd ever needed one for was his seed. Thanks to science, she got it without having to subject her body to the lust of a man.

It was enough for her, without having to sharpen the point with details, that she didn't like Cole. However, if Letty should ever mention him in conversation, Connie would be prepared with a response the girl could not refute.

She couldn't figure out why Letty had taken to this guy, had trusted him with her darkest secret, had healed under his care. These facts spurred her aggravation toward him. Cole Holloway had accomplished what she could not.

Connie used caution lowering to a seat at the table. Her awkwardness furthered her annoyance. "Yes, I would love some coffee. With cream."

Two bowls of dry cereal sat on the kitchen table, simple oak with no adornments. While he got her coffee, she took in the rest of the kitchen. The original design had been basic, probably built a very long time ago. There'd been a few nice touches added;

handcrafted carving in the crown molding, a clean, eggshell tile floor, and the appliances were modern, stainless steel, and of high quality. Some of the cabinets were fronted with diamond-beveled, glass panels, showing a lovely set of delicate dishes behind them.

The bright yellow paint on the walls was hideous, but not old. A creative art deco picture on the wall was pleasant enough. It was out of place in a mountain home but went with much of the other decor. She liked it. But she didn't like that she liked it. Hating everything about this place put it in a neater package.

The window over the sink was large and looked out to a view of fields and trees, giving the impression the wilderness beyond his property went on forever. Connie couldn't wait to get home to civilization.

Cole filled a teacup with coffee and set it, along with a matching saucer, on the table in front of her. He then took out the carton of almond milk and set it on the table along with a spoon. It was the kind of almond milk her daughter always used in her cereal, and in her cooking.

"Thank you," Connie said, wishing Letty had been there to witness her restraint. She'd asked for cream.

After pouring a splash into her cup and giving it a stir, Connie set the spoon on the saucer. It was a nice set. Not something she'd expect him to have. The stupid happy-face mug he'd been holding when she'd walked into the kitchen, now that looked more his style.

She stared at Cole. His back was to her, and he was gazing out the window. Her mind swerved from her original destination. In an uncharacteristic wave of uncertainty, Connie hesitated before saying, "Did she really try jumping off a cliff?"

****

Cole's vision was lost in the field of wildflowers where yesterday Letty had picked the autumn-blooming asters for their dinner table. He would always see her there when he looked out this window, thinking of her as the most ephemeral of flowers, and yet the most compelling.

After a short pause, Cole responded to Connie's question. "Maybe she was just thinking a little too close to the edge." Not until the words were out, did he turn around to face her.

He knew the truth, of course. If he hadn't happened to be in the right spot at the right moment, a rescue squad would have been removing Letty's body from a crevice a long way down from where she'd started. And only if someone saw her down there before the animals. His stomach churned at the thought.

But Cole was a parent, and he would have nightmares for the rest of his life if someone told him his son had come close to committing suicide. He might have them anyway, seeing as how he'd grown so attached to the girl. Besides, it might make life easier for Letty if her mother didn't know for sure, although, he suspected she already did. The woman was a lot of things, but naive wasn't one of them.

One look at her single, raised brow, and steady gaze, told him she was aware he was lying. She didn't call him on it. Instead, she steered their talk another way.

Connie wrapped her hands around one of Danielle's pretty little teacups. Her unpolished fingernails were short and neat. Her hands delicate, yet sturdy, like the plastic stem of an artificial flower.

"When Letty was born, I was sure I could never feel a lacking in my life because I had in my arms everything I could ever want. She was a beautiful baby, a beautiful child."

"Now she's a beautiful woman," Cole said, leaning back against the counter. He picked up his precious happy-face mug and took a sip of coffee.

"You don't know what it's like yet. Your son is still young. All of a sudden, one day, you realize your baby isn't a baby anymore; she's old enough, at least legally, to do things on her own. Except, you still see her playing with her toys, learning how to read and write, outgrowing her clothes, learning to drive. Then she's acting like she's all grown up, and you know she isn't. You're forced to give up your control a little at a time, and it kills you in bites because you know what's best for your child, but she won't listen. Kids think they know it all, when they've experienced too little to know much of anything."

Cole considered what she said before responding. "You do the best you can to teach them, but at some point, you have to let them put their knowledge to use, or what good is it?"

Connie shook her head. "My daughter wasn't ready to be on her own before. She isn't able now, not after what she's gone through. This...excursion of hers proves it."

"Sometimes wounds get worse before they get better. I think Letty's ready to get better."

Connie stiffened. "You hardly know her. You think spending a few days with Letty gives you some kind of special knowledge her own mother doesn't have?"

"I didn't mean to imply—"

"You are right about one thing," Connie said. "Letty will be just fine. I'll see to it."

It wasn't the least bit difficult to imagine her *seeing* to it. Although it was presumptuous, since he'd known her for so short a time, Cole held a certainty Letty needed a hand to hold for comfort, not to shove her toward any sort of goal. While he didn't doubt Connie's love for her daughter, it was a safe bet assuming she was not adept at passive support.

"Some things a person has to see to themselves," Cole said.

"How, Mr. Holloway, by running away from home, by getting drunk and telling a perfect stranger her most personal details?"

It was grating on her how Letty would talk to him about Danny, but not to her own mother. He could understand. He'd feel the same way if the situation was reversed.

"Like I said, sometimes wounds get worse before they get better."

Cole put those words to his own state of affairs as he drank from his mug. Maybe he had gotten worse over the last two years. He reran through his head the past days with Letty and Brett, how life had become less fraught than it was before she'd come into their world. Maybe now he was getting better, too. He would make an effort to adhere to the healing process, if not for his own well-being, then for his son's. For Letty had set Brett on a good path, too.

"None of this is any of your business, anyway," Connie said.

"No, it's not my business." Cole rinsed his mug and put it in the dishwasher. "I've got work to do." He left the kitchen and grabbed his jacket from the peg as he passed through the mudroom.

****

After he'd gone, Connie sat back in her chair and sank a little. For the next few minutes, she gave in to the multitude of aches assaulting her body. She lifted the delicate teacup and sipped. Letty had made the coffee. Connie recognized the mix. She should. Her daughter had expanded on the blend with her own touch, but it was her mother who'd taught Letty how to make it. She'd taught Letty everything the girl knew.

Letty had no living grandparents, no aunts, no uncles, and of course, no father. Connie had always been glad not to have those kinds of interferences. The last thing she would ever want was for someone else to tell her how to raise her daughter. She knew what was best for Letty. A mother knew.

Connie placed the cup back on the saucer. From somewhere outside blasted the course sound of a motor starting. It was too rough and too loud to be a car engine. Good Lord, it was probably a tractor of some sort. Her eyes rolled in conjunction with the slight shake of her head. She was on a damn farm. Glancing at her watch, Connie closed her eyes and rubbed her temples with her fingertips as the engine outside revved.

Two o'clock was much too far away.

Chapter 19

Cole stared down his driveway as his truck disappeared, a little too fast for the curve. No wonder Connie Norris had gone off the road. From what he could tell in the short time he'd known her, she was always in a rush.

Although he'd been acquainted with her for less than twenty-four hours, it was clear she was one of those people who focused on *getting* somewhere. She didn't take the time to respect or regard the journey. He couldn't imagine living in such a way. Letty's mother must miss a lot of wonders, hurrying through life with her tunnel vision. In that respect, he felt sorry for her.

She'd achieved a great deal in her life, made it on her own, started and maintained a business, and of course, raised a wonderful daughter. Cole couldn't help but wonder if the woman was even capable of enjoying what she had. Again, his thoughts swooped inward. A moment later, he wished they'd get out. These recent bouts with introspection were making him weary.

Letty's mother was angry again. Or maybe still. Since he had yet to see her much calmer than aggravated, Cole couldn't help but think maybe such a state was her regular mood. For Letty's sake, he hoped not.

At a quarter till two, when the rental car still hadn't arrived, Connie's vexation bloomed. She had asked, or rather, informed, Cole of her need to borrow his truck so she could go meet Eddie from the garage at the crash site. Cole had offered to take her, but he couldn't deny his relief when she insisted on driving. If good fortune graced him to never be confined in a car with her again, he'd be ever grateful.

After closing the door to his pole barn, Cole headed for the house. It was past time for lunch, and while he didn't have much of an appetite, his stomach was making its grumbles for food.

Inside, the house was as quiet as solitude, and he wondered if Brett had fixed himself a sandwich, or if Letty had made something for him to eat.

Come to think of it, he hadn't seen his son since this morning. On the days Brett didn't have school, after he finished doing his chores and his homework, he would come out to the pole barn, drifting in as if he hadn't been headed that way.

He'd help his father where he could, learned by doing, as Cole had at his father's side. Brett never gave the impression he was very interested in learning the mechanics of farming and maintaining the machinery. Cole had the feeling it was an excuse to spend time with his dad, and that was good enough for him.

He and Brett never delved into profound or intense conversations, both preferring to float on the surface in a more comfortable fashion. But they were working together, and the father-and-son time was what mattered. It's the way men did things.

It always astounded Cole how easy conversation flowed between women. They needed no preamble, no openings between broken distractions through which to thread their words. He envied the way they voiced their thoughts to one another, anytime and anyplace. Men could talk, but only while passing tools back and forth, tightening bolts and hammering nails. Or maybe at the end of the day, over a few beers. Even then, they kept the reins of their deepest emotions in their firm grips.

Cole hung his jacket on a peg in the mudroom. Maybe that was why he and Darrell Clayton always fought the way they did. It was their way of communicating. Then he almost laughed out loud. He and Darrell fought because they didn't like each other. They weren't layered folk.

Cole passed through the empty kitchen and then through the living room, on his way up to Brett's room to check on him. As he neared the bottom of the stairs, he stopped.

On the white tile near the front door, Letty's backpack was waiting, packed and ready to go. Her mother's travel bag sat beside the backpack.

Letty's sweet voice floated to his ears, as did the strumming of her guitar. She was sitting on the porch swing. Through the window, he could see her head of long, golden hair. He opened the door, quiet and slow, eased out, and leaned his shoulder against the frame.

Burt lay on the porch near her feet, his big head resting on his yellow paws. Scotty, their little terrier, was sniffing around in the yard. Burt had his eyes closed, but Cole suspected the old dog was awake, enjoying the private concert. He was proven right when the dog opened his eyes and shifted them his way, as if to shush him, before closing them again. Burt had never looked more content.

Following the dog's example, Cole hung his head and closed his eyes, listening to Letty play and sing for what would be the last time.

The music was rich, but the lyrics carried a lighter note than what she'd sung on the cliff the day he'd first seen her. Undertones of sadness still themed the song. Much like the singer, and it twisted his heart. Maybe it would always be so. He hoped not. Especially since after today, he wouldn't be able to do anything about it.

So lost in his thoughts was he, for a moment Cole didn't realize Letty had stopped singing, that her delicate hands rested on the strings, and her face was turned to him with the saddest smile he had ever seen.

"I'm sorry," he said when he opened his eyes to find her looking back. "I didn't mean to interrupt."

"You're not. It wasn't anything anyway."

Cole thrust away from the doorframe, crossed the porch, and sat on the top step facing Letty with his back against a post. One of his feet was flat on the next step below, the other propped up before him, knee bent, his forearm resting upon it. He took a moment to gaze around and soak up his surroundings before he spoke.

"What were you playing out on the cliff?" he asked.

She paused, her eyes straying out toward the woods, and Cole held his breath. He was afraid he might have breached a subject better left alone. They hadn't spoken of that time. That time. As if it had been so very long ago. Then Letty shook her head once, twice, as a bashful smile lifted the corners of her lips.

"The tune was floating through my mind on the bus ride," she said. "The words shuffled into my head as I was sitting there on the edge of the cliff. I don't even remember the music or the lyrics."

Cole didn't remember the words either, but the

resonance of the earnest melody would be with him forever.

"Why did you pick Montana? Why this part of it?" Cole asked.

"I didn't know where I was going. All I knew was I had to get away from Vegas. At least I had sense enough to know I was too upset to be driving, so I took a ride share to the bus station. I bought a ticket for the next bus out. It dropped me off in Pine Bluff, and I spent a night in a motel. The next day I started walking. This is where my feet took me. No reason, just happenstance."

Now Cole smiled. "I'm glad you came here."

"Me too."

"Will you be okay?" Cole asked.

"Yes, I think I will. I know it'll be hard, going back to Las Vegas. I'll have to deal with Danny. It'll almost kill me, but now I know it won't." Letty looked at him with a firm directness. "You don't need to worry about me, Cole. If ever in my life I feel myself falling, I'll picture you catching me. Or rather, tackling me," she said with a grin.

Cole grinned, too. He liked knowing she wouldn't forget him.

Something caught her eye. Letty shifted her head and peered out toward the woods. Cole twisted to see Scotty, their little terrier, sprinting from some underbrush. The dog dashed across the yard at full speed. Spencer, their golden tabby, was in pursuit not far behind. Cole and Letty laughed at the sight. Scotty ran around the house and out of their vision, the cat closing in. They were still laughing when Brett walked out from the same area.

The boy was halfway across the yard before he caught sight of them sitting on the porch. He stopped where he was, facing them.

Cole stared back at Brett. Something about the boy's expression raised his concern. For a moment, and for a reason too fogged with the moment's emotion to be clear, Cole feared he would return to the woods. Maybe it was because the boy was hurting, and he wanted his son close by. Oh, Lord, was he sounding like Connie Norris? Maybe the woman wasn't wrong about everything.

He took in a breath to call to Brett, to go to him if he didn't head this way. Then his son got back into motion and walked toward the house.

When Brett got close to the porch, the boy seemed unsure as to what he should do, stay and talk, or go inside. Then Letty made it easy for him to decide. She scooted over on the swing, like he always did for Teresa, and Brett sat down beside her.

"What have you been up to, Son?" Cole asked.

"Just went for a walk."

"Oh," Letty said. "We were going to walk to that lake today. I forgot."

Brett shrugged, shifting a quick peek her way before saying, "I don't think there's time now."

Letty glanced at her watch and then down the driveway. "No, we'd better not. Maybe you could email some pictures to me."

"Sure," Brett said, with somber undertones to his voice, as well as his posture. Then they were all three quiet for a while.

Sunlight gleamed across the land, uninhibited by the few distant fluffs of clouds. A temperate breeze scarcely ruffled the trees, the grass, the colored leaves drying on the ground. Indian summer had come to the mountain, and even in the shade of the porch, the day had grown warm.

Letty and Brett worked together, their feet rocking with the same amount of gentle force to keep the swing going. Cole removed his jacket and hung it on the post.

Beyond the porch, a host of free and wild birds harmonized in sporadic jamborees, enjoying the resurgence of summertime. Here and there, one of them chirped a solo. A couple of bumblebees hovered nearby for a few seconds before buzzing away. A soft, cleansing breeze wound through the land at an easy pace. The air was so clear it was like a lens.

Brett was the first to speak.

"Dad, can I get a new comforter? Mine has cartoon racecars all over it. I'm too old for that kind of stuff."

Cole studied his son before nodding. "Sure. We can go into town tomorrow. In the meantime, check some online sites. Maybe you'll see something there you like. Pick out whatever you want."

Brett nodded. "Okay. I'll do it later."

A robin landed on the porch railing in front of Brett and Letty. They all held still and gazed at it for a moment before it flew away.

"You could get a new comforter too, Dad."

Cole scratched his head and then shrugged. "The one I have is fine."

However, the suggestion snagged him. He'd never been one to get something new unless he needed it. His truck was twelve years old, but it still ran well, so he kept it. Comforters weren't something he'd given much thought to ever in his life.

No, that wasn't true. Every night he was aware of sleeping under a floral comforter he hated but kept because Danielle had chosen it, and she might come back expecting it to still be there.

"Actually, Son," Cole said. "I think I will get a new one."

"I think that's a good idea," Letty said. She was smiling his way. She understood.

Then a thought formed in his head, brazen and perfect, guided by the notes he'd made the night before. Notes about changes leading to other changes, in hopes of guiding them to a better future. His plans hadn't left the ground floor of the house last night. They did now.

Cole clapped his hands together once as he jumped to his feet. "I have another idea. A damn good one."

A thrill of youthful eagerness shot through his veins. It infused his core, grew fast, and electrified his thoughts, his life, igniting a glow at the end of what had been a long and treacherous tunnel.

"What is it, Dad?" Brett asked. His son leaned forward, a slight, but anticipatory grin lifting his face.

Cole said, "I think it's about time we light up our fire pit."

"The fire pit?" Brett said.

Cole gave him a meaningful nod. "Yeah. It's time to get rid of a few things."

Brett's face scrunched in confusion. Then his eyes grew large, his sudden smile on the verge of bursting. "Dad, are we going to burn our comforters?"

Cole chuckled through a grin and gave several quick nods.

Letty burst out laughing, and then Brett did, too.

"Can we do it now?" Brett asked. His palms were

already on his thighs, his body geared to leap into action.

In the exuberant tempo of "ready, set, go," Cole said to his son, "Go get your comforter. I'll go get mine."

Brett took off like Scotty running from the cat. Cole was right behind him, running as if he too were no more than a boy. A few seconds later, he popped his head back out the door and grinned at Letty, who was still sitting on the swing.

"Hey, Letty. Grab all those frilly little pillows on the couch. You know the ones with the tassels all around them?" His brow furrowed in disgust, but his grin held strong. "I hate tassels."

"You got it," Letty said, laughing again as she hurried into the house.

****

Brett walked out of the pole barn and handed his father the can of lighter fluid he'd requested. Their anticipation crouched like a jack-in-the-box, one turn of the crank away from popping.

Letty stood witness to the handover as if it was part of a ceremony. In a way, for each of them, it was. A page in their lives, so heavy it took all three of them working together to lift it, was about to turn to the next. Who knew what they would find? None of them, of course. But it would be better. It had to be better.

However, as they stood before the comforters and decorative pillows piled into the as-of-yet cold fire pit, another idea struck Cole. It set him something akin to giddy.

He paused for a minute, gazing at his unchained imaginings. The idea now blooming in his head was so terrific he had to take some time to savor it. His two partners had no such thoughts in their heads to distract them from their enthusiasm. Brett and Letty stood to his left, all shifting feet and giggles as they waited with great impatience for him to douse the past with lighter fluid and set it afire.

"Come on, Dad," Brett said. His fingers curled into his palms, making little pulses.

"Not yet, Son. I have another idea."

Cole set down the can of lighter fluid, then turned and strode into the pole barn. A minute or so later, he walked out with three pairs of work gloves, some large garden shears, and a few other tools cradled in his arms. He gave a pair of gloves to each of them. "Come on, you two, we're not ready to light this thing just yet."

Brett and Letty stuffed their hands into the work gloves without questioning him, ready to get to it, even though they didn't know what "it" was. All they were sure of was it would be something good.

They trailed Cole through the back door and then through the house. He didn't stop until he got to the tile entryway at the front door, just off the edge of the carpet, where he turned to face his followers. He held on to the garden sheers but dropped the rest of the tools beside him. Cole then tucked the shears under his arm while he put on his own pair of work gloves.

Lowering to his knees, he used the shears to cut along the edge of the royal blue carpeting that had irked him since the day Danielle had it installed.

After he'd made several good, long cuts, Cole tossed down the shears and jerked up a chunk of the carpeting. "Come on, you two," he said over his shoulder. "Do you think I brought you in here to watch me do all the work?"

In an instant, Brett and Letty got past the shock of seeing him slice up the carpeting, shared a burst of laughter, and then about tripped over each other in their rush to help him yank out the rest of it.

They shuffled furniture around. They cut, heaved, and piled the carpet until the floor was bared down to the padding. Then the three of them set to work on the stairs. Once at the top, they tore out all the carpet from the upstairs hallway, his bedroom, and Brett's. They didn't go into the guest room, as it had a wood floor.

Drunk on joy, their energy was boundless. By the time they had the carpet piled in scattered mounds throughout the house, they were all three glistening with sweat and prosperity.

Working as a team, trip after trip, they hauled the destroyed carpeting through the kitchen, the mudroom, and out the back door, where it all got tossed onto the pile in the fire pit. The pit overflowed by far upward and well out onto the grass. They kept heaping it on until every inch of it was out of the house.

When the last scrap was on the heap, Cole doused the whole thing with lighter fluid, circling the pile of yesterdays three times to make sure it was all good and soaked. The three of them stood there, out of breath and full of jubilance, waiting for their reward with excitement even their exhaustion could not diminish.

Cole dug into the pocket of his jeans for the matchbook he'd grabbed from a kitchen drawer during his first passing when his arms had been full with a flowery comforter. Then another idea skipped into his head.

"Hold on," he said. "I'll be right back."

A moment later, he marched out of the house carrying the abstract painting from their kitchen wall. He tossed it onto the pile, and Brett jumped up and shouted with glee.

"Hey, Dad," Brett said, his breath coming fast from action and exhilaration. "Will dishes burn?"

So Brett knew he hated those dishes. Maybe his son hated them, too. Cole laughed and said, "No, Son, all they'll do is turn black, break, and be ruined."

"Oh," Brett said, with no more than mild disappointment.

Cole stopped chuckling, but his smile held strong as he nodded at his son. "Let's go get them."

Laughing as they all ran back and forth from the kitchen to the fire pit, Cole, Brett, and Letty carried as many dishes as they could at one time, not being the least bit careful. Quite a few of the cups and saucers, the plates, and the bowls, dropped and broke along the way. The sound was music to their lively parade.

Using their gloved hands, they scooped up the broken pieces and tossed them into the fire pit as well, until the last of the set with the delicate yellow swirly pattern lay about the pile of carpet and comforters, and the throw pillows with tassels.

Cole removed his gloves and tossed them aside. Brett and Letty did the same.

Again, Cole retrieved the matches from his pocket.

"Wait a minute!" Letty shouted. "I have something I want to put on there, too."

Cole and Brett waited while Letty ran into the house. She returned a minute later holding a plain brown T-shirt. Cole recognized it as the shirt she'd been wearing the day he'd met her, the day she set out to end her life by taking a long, last leap off a cliff.

Letty tossed the shirt onto the pile. In response to Brett's questioning look, she said, "It has bad memories."

Brett accepted the answer without need of further explanation. After all, it was the same reason everything else was in there and about to burn.

At last, Cole lit the match. The scrape of the tip along the striker and the little burst of fire flared loud in the reverence of their anticipation. He held it between his thumb and forefinger for a second or two. When he tossed the burning match, it sailed through the air in a graceful, slow-motion arc.

The instant the small flame landed on the pile, the entire conglomeration of things they no longer wanted in their lives lit up in one monstrous *whoosh*.

Rowdy shouts followed. Their hoots and laughter were louder than the crackling flames. The three continued to yell, to laugh, and to cheer, with high fives all around. Fists punched the air, and they all had frequent distance between the soles of their shoes and the ground.

Smoke billowed and rose like exorcised demons condemned to banishment, dragging speckled tails of glowing red embers into the late afternoon sky. The sooty swells carried away the refuse of the magnificent flames, and everything they consumed.

Letty locked elbows with one, then the other, leading them in a bouncy do-si-do for a few turns before they all leapt about the yard again until their bodies tired and their voices threatened to go hoarse.

Then, when calmed by relief and their physical exertions, they drew a deep, collective breath and exhaled their cathartic goodbyes to a past now in exile.

The three of them stood close together near the heat, drained and elated, optimism settling into the space once too crowded with grief to hold anything else.

Quiet now, Cole, Brett, and Letty gazed at the fire while catching their breath, and beheld the beautiful destruction.

The royal blue carpeting turning black, the edges curling up like the toes of the wicked witch as she lay crushed and powerless beneath Dorothy's humble house. The painting from the kitchen was already gone. Flames danced across what was left of its charred, gilt frame. Letty's T-shirt melted into the sizzling carpet. The dishes were not aflame, but they were turning black, and they were broken and finished.

The fire had the three of them transfixed. They stood witness to the change, watching a past that had haunted and daunted them become a harmless mass of ashes.

So lost in their thoughts were each of the three, they didn't hear Cole's truck until it was almost upon them.

The driver's door swung open, and Connie stepped down from the cab in her heeled boots, gaping at the huge fire. Once she got close enough, she had a good look at what was burning.

"Is that your carpeting?" she asked without taking her eyes from the flames and what they were consuming. She studied it like it was a puzzle of great importance.

Brett giggled, followed in an instant by Letty. Giggling wasn't very manly, so Cole outright laughed.

"Yes," Cole said with a proud nod. "It sure is."

Brett and Letty's giggles exploded into laughter.

The picture frame near the top of the burning pile pierced their merriment with a resounding snap and partial tumble. Connie got an eyeful of what was left of the frame. "Is that the painting from your kitchen wall?"

Another round of laughter erupted from all three before Cole gave her an answer. "Right again, Miss Norris."

Connie surveyed the burning pile with more scrutiny. "Are those..." Her voice rose on a note of disbelief. "Are you burning your dishes?"

Laughter burst again from the three of them.

Brett said, "We're trying to, but Dad says they won't burn. They'll just turn black, and break, and be ruined."

At the boy's explanation, the three cracked up so hard they almost couldn't stand. Brett and Letty leaned on each other. Cole wiped his eyes, laughing harder still, finally bending over with his hands on his thighs for support. When he straightened, still chuckling, he rubbed his shoulder where he'd pulled a muscle yanking up the carpeting. It was going to give him hell tomorrow. Yet he'd never felt so good in his whole life.

"You're all nuts," Connie said. Her voice held not a speck of amusement. "You've all gone insane!"

Letty made a go of reining in her laughter as she spoke to her mother, but the effort gained her little. "It's okay, Mom. Really it is."

"You're welcome to throw something in if you'd like," Cole said as his eyes shifted from her face to her snug fashion boots with the three-inch heels. "Those shoes you're wearing don't look very comfortable." This produced another round of raucous laughter from his punch-silly cohorts.

Connie glanced down at her boots before casting her appalled expression upon all three of them in turn, ending with Cole. "Burn my boots?"

The trio sailed along in their mirth, maybe never to stop, until a dark blue Toyota Camry rounded the curve of the driveway and parked a few feet behind Cole's truck. The rental car Letty's mom had ordered. An identical car followed and parked beside the first. Why two, though? Oh, right. Because the person who drove the car up here would need a ride back.

"Thank goodness," Connie said. Then to her daughter, "Are your things packed and ready to go? I need to get you out of here before you completely lose your mind."

Though its rewards would last well into the future, the laughter of the three did a fast fade. The fire still blazed. It crackled, it consumed, expelling heat and ash upon its instigators.

Letty tipped a bare nod to her mother as she stood in the puddle of her melting glee. She paused in her glance at Cole, and then Brett, before going into the house to retrieve her things.

"You take the guitar, Letty!" Cole called to her before she stepped inside the house. "It's yours to keep."

Letty smiled back over her shoulder, but now it was sad and grateful.

A minute or so later when she walked out again, her mother was talking to one of the two young men who'd delivered the rental car. His coworker was standing beside the other car, stretching and checking out his surroundings. Both guys were dressed in navy blue polos and khakis. Letty walked to where Cole and Brett stood and set her backpack, her mother's travel bag, and the guitar case on the ground.

"Brett," she said, her voice strained. "You're such a great kid. I'll never ever forget you."

"I won't forget you either," Brett said. His eyes were watering, but not from the smoke. Cole knew this because he was suffering the same.

Letty hugged Brett. Tears flowed down her face, leaving a damp trail in the dirt and the dust. Brett wiped his eyes when she stepped back. Letty didn't bother to stem her tide. She made the short journey to Cole a slow one.

"Thank you isn't anywhere near enough," she said.

"Letty," Cole said. "You gave far more than you took."

Letty afforded him another grateful smile and then folded her arms across her middle and squeezed. She sniffed and looked Cole in the eye.

"Cole, I never knew my father, never knew anything about him other than a basic physical description, some medical history, and that he played piano. If you don't mind, I'd like to spend the rest of my life thinking he was like you."

Cole would never know how he managed to get the words through the tightness in his throat, but he did. "I'd be honored."

Letty's tears fell free. She slanted a quick peek over to where her mother stood waiting. Cole shot a glance toward the woman, too. She was watching them, watching as if they were up to something. He stuffed his hands in his pockets in an effort to appear less threatening.

"You'll always have a place here, Letty," he said. "I mean it." Then he was able to wrangle a smile. "I'd love to hire you as a full-time cook. God knows we need it."

Letty laughed as she wiped at her tears and smeared her face. "Maybe someday I'll take you up on that." Then Letty rushed into his arms.

She hugged Cole with a fierceness he couldn't help but return. He yanked his hands out of his pockets and wrapped his arms around her. Her tears soaked into the plaid of his shirt. Cole blinked and was warmed when from the corner of his eye, he caught her stretching out her right arm. In an instant, Brett was there, hugging her too. Against his side, his son gulped a couple of times as he clung to Letty.

"Thank you, Mr. Holloway, for your hospitality," Connie said a moment later, now but a few feet away from the three. Her words were polite. Her voice was not.

Cole backed away from Letty. Brett stepped back, too, but stayed beside him. Cole draped an arm across his son's shoulders, but he didn't shame him by watching as Brett used both hands to swipe at the tears on his face. The sound of car doors closing cut through the silence when the two young men who'd delivered the rental car got into the second car. The engine started, and they turned around and drove away.

"We have to go now, Letty," Connie said, all businesslike. She slanted a glance at her daughter and grunted. "You're filthy. We'll stop somewhere along the way so you can clean yourself."

Letty didn't respond. She didn't say another word to anyone. She picked up her bag and the guitar case and walked to the remaining car, her mother right behind her dragging her travel bag. Letty put her things in the back seat. Connie put her bag in the trunk. Then they both stood at the driver's side door.

The two women engaged in a debate. From what Cole could hear, Letty wanted to drive. After a moment, they got in the car, Connie behind the steering wheel.

As the car made a U-turn, Letty shifted her head and looked out the window of the passenger side. Cole was standing beside Brett, his arm still around his son's shoulders. Behind them, the fire heated their backs as it continued to burn big. Brett lifted a hand and waved. Letty waved back. And then they were gone.

Cole and Brett stood there until the car had been out of sight for a good minute or so. Then Cole strolled into the pole barn. He walked out with two lawn chairs. He set them near the fire pit, not too close, though, as it was still a monster of a fire. They sat and gazed into the flames, sharing in silence their grief and their gladness.

Sometime after the pile had collapsed in on itself, when the sun was setting low behind the trees, when the air was cooling and their stomachs grumbled, Cole got out the hose and gave a good watering to what was left of the fire. It was a giant, wet, black ball of nothing now. He'd have to use some equipment to get it all cleaned out. It could wait until tomorrow. He put his arm around his son, and he and Brett walked into the house together.

They ate peanut butter and jelly sandwiches on paper towels, and even laughed a little when Brett said, "Don't worry about the dishes, Dad. I'll take care of them tonight." Then he threw the paper towels in the garbage.

Chapter 20

"Well," Brett said to his father, "if you're going to help Teresa clean the kitchen, I'm going to study. Finals are coming up soon."

"Finals already?" Cole asked as he picked up three plates and carried them from the dining room to the kitchen, Brett behind him with three glasses.

The thick plates were a simple white with forest green trim around the edges. He and Brett had picked them out together the day after they'd burned the old ones. The memory of their unconventional fire still made them both smile whenever one of them mentioned it. Cole appreciated the knowledge the memory always would.

Although the new set of dishes they'd chosen had come with matching mugs, mugs Cole did like, he continued to drink his coffee from the happy-face mug Letty had given him. The bittersweet memory of her over his morning coffee replaced the ones that were just bitter.

Teresa thanked Cole for the dishes he'd handed her at the sink. They shared a smile for no particular reason, and then he followed his son back to the table for more dishes.

"Yeah," Brett said. "It's almost time for summer vacation to start."

He was right. The realization struck Cole with no

small amount of surprise. This school year had gone by so quick. It wasn't just the school year, either. It was as if time itself was scooting along at a faster pace than usual. Maybe faster wasn't the right word. Their lives were moving along at a *happier* pace. The old saying about time flying when you're having fun popped into mind. It was true.

"You go on and study now," Teresa told Brett when he and Cole walked back into the kitchen with the rest of the dishes. "That's more important. We've got this."

Brett smiled at Teresa. "Thanks," he said. "And thanks for dinner too. The spaghetti was good."

Teresa beamed. "You're welcome, Brett."

Cole nodded in agreement. The spaghetti had been bland and a bit undercooked. But he had enjoyed the meal.

When they had the dinner mess cleaned, Cole and Teresa sat at the kitchen table, each with a beer. Teresa used a glass. Cole was fine with a bottle. They began sitting inside not long before the first snowfall, when the temperature had dropped to below comfort. The weather was warm now. Cole figured they should go sit outside. Maybe after this beer. Right now, he was comfortable in his kitchen.

The walls were now painted a pale peach, and a new picture hung on the wall beside the table. The picture was the only new thing he'd picked out without any input from Brett. The instant he saw it, it was his. He didn't even look at the price, didn't care. He glanced up at it. The artist had done an outstanding job painting the field of asters in autumn.

"Letty called yesterday," Cole told Teresa.

"Did she? How is she doing?"

"She's doing well," Cole said, nodding. "She's going to start her own business. Said she's worked with her mother her whole life, and now she's ready to stretch her independent wings."

Teresa smiled. "To be young, living with so many possibilities. What kind of business does she plan to start?"

"She's going to open her own restaurant and eventually branch out into catering. Aside from taking some business classes, she's been working at two different restaurants, learning everything she can."

"Oh, how wonderful," Teresa said. "She's such a go-getter. What kind of restaurant is she going to open, did she say?"

"She's mulling over some possibilities. Probably a place specializing vegan food." Once, the very idea of such a thing would have made him cringe. The dinner she'd cooked for them, though, damn, it had been good.

Teresa laughed and shook her head. "I still can't believe I was giving cooking tips to a professional."

Cole chuckled. "She asked about you, told me to say hi."

"Be sure and tell her hi back for me when you talk to her again."

"I'll be talking to her in a couple of weeks," Cole said as he set down his beer. "She's coming out."

"Terrific! Brett must be so excited."

"He doesn't know. Letty wants to surprise him."

"I won't say a word. I hope I get a chance to see her while she's here."

"You will. She plans to open her restaurant here."

"In Pine Bluff?"

A wide grin split his face. "That's right. I told Letty I'd go with her to look at some places in town. She's already set it up with a realtor. I made it clear to her I'd love to be an investor. Any restaurant of hers is a sure thing."

"So you're going to be in the restaurant business."

"No. I made the offer, but Letty is determined to do it on her own. Apparently, she's squirreled away quite a bit of money. We won't be financially invested, but we'll be regular customers."

"This is such great news! We sure could use a good restaurant. A lot of the surrounding towns are so small there isn't much in the way of choices to go out for a meal. People come into Pine Bluff all the time to eat. Did you tell her that?"

"I did," Cole said.

"I think she'll do well."

"So do I. I told her that, too."

"Gosh, maybe I can even pick up a few cooking tips from her."

"I'm sure she'd be happy to teach you," Cole said, hope in his heart and his stomach.

They continued to drink their beers in the quiet pleasantness of each other's company. For months now, instead of finishing his Sunday dinner and going straight out to the porch or to the couch to watch television like he used to do, Cole stayed to help Teresa clean up the kitchen. What's more, he enjoyed it.

Their conversations were no longer stifled or one-sided. He spoke without prompting, and Teresa didn't ramble anymore. Every now and then, over the last few months, Cole stopped by her house to visit her during the week, maybe bring her some flowers or a box of candy, maybe do some repairs for her, or just visit for a while. Sometimes he and Brett took her out to dinner or to a movie. They had become, at the very least, comfortable companions.

Teresa stared at the painting on the wall. Cole followed her gaze.

"It's a beautiful picture," Teresa said. "It reminds me of your field of wildflowers in the fall when the asters are in bloom."

Cole nodded, pleased she liked it. "Me too. That's why I bought it."

He had come to value Teresa's opinion. Once the woman had relaxed a little, she was nice to have around. She was...good company. She liked the things he liked, appreciated this land and all it had to offer. Maybe he'd ask her to go camping with him and Brett. She might enjoy that.

"The painting looks right in here," Teresa said, still gazing up at the picture on the wall. "It's perfect for this house."

Cole nodded and broached the subject of camping to see how she'd react. The more he thought about having her along, the more he liked it. "Yeah, I think so, too. The wilderness makes me think of being a kid and camping with my father. In fact, this painting inspired Brett and me to plan a trip when school gets out. We haven't gone camping in a long time."

Too long. Though they had reclaimed their winter activities over the season, even built a snowman, they still had two years of life to catch up on, and time kept marching.

Teresa got a faraway smile. "Teddy and I used to camp out at Lake Swanson. Gosh, I haven't been there in ages."

"Lake Swanson? Haven't been out that way in years. I think the last time we were there, Brett was a toddler. We usually go to the woods by Caskon Ridge. There's a wide stream running through there. Maybe we'll give Lake Swanson a try."

"There's a nice path circling the entire lake, and the lake is small enough to walk all the way around."

"Hmm, right. I forgot all about that."

"At least, there used to be. Like I said, I haven't been there since Teddy. If it's anything like it used to be, I think you guys would have a good time."

"Sounds like. Why don't you come with us?"

"Camping? Really?"

"Sure. You enjoyed it, didn't you?"

"Loved it. But, Cole, don't you want to go with just you and Brett?"

"Oh, we'll do plenty of father/son camping trips. I thought you might like to come with us every now and then. I know Brett would like that, too. Maybe we could get Letty to join us. Make a party of it. I'll bet she's never been camping before."

"Cole, that sounds like a great time."

They sipped on their beers for a while. Evening settled. A full moon took up a good portion of the window over the sink.

"I have the compass my dad gave me when I was a boy. I think I'm going to give it to Brett while we're camping, you know, go for a walk with him, maybe on that path around the lake, stop and skip a few stones first, make it a special moment when I hand over the compass."

"Why, Cole Holloway, I never would have guessed

you to be so sentimental."

He peered over at Teresa. "Why not? You know how I feel about this land, how I've always felt."

"That's different. Land is substantial and valuable."

"So is the compass."

"That's not the same. It's an item. Men aren't usually sentimental about items."

"That's ridiculous. Men can be sentimental about items."

Teresa took in and released a long breath. "Well, I suppose since it's an heirloom, something your father once owned and gave you, that makes it different."

"Different from what?" Cole asked. He leaned forward on his elbows, folded his hands on the table, and looked closer at Teresa. She had her hair tucked behind her ears, and it curled in fat swoops against her neck. She always kept her hair so pretty. He wondered if it felt as soft as it looked.

Teresa sipped beer from her glass before speaking. "You know I have the first birthday card Teddy ever gave me. I have the first flower he ever gave me pressed into a book."

"So you think men don't care about those kinds of things?"

Teresa laughed. "No, I don't. It's all right. You're different creatures. Your minds are incapable of attaching value to certain things."

Cole sat up straight. "Incapable?"

"Don't take offense, Cole. It's the way men are. You know, I'll bet if Teddy was still alive and you asked him what color my eyes were, he wouldn't be able to tell you." Teresa covered her eyes. "Can you?"

"How the hell would I know what color your eyes are?"

They were blue, Cole well knew, like a mid-summer sky on a cloudless day. But for some reason, he couldn't tell her he knew. He suspected it was because of her late husband, Teddy. A part of him rebelled against that kind of encroachment.

They'd all been friends for so long. At times, he still thought of Teresa as a woman not just married but married to one of his friends. Over the winter months, the way he looked at Teresa had undergone a gradual change. Maybe it was time to complete the transition. He'd invited her to go camping, so it appeared the change had already begun. He opened his mouth to say blue, but she beat him to it.

Teresa uncovered her eyes. "Blue. They're the same color as yours. Oh, Cole, don't frown at me. Men don't hold on to things like eye color and sentimental gifts because they're not important to you. I accept that."

Scowling, Cole got up from the table, marched through the mudroom, and left through the back door. A few minutes later, he strode back into the kitchen holding a bundle of clean rags in his hands. He set them on the table.

"What's this?" Teresa asked.

Cole answered her by showing her, unpeeling the rags with a slow reverence. He lifted the last cloth and revealed they were more than a ball of rags. They were layers of protection.

"Oh, Cole," Teresa said, her hand over her heart. "Is that what I think it is?"

"Of course it is. What do you think; I buy these

things for myself?"

With wonder, Teresa lifted the snow globe, the one she'd given him for his eighteenth birthday. It was in perfect condition. Not a single scratch or chip marred the glass. She turned it upside down and gave it a gentle shake before setting it upright on the table. Snowflakes fluttered around the log cabin still sitting firm upon the little plastic mountaintop after all these many years.

"I can't believe you saved this," Teresa said, her gaze stuck on the flurry of flakes busy inside the snow globe.

In cantankerous defense, he said, "I knew you spent your babysitting money to buy a gift for me. What was I supposed to do with it, throw it in the garbage?"

"You took such good care of it."

He dropped back into his seat. "Well, it's not like I used it for anything. It's been all wrapped up and sitting in the pole barn for years."

She gazed at Cole, a bit of mist in her eyes. "I guess I was wrong. Men can be sentimental."

While embarrassment warmed his ears at having brought it out for her to see, he didn't mind if she thought of him as sentimental. In fact, as long as it didn't get around, he kind of liked it. He and Teresa sipped their beers while the snowflakes settled on and around the little cabin inside the snow globe.

"I saved something else, besides the things Teddy gave me over the years," Teresa said.

"What?"

Her lips parted, but after a second or two, she huffed instead of spoke. Her gaze broke away from his, pausing on the snow globe before returning. "A wrapper from a stick of gum."

"A stick of gum?"

"A wrapper from a stick of gum you gave me when I was seventeen years old."

Cole leaned back in his chair, gazing at her, grinning a little bit.

"Don't you dare laugh at me, Cole Holloway."

"I wouldn't dream of it," he said. He picked up the globe and shook it. A snowy commotion swirled inside the glass ball. He set it on the table, and they shared the small joy of the show while finishing their beers.

Twenty minutes later, Cole helped Teresa gather her things and walked her through the house, across the carpet of deep marbled oat and charcoal gray, and out to her car. After setting her bags in the back seat, he closed the door and opened the driver's side door for her.

"Thanks again for dinner, Teresa," he said.

"You're welcome. Any requests for next week?"

"It doesn't matter. I just like having you here."

Her jaw lowered a little. Then she formed her sentence. "Would you mind saying that again?"

He scowled. "You heard me."

"Thank you," Teresa said on a little chuckle. "I enjoy being here."

Above them, stars packed the vast night sky, glittering with charm and magic. The moon was a solid ball amongst the endless array of tiny, twinkling lights. Cole gazed down at Teresa, and for a moment, she appeared to glow beneath the enchanting luminosity of the Montana night sky. He couldn't help but stare at her lips. It's where he was gazing when she spoke.

"Cole Holloway?" Teresa asked, placing her hands

on her hips.

"What?"

"It's been years. Are you ever going to kiss me?"

Cole's frown softened, and then he grinned. "Of course I am. I didn't want to rush you."

As their laughter faded, Cole lowered his head and gave Teresa the kiss he'd been thinking about ever since she was too young for him to kiss.

A word from the author...

I lived most of my life in the wondrous city of Las Vegas, Nevada. For a while, I lived in an RV with my husband, and I was fortunate to see every state in this amazing country. Now I live in beautiful Michigan, where I've learned about layering clothes and that boats don't have brakes.

~

Visit Micki at:
Twitter: @millermwriter

Instagram: micki.miller

https://www.facebook.com/mickimillerwriter